"YOU'RE RIGHT. THIS IS A BAD IDEA."

His brows came together. "Sorry?"

She opened her eyes at this and allowed her hands to smooth tenderly over his bare skin, over his shoulders, across his chest. "I want you, Jack," she told him. "My *God*, I want you. But I don't want to just fall back into bed with you. It's far too easy to slide into our old pattern. It's not fair to use you just to satisfy my libido."

He caressed her cheek with the back of his fingers. "Really? That would be such a terrible thing?"

She shook her head. "No. It would be beautiful and thrilling and amazing—just like it was before. But, ultimately, heartbreaking. At least, that's my fear. That seems to be our track record."

"I can't promise you that we'd live happily ever after, Maddie," he admitted even as he realized that's exactly what he wanted . . .

More from Kate SeRine

The Transplanted Tales series

Red
Grimm Consequences
The Better to See You
Along Came a Spider
Ever After

The Dark Alliance series

Deceived

CONCEALED

KATE SERINE

ZEBRA BOOKS
KENSINGTON PUBLISHING CORP.
http://www.kensingtonbooks.com

ZEBRA BOOKS are published by

Kensington Publishing Corp.
119 West 40th Street
New York, NY 10018

All Kensington titles, imprints, and distributed lines are available at special quantity discounts for bulk purchases for sales promotion, premiums, fund-raising, educational, or institutional use.

Special book excerpts or customized printings can also be created to fit specific needs. For details, write or phone the office of the Kensington Sales Manager: Attn.: Sales Department. Kensington Publishing Corp., 119 West 40th Street, New York, NY 10018. Phone: 1-800-221-2647.

Zebra and the Z logo Reg. U.S. Pat. & TM Off.

First Printing: April 2017
ISBN-13: 978-1-4201-3779-8
ISBN-10: 1-4201-3779-4

eISBN-13: 978-1-4201-3780-4
eISBN-10: 1-4201-3780-8

10 9 8 7 6 5 4 3 2 1

Printed in the United States of America

For N. R.
Whose faith in me never wavers

Chapter One

Jack Grayson took a sip of his beer and covertly adjusted the earpiece he wore, trying to ignore the bead of sweat trickling down his back. A childhood spent in London had hardly prepared him for tropical climates.

He spared a glance toward the third-story window of the building across the street and saw a glint of light, reassuring himself that Luke Rogan, the Alliance's deadliest sniper and one of the few men he knew he could trust unequivocally, was still in place in case they needed cover.

"Where the hell is Ralston?" Luke murmured over the comm, his deep voice gruffer than usual. "This op's been pissing me off from the start."

Jack could relate. He'd spent the last eight months gathering intel on a man named Eric Evans who'd been hired to take out Luke and the woman who was now Luke's fiancée, in the hopes that the trail would lead them to Jacob Stone—the traitorous son of a bitch who'd been behind it all.

The trail had taken Jack from Luke and Sarah's home in Wyoming to a rogue assassin's villa in Cuba to a drug runner's warehouse in Miami and now to this shitty hotel in Mexico City, where someone working on Jacob's behalf had made contact with the local drug cartel, presumably setting up a deal to help fund Stone's operations now that his political career was over and he'd been burned by every reputable agency and organization in the United States. The man they'd once trusted as a friend—a brother—had been blacklisted by those eager to distance themselves from his fall from grace. At least, that was how it appeared on the surface. But Jack knew that, in reality, there were most likely many still clamoring for Stone's favor, clinging to his coattails in hopes of still furthering their own ambitions.

Unfortunately, Jack had no idea where the hell Stone himself had holed up when his bid to steal the Templar treasure was thwarted. But as soon as Stone's lackey returned, Jack sure as hell intended to find out.

He took another sip of his beer, surreptitiously taking in his surroundings at a glance. The slowly whirling ceiling fans attached to the vine-covered pergola did little more than stir up the oppressive, moist air that hung about the incongruously heavy European tables packed in among the potted palm trees and suffocating heat of the hotel's outdoor café.

Most of the other patrons were obviously tourists, laughing and talking too loudly as their margaritas took effect. To his experienced eye, the only one who didn't seem to fit was a lone man tucked in the corner who looked like he was heading out on safari, his khaki pants and cotton shirt a little too *turista* to be legitimate. He was also trying far too hard to blend in with the crowd, standing out more conspicuously for the effort and setting off Jack's finely tuned internal shit-storm alarm.

"Look alive, ladies and gentlemen," Jack announced, experiencing a familiar heaviness in the air that was independent of the intense tropical heat as his muscles tensed, preparing for action. "Looks like we have company. Three o'clock. Safari hat."

"Got him in my sights," Luke confirmed.

"Don't take a shot unless I give the word, even if he moves in on Ralston," Jack ordered calmly. "Let's just see how Dr. Livingstone here plays into our little drama, shall we?"

"Dr. *who*?"

At the sound of Ian Cooper's Texas drawl over the comm, Jack glanced toward where the man lounged on a bench across from the café, pretending to read the local newspaper. The former U.S. Marshal was one of their own, having been recruited to the Alliance several years earlier. He'd proven to be a tremendous asset in the field and a shrewd negotiator in the boardroom when acting for their front company, Temple Knight & Associates. But there were days he seemed seriously damned young. Of course, the older Jack got, the younger and younger *all* the newer recruits seemed . . .

"*Livingstone*," Jack said. "The nineteenth-century explorer who went missing in Africa? 'Dr. Livingstone, I presume?'" When he was met by only silence, Jack added, "You've seriously never heard of him?"

"Sorry, brother, not ringing any bells," Ian told him.

"So, Jack, you think this 'Livingstone' guy's cartel?" Luke interrupted.

Jack's gaze flicked toward the subject of their conversation, taking another look. "If so, he's not local. Regardless, we're clearly not the only ones who'd like to chat with Ralston. Ian, can you get a facial rec on our friend?"

Ian casually rose from the bench and strolled into the café with his cell phone to his ear. He lingered near the bar as if waiting for a seat and pulled his phone away from his ear, fiddling with it as if texting, but Jack knew he was snapping a photo of the man in the safari hat to send back to their tech team at headquarters. "Sending it through now," Ian murmured. "Stand by."

"Watch your back," Jack murmured, scanning the patrons in the café once again. There were some new faces among the crowd—and they didn't look like they were there to tie one on. "Two spooks three o'clock."

"Copy that," Ian affirmed.

Jack allowed his gaze to casually drift back toward the hotel. "Maddie? What's your twenty? Do you need backup?"

Maddie Blake, the only female member of the team, heaved a sigh over the comm. "I'm in position. And, no, I don't need any backup, Jack."

"Is there a problem?" he asked, slightly taken aback by her obvious offense at his question.

"Yeah, there's a problem," she snapped. "I may be new to the Alliance, but I'm a big girl, Jack. I don't need you to babysit me."

Her no-nonsense attitude was one of the things that had first drawn him to her all those years ago, and he'd fallen in love with her before he'd even realized it. Unfortunately, he'd had to walk away from her without a word of explanation, thinking he'd been protecting her when really he'd been too much of a fucking coward to explain the truth. And now he was paying for that with the daily torture of having her within arm's length since she'd joined the Alliance, yet forever out of his reach.

He ran a hand through his hair and took a moment to consider his response. The last damned thing he wanted to do was hash out their issues in front of the others. There was little that was private in the Alliance, but what he'd once shared with Maddie was too precious to him to open it up for discussion. "I'm not babysitting, Maddie. I'm just ensuring that a member of my team is safe."

There was a long, tense pause over the comm, neither of the others apparently wanting to be the first to break the silence. Finally, there was a quiet cough and Ian asked, "So, how's the housekeeping uniform workin' out? Anyone give you a second glance?"

Maddie grunted. "Only because the shirt is about two sizes too small. One false move and the girls are gonna burst out. And these shorts are ridiculous."

"Sorry 'bout that," Ian admitted. "Didn't get much notice you'd be joining us on this little excursion. I had to guess at your size. But I'm happy to gather that intel first-hand next time, Maddie, if you're up for it."

"Lock that shit down, Cooper," Luke growled, "and show some fucking respect."

But Maddie just scoffed at Ian's insinuation. "Gee, I don't know, Ian . . . From what I hear from the other guys, your hand is probably otherwise engaged . . ."

Ian chuckled. "Ah, honey, don't you listen to their jaw jackin'. They're just jealous 'cause they're all hat and no horse—"

"Stay on task," Jack cut in, his British accent, normally just a hint of what it had once been after so many years of living in the U.S., growing thicker in his irritation.

The thought of Maddie being with another man made him want to put his fist through a wall. But as Maddie had reminded him not too long ago, he'd given up the right to an opinion where she was concerned. He'd been the one who'd walked away all those years ago.

Jack inhaled deeply, sucking in the damp, heated air that was the calling card for Mexico at this time of year, then rubbed the back of his neck beneath the dark waves of hair clinging to his nape, in an attempt to remove the thick paste of perspiration and grime that had gathered there. The pungent odor of his own sweat assaulted his senses, pissing him off even more.

God, I hate the tropics.

And the heat didn't help his already low tolerance for bullshit. Normally, he didn't mind a little trash talk among his team in the Alliance when they were on a mission. He knew when it came down to it, he could count on them. But he didn't have the patience for it today. If they fucked up this mission, his months of tracking Jacob Stone would be for nothing.

And the trail ran out here, with one Tad Ralston. If Jack didn't get anything out of the congressional aide, then he had nothing more to go on, thereby bringing an end to their attempt to link Jacob Stone to the Illuminati and finally convince the Grand Council that their old enemies were a threat once more. Without Stone, the Alliance lacked the proof that the Illuminati had not been eliminated as they'd thought, and were in fact growing in strength, preparing to make their next move.

"Any progress on that facial rec, Ian?" Jack demanded, his tone harsher than he'd intended.

"Nothing yet." Ian sauntered over to a vacant bar stool and flashed a wide grin to a gorgeous brunette and her friends. Livingstone's gaze drifted away, apparently satisfied that Ian wasn't a threat.

"Heads up," Luke announced, his voice carrying that no-bullshit, steely edge Jack relied on. "Ralston's moving your way."

Jack glanced up and down the street, studying the sun-bronzed faces of the locals who scurried about, tending to their shops and barking sales pitches at sunburned tourists who weren't discerning enough not to buy the cheap, brightly painted souvenirs that were actually made in China. A few minutes later, he saw a man fitting Ralston's description hurrying toward the hotel, his gaze darting about nervously, his shoulders hunched a little as if expecting to be jumped at any moment.

He knows he's being followed . . .

There was no way he was on to Jack's team. They were far too experienced in surveillance, too accomplished at hiding in plain sight—it was the reason the Templars had survived after the order was dissolved in the Middle Ages and the Alliance had been formed to continue their mission to guide and protect.

No, Mr. Ralston was afraid of someone else.

Rising to his feet, Jack dropped a handful of pesos on the table for the waitress. "Here we go, folks. Maddie, love, you're on."

Jack didn't miss the way Livingstone's body stiffened with sudden interest the moment Ralston came into view. As the guy lurched to his feet, his gaze trained on the congressional aide, Jack picked up the pace, quickly darting through the network of café tables to intercept him.

"Livingstone's on the move," Jack barked, not bothering to keep his voice low.

He glanced back and forth between Ralston and Livingstone and saw Ralston's horrified expression of recognition before he sprinted toward the hotel's front door.

"Shit," Jack spat, bumping into one of the waitresses and sending her tray of drinks flying. He muttered a quick apology as he grabbed her shoulders and moved her out of his way. "Ralston's running."

Finally clear of the tangle of café patrons, Jack double-timed it to the hotel entrance, reaching the door just as Livingstone's hand grabbed the brass handle.

The guy's eyes narrowed menacingly. "Out of my way, asshole."

Livingstone was one hell of a lot bigger than he'd appeared from across the café. He towered over Jack's six feet and had at least fifty pounds of muscle on him. But even more interesting was his thick accent; Russian if Jack had to hazard a guess.

Jack gave him a guileless grin. "Why must we resort to name-calling? You just met me."

Without warning, the guy grabbed Jack by the front of his shirt and lifted him off his feet, sending him flying backward with ease before taking off around the side of the hotel. Jack grunted with the impact as he ass-planted in the hotel's flower beds—but not before catching a glimpse of the tattoo of a pyramid surrounded by a stylized starburst and the all-seeing eye on the man's forearm.

Jack hissed a curse as he scrambled to his feet and ran in the same direction the other man had gone, drawing his weapon from where it'd been hidden at the small of his back. He was just turning the corner when a bullet zinged past his head, narrowly missing him as it hit the bricks of a neighboring building.

He darted behind a trash Dumpster, taking cover. "Change of plans, Maddie. Get Ralston the hell out of here." He peeked out from behind the Dumpster and fired off two rapid shots before pulling back as bullets zinged off the metal Dumpster, sending up sparks. "And take care, love. Livingstone's Illuminati. His friends are probably already heading your way."

"More bad news, Jack," Luke cut in. "About half a dozen dudes carrying big fucking guns and not giving a damn who knows it just showed up. And they look seriously pissed off . . ."

Fear shot icy-hot through Maddie's veins when she heard more gunshots over the comm. She instinctively felt for the small Templar-cross pendant she normally wore around her neck, which was now tucked into the pocket of her shorts. Finding it still safely where she'd hidden it while changing into the uniform, she felt her fear subside ever so slightly.

But then another burst of gunfire erupted. Then silence. Complete silence.

Her fear for Jack's safety rushing to the surface once more, she grabbed her Glock from beneath the stack of towels where it was hidden on the housekeeping cart and quickened her pace toward Ralston's hotel room. "Jack? Do you copy?"

Nothing.

"Anybody have eyes on Jack?" she called out.

"Negative," Ian replied. "He's not in the alley. Stand by."

Maddie squeezed her eyes shut for a moment and blew out a harsh sigh, struggling to tamp down her dread and keep her attention focused on apprehending Ralston.

She tried to tell herself that she'd be just as worried about any of the other guys in the Alliance if they weren't responding, but she knew it was a lie. Jack was far more than just a colleague and friend—at least, he'd been far more to her for a time.

She gave herself a quick mental shake and forced her thoughts to focus on her redefined objective—apprehending Tad Ralston and bringing him in for questioning. After all, hadn't she just jumped Jack's case about him being over-protective of her? He'd been doing this one hell of a lot longer than she had. He would be okay. He had to be.

Maddie left her supply cart parked a few doors down and crept toward Ralston's room, her weapon held down at her side near her thigh, keeping it hidden from sight as much as possible in case anyone was to suddenly step into the hallway.

Another wave of dread washed over her when she reached Ralston's door, which stood slightly ajar. She darted past the opening to the other side of the doorway and peered into the room, taking in what she could in a glance. Not seeing anyone, she pressed her palm against the wood and slowly swung the door open, her gun raised as she swept inside, quickly clearing the room of any threats.

The place had been tossed, Ralston's clothes scattered on the bed and floor. The drawers to the dresser and nightstand stood open, their contents emptied in a hurry. She made her way through the debris toward the bathroom, careful not to step on anything and disturb the scene—habit from her days in the FBI.

When she entered the small bathroom she encountered more of the same—toiletry items scattered and broken, the overwhelming odor of spilled aftershave burning her nose. But there was no sign of Ralston or whoever it was who'd torn his room apart.

She cursed under her breath and wiped the perspiration from her forehead with the heel of her palm. The heat in the tiny bathroom was stifling, and the stench of Ralston's aftershave was making her stomach roll.

"Ralston's not here," she whispered as she came back into the bedroom. "I'm just going to—"

Her words died on a gasp as a figure in rumpled khakis and a sweat-soaked button-down suddenly appeared in the open doorway. She brought her gun up and the man's eyes went wide with fear behind his round spectacles before he bolted.

"Stop!" she barked, racing after him. "Ralston!"

He threw open the door to the stairs and dashed into the stairwell. Maddie was right on his heels, sprinting down the steps and closing the distance between them. "Ralston!"

He sent a panicked glance at her, then slammed open the door that exited to the outside.

"No!" she cried. "Don't—"

The loud crack of a gun cut across her words and Ralston fell back into the stairwell, blood spreading across his shoulder.

Maddie fired off a round as Ralston's assailant pulled

open the door and stepped inside to finish him off. The assailant flinched as her bullet nailed him in the side. He spun around to return fire but Maddie was quicker, nailing him twice in the chest. He hit the wall and slid down to the ground next to Ralston, who was alternately whimpering and groaning in fear and pain.

She bent and grabbed Ralston's good arm, helping him to his feet. "C'mon," she ordered, draping his arm across her shoulders. "We've got to get you outta here."

"They won't let me live," he blubbered. "It's over."

"What's over?" she huffed. The guy was a hell of a lot heavier than he looked. "Who wants to kill you—cartel or Illuminati?"

Ralston sent a startled glance her way. "How'd you . . . ?" Then his expression went slack as he realized the truth. "You're Alliance. But . . . you're a *woman*."

"Yep," she said, pushing open the door and helping Ralston into the alley. She tapped her comm. "I have Ralston, but he's hit. I need an evac from the alley on the west side of the hotel *now*."

"Uh, that's a negative on the evac," Ian replied, the sound of gunfire in the background. "I've got cartel on my ass—had to draw them away from Jack where he was pinned down with that Illuminati asshole. I'll meet up with you guys at the rendezvous point."

Luke joined in. "I'm on my way, Maddie." His voice was uneven, as if he had already abandoned his position and was on the move, the rhythmic pounding in the background telling her he was even now racing down the stairs of the building across the street. "Be there in two minutes."

"Better make it one, Luke." She then cursed under her breath and sent a sidelong glance toward Ralston, who was growing increasingly pale. "What the hell did you *do*? I thought you were supposed to be setting up a deal with the cartel."

He shook his head a little. "I was. But it went to hell. We were in the meeting . . . and someone opened fire. Killed Escobar and his men. They must think it was me."

"Okay, that explains the cartel wanting you dead," Maddie muttered, scanning up and down the alleyway searching for a way to get Ralston the hell out of there as soon as Luke arrived. "But why are your bosses in the Illuminati trying to delete you?"

The sound of squealing tires brought Maddie's head around and her gun up. But she heaved a sigh of relief when Jack lunged out of the Jeep and spread his arms wide, a gun in each hand as he covered the street. "Get in!"

Maddie half dragged Ralston toward the Jeep as quickly as the man's weight would allow. He was going limp, weak from blood loss. "Hang on, Ralston. We're almost there."

Sirens sounded in the distance, earning her an impatient glance from Jack. "Maddie, I don't mean to rush you . . ."

Maddie groaned as the man sagged against her. "C'mon, Tad, keep those feet moving. Trust me, a guy like you does *not* want to end up in a Mexican prison . . ." That seemed to rally the sagging Ralston, but when she glanced up she saw Luke had arrived, and had slipped in beside her and grabbed Ralston's belt, lifting him off his feet to hurry him along. She offered her future brother-in-law a grateful grin. "About time."

Luke returned her grin and opened the Jeep's back door. "One minute was *your* suggestion, not mine."

Maddie shoved Ralston into the backseat of the Jeep and jumped in after him just as the *policía* came into view. Luke slammed the door and dove into the front passenger seat. "I'm in!"

"Go, go, go!" Maddie yelled, punctuating each word with a slap on the headrest of Jack's seat as he stomped on the accelerator.

"Are you all right?" Jack demanded, sending a worried glance into the backseat. "Are you hit?"

She shook her head, turning her attention to Ralston's wound. "I'm okay." She sent a frantic glance around the inside of the Jeep, searching for a go-bag. Seeing none, her head snapped up. "This isn't our Jeep."

"Indeed," Jack agreed, taking a sharp corner and sending Ralston slamming into the door with a groan. "I borrowed it from our Illuminati friend."

Maddie braced herself as they flew over a bump, sending them airborne for a moment before they crashed back down. She tore off the uniform shirt, leaving her in just the sleeveless tank she'd been wearing underneath, and pressed the shirt to Ralston's wound to stanch the bleeding. "Where is he?"

"Dead." Jack glanced in the rearview mirror, checking the distance between them and the police before jerking the wheel to the right and taking a turn into a narrow street just wide enough for them to jet through. He shot out the other end, barely missing the cars speeding toward them. Horns blared as he briefly fishtailed, then wove in between the other cars.

Ralston cursed weakly, drawing Maddie's attention back to him. "I fucked up. Oh God, I totally fucked up."

"Luke, see if you can reach Ian," Jack said, turning the wrong way onto a one-way street and leaping the median to cross into the traffic on the other side. "I've not heard him on the comm in the last couple of minutes." He then glanced up into the rearview mirror. "We already know that you work for Congressman Hale and that you were sent down here to broker the deal with the cartel. Now, I'd like to hear what else you were up to, if you please, Mr. Ralston."

When Ralston hesitated Maddie said gently, "We can protect you. Just tell us what we need to know."

He swallowed hard. "There was more going on than just the deal with the cartel. Before I came to Mexico I got a call from a former KGB operative named Sergei Antonovich—"

"Antonovich?" Jack glanced into the backseat, frowning.

"—said he had something he wanted to sell. Information about a hit on an Alliance operative in Moscow and another one in London. He said he'd turn it over to the Alliance if we didn't pay him what he was asking."

Maddie's gaze flicked toward Jack, wondering what exactly he knew about the former KGB operative. "And your bosses in the Illuminati knew about the deal you'd made?"

Ralston nodded, wincing as they bounced over a pothole. "Of course. I don't have access to that kind of money."

Jack muttered a curse. "Did you get the information?"

Ralston nodded again. "Yeah. I was supposed to turn it over to my handler, but . . ."

"But you double-crossed them," Maddie guessed. When he nodded, she sank back against the seat for a moment. No wonder they were trying to kill him. "Who did you offer the information to?"

"A reporter named Claire Davenport," Ralston said.

Jack's brow furrowed into a deeper frown. "How do you know Claire?"

A better question might be how Jack *knows this Claire Davenport . . .*

Ralston had to take a few breaths before he answered. "We went to college together, so I reached out to her when I realized what I had. She said the paper she works for would pay me for the story."

"Where's this information now?" Jack demanded, his tone harsher than Maddie had ever heard it. "Do you still have it?"

She sent a baffled look Jack's way. *What the hell is his*

problem? With an exasperated sigh she said to Ralston, "Is that what they were looking for in your hotel room?"

"Yeah," he told her, his eyelids growing heavy. "But I already mailed the flash drive to Claire. She's going to confront Congressman Hale about it at his Fourth of July gala in Boston."

"I can't raise Ian," Luke interjected, pocketing his phone. He and Jack exchanged a glance. Maddie could see their concern in their expressions, even though Luke added, "I'm sure he's fine. Dude knows what he's doing."

Jack gave a terse nod and jerked the wheel, spinning the Jeep around in a U-turn and earning more infuriated honking and more than a few crude gestures. "We've got to get that flash drive before Hale gets his hands on it. What else can you tell us?"

But Ralston's lids had fluttered closed.

"Ralston's losing a lot of blood," Maddie said. "How long before we reach the airstrip? He needs medical attention."

Luke turned back to assess the situation, but his face was grim. "We're still—"

The window in Maddie's door shattered, cutting off Luke's words. She cried out and ducked down, shoving Ralston onto the seat and shielding him as the car next to them slammed into the Jeep.

Jack hissed a curse and jerked the wheel, returning the assault as Luke fired out his window at another car that was accelerating to ram them from behind. Then, with the steely calm Maddie was accustomed to, Jack held a hand out. "Maddie, your weapon, please."

Maddie shoved her Glock into his hand. Without missing a beat, he aimed it out the window and fired with barely a glance. Immediately, the car swerved away as the driver slumped over the wheel. Maddie lifted her head in time to see the sedan crossing into oncoming traffic and onto the opposite curb where it slammed into a concrete wall painted with a brightly colored mural.

She ducked back down with a sharp curse when the Jeep's back window shattered.

Luke fired off two more shots. "Clear," he announced a few seconds later.

She lifted her head and glanced behind them to see the other car had come to a stop in the middle of the street, several bullet holes in the windshield. She closed her eyes on a sigh, then turned back to check on Ralston.

Her stomach sank when she saw his wide, vacant expression. "Damn it!" She slumped back against the seat, her shoulders sagging as she met Jack's gaze in the mirror. "Ralston's dead."

Jack nodded, his jaw going tight. Then he jerked the wheel, hopping the median to head back in the opposite direction.

"Where are we going?" Maddie asked. "The airport is in the other direction."

"We're going back for Ian," Jack told her. He turned to Luke. "Get on the phone with headquarters and get a lock on Ian's location."

"He said he'd meet us at the rendezvous point," Maddie reminded him. "Shouldn't we go wait for him there?"

When Jack didn't immediately respond, she glanced between Jack and Luke, their grim expressions telling her all she needed to know. "He's down."

Jack's grip on the steering wheel tightened. "I'm not leaving a member of my team behind."

Chapter Two

Commander Will Asher paced his office, his scowl deepening. Jack had been vague when he'd called to report in about events in Mexico City. Will didn't like vague. In fact, it pissed him off. He wanted facts, details. And Jack fucking knew it. Which was what had him worried.

Jack was not only one of his most trusted men, he was Will's oldest friend. They'd grown up together, their fathers both having served the Alliance and brought their sons up to eventually take the oath as well. Jack knew Will better than anyone else. So if Jack was hiding something from him with a promise of more info when they returned to Chicago, it had to be some serious shit.

A knock on the door brought Will up short. "Enter."

Adam Watanabe strode in and bowed in greeting, then stood at attention directly in front of him—not because Will demanded it but because Adam's code of honor and sense of duty required it. He was the most disciplined of any Templar Will had ever known, but Will hoped that Adam might eventually feel like he wasn't just a guest with them in Chicago. Hell, maybe one day the guy would eventually even call him by his name instead of his rank.

"I've taken care of the arrangements with Hale's office

for returning Tad Ralston's body, Commander," Adam assured him.

Will crossed his arms over his chest and leaned back against the edge of his desk. "What story are we telling?"

"Wrong place, wrong time," Adam told him. "Caught in the middle of crossfire between two rival drug dealers while on a business trip to Mexico City. Not entirely untrue."

Will nodded. "And his remains?"

"They will be sent to his family in Rhode Island," Adam informed him. "We have already notified his parents and sister."

"How about Congressman Hale?" Will prompted. "What was his reaction?"

Adam's mouth curved up at the corner—which was about the most Will had ever seen the man smile. "He was appropriately saddened to learn of the 'tragic death of a young man who had such a promising career.'" Adam lifted a sardonic brow. "I imagine you will hear the same statement in the press release tomorrow."

Will's mouth twisted with disgust. "The bastard probably had a statement prepared before he even got the call."

At that moment, a man with shaggy, sun-bleached hair and wearing a horribly gaudy Hawaiian shirt, ratty jeans, and well-worn red Chucks sauntered into the office. "Right you are, boss-man." Elliot "Finn" Finnegan—their tech specialist and resident genius—offered Will his wide, easy grin, a striking contrast to Adam's formality. "Your third eye is totally rockin' today, brah."

"Don't need a third eye to see bullshit a mile away," Will assured him. He jerked his chin at the device Finn held. "What'd you find?"

Finn tapped his tablet and then swiped a finger across the surface, throwing an image up onto one of the monitors on Will's wall. "Congressman Hale sent out an email message to his staff within two minutes of Adam's call to his office. Another went out to the press immediately after. The messages were already written and waiting in his drafts folder. All he had to do was add a vague statement based on the misinformation Adam provided."

"They never planned to let Ralston live," Adam said. "They were going to eliminate him no matter what happened."

"Where's the flash drive that Jack was talking about?" Will demanded. When Adam and Finn traded a cautious glance, Will raised his brows. "Well?"

Adam cleared his throat. "Jack said Ralston had already sent the flash drive to a reporter."

Will frowned. "Okay . . . So who's the reporter?"

Finn studiously avoided Will's gaze, pretending to fiddle with his tablet. "Dunno. Sorry, boss."

What the hell is their problem? "I've seen you track tougher shit than this, Finn," Will insisted. "Finding out where Ralston mailed the package should be cake. Why is this person's name not already on the screen?"

Finn squirmed a little before explaining, "So, here's the thing . . . Jack wouldn't tell us the name of the reporter and told me not to look into it. He said he wanted to talk to you about it personally."

Will lifted a brow in challenge. "Last time I checked, you reported to *me*, Elliot."

Finn winced at Will's use of his first name, but then dipped his chin slightly. "Uh, yes, sir, I do. And I certainly prefer that to sitting in the federal prison where you found me, trust me. But I figured if Jack was asking me to keep something from you, he had a damned good reason."

As much as Will hated to admit it, Finn had a point. Will pegged Adam with a pointed look. "How about you? You get the same impression?"

Adam inclined his head slightly. "I have only been among my brothers in Chicago for a short time and am still learning your dynamics, Commander. But I must trust that if one of you wishes to keep something from another, he has a good reason, and it is not my place to interfere."

Will crossed his arms over his broad chest and heaved a harsh sigh. "What about the photo Ian sent of the Illuminati's spook? Can you at least give me something there, or is that top secret too?"

Finn swiped his finger over his tablet again. "That I can help with." He nodded toward another monitor. "Meet Egor Poleski. According to my pals at Interpol, this was one scary dude. Hired muscle for the Russian mob most recently, but was making friends all over Eastern Europe long before that. If it's nasty and violent, this guy has been accused of it. After his mob employers were taken out when an arms deal went south, he went freelance. I'm guessing that's how he came to the attention of our Illuminati friends."

"And his status is confirmed?" Will prompted.

Finn threw another couple of images up on the screen. These appeared to be crime scene photos. Poleski's body was sprawled out in an alleyway, his eyes vacant, his mouth agape, a bullet hole in the center of his chest and another in the center of his forehead. "Yep. Dead as a doornail."

"And the others?" Will asked.

"Well," Finn said, "I got a German, an American, a few locals, and a Colombian, but all appear to be hired guns with no connection to the Illuminati that I can discern. My guess is they're mercs Poleski hired."

Will's phone began to buzz at his hip, drawing his attention away from the monitors. He snatched it from his belt and glanced at the number.

Shit. "I gotta take this," he said to his men. "Keep digging on the mercs and make sure we can't connect them to any known operatives." He waited a beat until after they'd left his office and closed the door before he answered his phone. "Asher."

"I thought we had agreed that you would not pursue this obsession you have with the Illuminati."

"Good evening, Grandfather," Will replied to the Alliance's High Commander, forcing his voice to remain even and unconcerned. "I figured you might be calling."

"William, I have warned you about what could happen if you continue to persist with this nonsense. And now I find an urgent email from you to the Grand Council on this very topic."

Will's stomach churned at his grandfather's words. The man had been instrumental in destroying the Illuminati's stranglehold on the world, decades earlier. And they'd all believed the Illuminati to be defunct, never questioning the High Commander's insistence that the problem had been taken care of. Not until everything had come to a head with Jacob Stone, and evidence pointed to the man being in league with the Illuminati organization.

But in spite of Will's assertions to the Grand Council that their enemy was thriving and making a play to regain their ruthless grip on the world, there were only a handful taking the threat seriously. He wished his grandfather, as High Commander of the Alliance, was among them.

"And I've warned *you* about what is going to happen if we don't act," Will returned. "We've confirmed that the man who went after Tad Ralston was Illuminati."

"Have you now?" the High Commander drawled. "And how exactly did you confirm this theory of yours? A *tattoo*? He could've had it done at any tattoo parlor. The symbol is hardly a secret."

"You think I don't know the difference?" Will demanded. "After all the years of studying those assholes and what they did to my father?"

"Have you considered that Jacob Stone has created an

elaborate little charade to make you think there is a threat? To keep you chasing phantoms and shadows instead of the very real threat that is a spoiled, pampered little bastard who feels he's entitled to my position within the Alliance because of some imaginary wrong against his family?"

Will held back a sigh and ran a hand through his sable hair. "Perception is reality. Regardless of whether he has revived the Illuminati himself and fooled others into believing him, or if the remnants of the Illuminati have re-formed and are using Jacob as their poster boy, there's still a threat that we can't continue to ignore."

"I will not order additional resources to aid this quixotic little endeavor of yours, William, until I have undeniable proof that the Illuminati are among us—in the truest sense, not some trumped-up smoke screen for Stone's ambition."

Will's grip on his phone tightened as he attempted to keep his frustration in check. "Sir, all I ask—"

"If I hear another word on it, I will be forced to set aside the fact that you are my only remaining grandson, and respond accordingly," the High Commander interrupted. "I will not be challenged and humiliated in this manner. Are we clear?"

Will ground his back teeth together, his jaw muscles twitching from the strain. Finally, after a long, tense moment, he ground out, "Of course, sir."

The moment the call disconnected, Will stormed from his office, his heavy footsteps echoing through the concrete tunnel that connected their ops center to the homes aboveground.

"Where ya headed, boss-man?" Finn called out from behind him.

Will glanced back to see Finn leaning out the door to his situation room, a concerned frown creasing his brow. "I'm going out."

"Want some company?" Finn asked.

"No," Will snapped, not bothering to offer any other explanation. After all, he didn't want Finn tipping off Jack to the fact that Will would be waiting for his team the moment they deplaned. No point giving Jack time to figure out a way to avoid him. There were only a couple of reasons Will could think of for Jack to keep intel from him, and none of them were particularly pleasant options. But he didn't give a shit. Whatever the reason, Will was determined to get some goddamned answers.

Jacob Stone rose naked from his bed and silenced the ringer on his cell phone as he glanced behind him, ensuring the call hadn't wakened his wife. He strode into the adjacent sitting room, which was bathed in moonlight, adding an eerie quality to the already heavy silence.

"Do you have it?" he demanded by way of greeting.

The caller hesitated a moment, telling Jacob all he needed to know before he even answered, "No, Master. The Alliance intercepted Ralston before we could."

Jacob clenched his fist, his manicured nails digging into the palm. "And the team responsible for this ineptitude?"

"Dead." There was no hesitation this time.

"At whose hand?" Jacob pressed. "*Please* tell me that they were executed before an audience of their peers to illustrate what happens to the Faithful who fail me."

Jacob could practically feel the man's balls tightening with fear. And he definitely heard his hard swallow. "Unfortunately, they died in pursuit of the Alliance team who intercepted Ralston."

Jacob paced the moonlit room with furious strides, clenching and unclenching his fist. "Who led the team? Was it Asher?"

"No, Master. I believe it was Jack Grayson."

Jacob's pacing slowed. Jack. His old friend. He felt a

brief stab of guilt for the betrayal he'd perpetrated against his former brethren. He had once called them all *brother*, had fought alongside them as a member of the Alliance, bled alongside them. But it was he who was betrayed first, wasn't it? He'd been meant for greatness, destined for the highest office within the Alliance. And they'd ousted him, forced him into the indignity of becoming a *confrere* against his will, to *oblige* them. Like a fucking *servant*.

His gut twisted with disgust and fury, supplanting his guilt. "Who was with him? I want their names."

Jacob heard tapping on a keyboard as the man apparently looked for the information requested. "Luke Rogan, Ian Cooper, and the new woman . . . Madeleine Blake."

Jacob hissed a curse. *Maddie*. The woman who was his mentor's eldest daughter—she'd been like a sister to him most of his life. Her sister, Sarah, had been a regrettable target of Jacob's failed plan several months earlier. Now it seemed he would have Maddie in his crosshairs as well. The ache of this realization was far worse than his regret about Jack.

He ran a hand through his hair with a sigh. "Where is the flash drive Ralston was supposed to have intercepted?"

"We're not entirely sure, Master," the man admitted. "It wasn't in his hotel room."

"If he handed it off to the Alliance, they'll be moving quickly to act upon the data," Jacob mused. "And if he didn't, they'll most assuredly know where he hid it. I want someone monitoring Jack Grayson's every move."

"Yes, Master."

Jacob disconnected the call, his shoulders sagging. He'd been given a second chance to prove himself after the debacle with the treasure. The last damned thing he needed was for the proof of the Illuminati's existence to fall into the hands of the Alliance. The Illuminati weren't yet ready. They were still positioning themselves, putting all of their pawns upon the board.

But soon.

And when that happened, Jacob would unseat his son of a bitch grandfather and take control of the Illuminati himself. His Faithful would see to that. They recognized that Jacob was the One True Master—not the asshole who called himself Jacob's family.

When Jacob had been de-cloaked, forced from the Alliance after screwing up a mission, his grandfather hadn't bothered to offer any support. He'd been too ashamed to show his face at Jacob's de-cloaking—never mind that the son of bitch was even then plotting against the Alliance to restore the Illuminati to power.

Angus Stone had betrayed everyone in his life that supposedly mattered to him. It wasn't exactly a shock to Jacob that the hypocritical asshole would betray him too. That bastard would've put a bullet in Jacob's head a few months earlier had it not been for the beautiful woman lying in his bed.

The quiet creak of floorboards behind him brought Jacob's head around. As if sensing his thoughts, his new bride had awakened and was gliding toward him, every sway of her hips meant to seduce him into submission.

"Who was that?" she asked, draping her arms around his neck.

"One of the Faithful," he told her, not bothering to suppress a shiver of desire as he pulled her close. "The mission failed."

Her expression went instantly hard. "And they paid for their incompetence, I presume?"

"Of course," he assured her, leaving out that the Alliance had been good enough to take care of the problem for him. "I was weak before, Allison. I was too merciful. I realize I allowed sentimentality to get in the way of our vision.

But no longer. Those who have wronged us will pay for their transgressions."

"Call in the twins," she urged. "They have offered their allegiance to you already. All you have to do is ask for their assistance and it's yours."

The men she spoke of—Stefan and Demetrius Shepherd—were among his grandfather's trusted circle of assassins. They'd been deployed on numerous occasions with maximum effect. But they were dangerous. And not people Jacob wanted to be beholden to.

Jacob shook his head. "No, not yet. They may have said they will side with me when I take control, but I don't trust them. I'll handle this myself."

This brought a smile back to her lips. "Soon, Jacob, you will be the most powerful man in the world. And I will be right there beside you, guiding you to greatness . . ." She brought her lips close to his ear. "Fulfilling our every desire."

He pulled back, peering down at her, studying the coldness in her eyes, surprised he'd never seen it there before. "And what do *you* desire, my darling? You can't tell me that you'll be content to just hang on my arm when I take control."

Her smile grew, a hungry look coming into her pale blue eyes, making them gleam in a way that honestly made Jacob a little nervous. "I want what *you* want, Jacob—power, influence, the world at my feet. I saw that ambition in you the moment your grandfather sent me to your office and have seen it every day since. It's why I fell in love with you."

He brought her hand to his lips and pressed a kiss to her fingers. "Then you shall have it, Allison. You shall have all your heart desires and more."

Chapter Three

"Mind if I join you?"

Jack's gaze came up from the book he'd been reading during the journey from Mexico City to Chicago. He hated flying, hated it with a passion that compared to little else, so burying himself in some book or another was about the only way he could manage a trip of such duration. Well, that and an ounce or two of well-aged scotch. And, up to then, none of the others had interrupted him, knowing well the ritual he depended upon to maintain his sanity.

And yet now he found himself looking into Maddie's sympathetic forest-green gaze and not minding the interruption at all, even though he clearly was the object of her pity. "Pardon?"

Maddie gestured toward the vacant seat next to him. "Do you mind?"

"Of course not," he said, forcing a weak smile. As welcome as her presence would always be, having her so near was torture. And it was especially difficult at the moment, when he desperately wanted to feel her arms around him, to seek the comfort and peace he'd only ever known in her embrace.

They sat in awkward silence for a long moment before she said softly, "I'm so sorry, Jack."

Jack took a deep breath and let it out slowly before dropping his gaze to the body bag lying in the aisle of the Alliance's private jet. They'd found Ian lying facedown in a pool of his own blood, inches away from the vehicle that would've taken him to safety. A few seconds sooner and he would've escaped the assholes who'd shot him in the back.

"Ian was a good man," Jack told her.

"I didn't know him very well yet," Maddie said, her hands clasped between her knees. "Did he have any family?"

Jack shook his head. Hell, most of them didn't. The Alliance intentionally recruited from among those with few connections to tie them down and distract them from their missions. There were a few exceptions—Luke being one of the few who'd found love and happiness and was successfully managing to balance his new family and his duty to the Alliance. The others—like Jack and Will—had family ties only because of their families' legacy with the Alliance. Having witnessed the heartache—and tragedy—his own family had experienced, Jack would never have asked a woman to join him in this life. The risks were too great.

Which made it all the harder to have Maddie join the Alliance as the first female initiate. The thought of someday having to bring *her* home in a body bag had been haunting his nightmares every night for months, tormenting him to the point of madness.

"I think you should reconsider your association with the Alliance," he announced. "After what happened today—"

"I am a trained law enforcement agent, Jack," Maddie reminded him. "I can take care of myself. I don't need you treating me different from any other member of your team."

He closed the book and set it aside, taking a moment to consider his words. "I am well aware of your capabilities, Maddie. I witnessed them firsthand—as I'm sure you recall."

She flushed, no doubt remembering the case that had reunited them briefly a few years after their initial affair, when Maddie had been a rookie agent with the FBI. Jack had been called in to assist by their *confreres* in the Bureau when the case got a little too close to the Alliance's interests. Once again they'd been unable to resist the attraction between them. But this time it'd been Maddie who'd walked away.

"Of course I do," she said, her voice losing its hard, angry edge, her gaze growing softer. "But . . ." She glanced around to make sure Luke was otherwise occupied and not listening in, then took a deep breath and let it out on a long sigh that sounded surprisingly mournful. "I know it's only because you care, Jack. And I appreciate that. You're my best friend—"

Friend. The word stung like venom, her accent upon the word so slight he couldn't even guess as to whether it was intentional or an unconscious reminder of where things stood between them.

"—but you have to let me do my job. I need the others to see me as their equal."

Her hand covered his, her fingers pressing lightly against his skin when she squeezed. It seemed meant to be an innocent touch, a gesture of friendship. And yet his lungs went tight in an instant, as desire for her gripped him. He closed his eyes before she could see how much he wanted her, and dipped his head, hoping to compose himself.

But when he opened his eyes, he saw her peering down at their hands. Her full lips parted just enough to expel a sharp gasp when he smoothed his thumb over her skin, her lids dropping just enough to shield her eyes from him. He studied her lovely face, from her flushed cheeks to her delectable lips to the smattering of freckles across the bridge of her nose, which he'd always found so adorable.

He leaned in toward her, bringing their heads so close together that when he whispered her name and she lifted those remarkable eyes to his, it would've taken nothing more than a fraction of movement from either of them to end their suffering with a kiss.

"I will try to be what you need me to be," he murmured, "if you give me the chance."

Maddie's gaze held his for a long moment before she finally said, "I can't."

He blinked, startled by her flat denial of his offer.

His brows came together in a frown. "Sorry, what?"

"I can't work another mission with you, Jack," she insisted, slipping her fingers from his grasp. "Working on this op together was a mistake. I'll make sure it doesn't happen again."

"And how exactly do you intend to do that?" he pressed. "Will isn't going to continue to make accommodations for us because of our history. That was one of the conditions of your joining our team. And I think he's been far more sensitive to the situation than most in his position would've been."

She leaned back and stared hard at the back of the seat in front of her. "I think it might be best if I transferred to another team."

Jack's frown deepened. "You can't be serious."

She sighed, keeping her eyes averted. "I'm going to talk to the commander when we get back to headquarters to see if he can place me with the team in Seattle. I already know the men there because of my father, and—"

"Twenty minutes until we land," Luke announced abruptly from where he was stretched out on the plush leather sofa across from their bank of seats. "If you've got any unfinished business, better take care of it now. Just got a text from Finn letting us know that Will's meeting us at the hangar."

Jack's attention abruptly shifted to Luke, even as he made a mental note that this conversation was far from over. "Will is coming out to meet us? Damn. He never debriefs until we get back to headquarters."

"He's gotta know we're keeping something from him," Luke said. "I understand not telling him about Ian over the phone. But why not share the name of Ralston's reporter friend?"

He'd known Will for far too long to deliver that kind of bombshell over the phone. And, lucky him, he'd have to break that shitty piece of news to him right after telling him one of his best hadn't made it home.

Jack leaned back in his seat and closed his eyes, walling himself off from both Luke and Maddie, dreading the moment when he'd have to face his commander and best friend and tell him why only three of them got off the plane . . .

Maddie sat in silence the rest of the flight, even though she was dying to know what it was about Claire Davenport that had Jack frowning so fiercely that he forgot all about his fear of flying—or their conversation about her leaving the Chicago commandery. At that moment, though, she had her own thoughts to untangle.

Reaching for Jack's hand had been instinctive, a simple gesture of friendship. But she hadn't expected it to affect either of them as much as it clearly had. After all, she'd been the one to put the brakes on their relationship last time. Too afraid to have her heart broken again by a man whose top priority was his vow to the Alliance, she'd decided it would be better for both of them if she insisted that they keep their relationship platonic.

And it had worked—to a point. She'd at least had the benefit of his friendship for the last several years. Long-distant though it was, it had been *something*. And she'd told herself that it was enough, that what they'd shared had been amazing, but it was over. Then one touch had dispelled all of her flimsy self-delusions. She was as much in love with Jack as ever.

Her determination to ask Commander Asher for a transfer had been a spur-of-the-moment decision. She'd just thrown out the first idea that had come to mind. She needed to put some distance between her and Jack. And fast. She could feel his desire for her in the warmth of his gaze, the gentleness of his touch as he'd smoothed her skin.

And it was torture.

Maddie was trying desperately to ignore the nearness of him and how it made her heart pound and her senses come alive, when the slight lurch of the plane landing forced her to get her shit together and shove her emotions down deep. Everyone was already talking, she knew, speculating about what was going on between her and Jack. They didn't need any more fuel for *that* fire. She just needed to walk away. Maybe then they could just go on pretending that they were over each other . . .

"Maddie?"

She glanced over to see Jack staring at her expectantly. "Yeah?"

"We've arrived," he informed her.

She glanced around to see Luke had already left the plane. She gave herself a mental shake and stepped into the aisle to grab her bag, but, ever the gentleman, Jack rose to his feet and reached for her bag at the same time, his body brushing against hers. They both paused, the contact bringing them up short.

Maddie raised her eyes to Jack's, her gaze holding his as he lifted her duffel bag from the bin and slowly brought it down. Maddie swallowed hard, suddenly finding it hard to breathe. And for one crazy, dizzying moment, Maddie thought he might actually kiss her. Dear God . . . she *hoped* he would, longed for it. The thought of his lips against hers again consumed her in those few, heavy seconds.

But a quiet cough broke the spell and she jumped away as much as the narrow aisle would allow, practically sprinting toward the door, where Luke stood looking a little embarrassed at intruding upon their moment.

"We're coming," Maddie mumbled. As she tried to squeeze by him, her future brother-in-law gave her a searching look, asking a question she didn't even know how to answer.

As she raced down the steps the landing crew had provided, she nearly collided with their commander, his unshakable, muscled frame making for an impressive barrier to her escape.

"Jack and Ian coming?" he demanded, his scowl far more ferocious than usual.

She hesitated, then nodded, knowing it should be Jack who broke the news to their commander about losing a member of the team.

"You and Jack good?" he asked, apparently misreading her hesitation.

Maddie cursed the heat she could feel creeping into her cheeks at his question. *Great.* Now she *really* looked guilty of something inappropriate. What the hell was her problem? She'd been able to go up against suspects who would make even the most hardened law enforcement officer nervous, and yet she was acting like a silly schoolgirl with a crush on the captain of the football team.

Fortunately, before she had to answer Will's penetrating gaze shifted above her head to where Jack was unhurriedly coming down the steps behind her. "What the hell's going on, Jack? What's with all the cloak-and-dagger bullshit?"

Jack met his old friend's furious gaze and held it for a moment. "Ian's dead, Will."

A myriad of emotions seemed to play out on Will's face in the next few seconds before he finally hung his head, his hands on his hips as he took a moment to absorb the information. Finally he hissed a series of curses and lifted his gaze. "How?"

"Shot by the cartel," Luke supplied. "He got separated from us trying to draw them away from Jack."

Maddie's attention shifted briefly to Jack. The implication that Ian had lost his life in order to save one of his brothers wasn't lost on him. She could see it in the way his eyes clouded over with regret and sorrow.

When she turned her attention back to their commander, Will was nodding solemnly. "I'll alert the Grand Council."

"You want me to take care of the arrangements for his funeral?" Jack asked.

Will shook his head. "No, I'll handle it."

Maddie was still learning the customs and traditions of the Alliance, but based on the look of surprise that passed between Luke and Jack, she gathered that it wasn't typical for the commander to handle the arrangements for a fallen brother.

"Now," Will continued, "you want to tell me what the hell else was worth keeping from me?"

Maddie turned in time to see Jack lift a brow and tilt his head to the side in the way she knew indicated now was not the time and place for whatever discussion the two men needed to have.

"Why don't we wait until we return to the compound?"

Jack suggested, glancing at her and Luke. Maddie wasn't sure about Luke, but she sure as hell wanted to know the connection to the reporter and why it was such a delicate matter with their commander.

When Jack started to go around his commander to where a pair of black Hummer H2's waited to take them home, Will smoothly stepped in front of him, crossing his arms over his chest. "Who's the reporter? We're not leaving this hangar until I get a name. Now quit dicking around, Jack." His tone softened a little as he added, "I already know Antonovich is involved. What could possibly be worse than that?"

Jack heaved a sigh and sent another glance around the group. "It's Claire Davenport."

Will's face went slack, his crossed arms slowly drifting down to hang loose at his sides. He was clearly shocked by the name. Then his expression morphed into what seemed to be a mixture of anger and concern. "Of all the hard-headed, stubborn, pains in the ass . . . She has no idea what she's up against. She'll end up getting herself killed! What the hell is she *thinking*?"

Maddie looked to Jack for an answer, not sure if Will's question was rhetorical or if he thought maybe someone had the answer. To Maddie's surprise, Jack actually *did* have a theory.

"I imagine she thought it might lead her to you."

Will shot a look Jack's way that would've made anyone else under his command wither—Maddie included. But Maddie had learned long ago that Jack wasn't the kind of man to shrink from anyone. And from what she'd heard, the two men had been through a lot together over the years. She didn't know the details—just the references the other, longer-serving members of the team had alluded to as if she should know the story because of her association with

Jack. Regardless, it was clear to her even as a newbie that Jack was a valued friend to a man who seemed to intentionally keep everyone at a distance.

"Where's Claire now?" Will demanded.

Jack shrugged a shoulder casually. "I have no idea. Set Finn on her now that you have a name, and I'm certain you'll discover she's headed to Boston—if she's not already there. Ralston told us Claire plans to confront Hale at his Fourth of July gala."

Will gave a sharp nod, then jerked his chin at Luke. "We're taking Ian back to the compound. Hope you got a little shut-eye on the plane because I want a full debrief on the mission in Mexico City when we get there." When Luke returned to the plane to retrieve Ian's body, Will nodded toward Jack and Maddie. "You two get back to the compound and grab some fresh gear. I want you on a plane to Boston ASAP."

Maddie's eyes went wide at the order. "Wait. What?" Will turned and took a few long strides toward the waiting H2's, but Maddie hurried after him. "Will, I can't go to Boston."

He pivoted, giving her the same look he'd given Jack only moments before. "I'm sorry. What was that, *initiate*?"

This brought Maddie up short. True, she was the daughter of a U.S. senator who was one of the most powerful and influential *confreres* to the Alliance. Also true that she was a former FBI agent who'd proven herself over and over again in her training with her Alliance brethren. But all of her family ties and credentials meant precisely *shit* until she officially took her vow to the Alliance and became a Templar.

She took a bracing breath and tried a different approach. "Commander Asher, could I please have a moment to speak with you about this mission? In fact, about my assignment to your commandery? I don't think it's a good idea to put me on another mission with Jack. I need—"

"You *need*?" he interrupted. "Ms. Blake, you understood what you were asking when you petitioned me to join the Alliance, correct? I broke centuries' worth of rules by accepting a woman as an initiate—not just because I thought it was about damned time the Alliance allowed women to take the oath but because I also thought you would be one hell of an asset to this team. But you knew there would be sacrifices, that sometimes we would have to put our own personal needs and desires aside for a greater good. Am I right?"

She pursed her lips for a moment, knowing he was right and feeling like the most selfish, childish bitch on the planet. "Yes, sir."

He jabbed an angry finger at Luke, who was coming down the steps from the plane, the body bag containing Ian's corpse draped over his broad shoulders. "Because if that message is a little hazy, you can see the evidence of it right there in a fucking body bag! I guarantee you Ian knew that he might not make it out when he drew off those assholes trying to take out you and Jack. You want to talk to me about what you can and can't do? What you *need*?"

"No, sir," she choked out. "Forgive me for even mentioning it."

"I want that flash drive retrieved before Claire Davenport digs too deep and gets herself killed," he ordered, addressing both her and Jack now. "I don't need more deaths on our heads."

Clearly, Will meant that to be the end of their conversation, but Maddie wasn't quite ready to give up. If Will was going to keep her on this assignment, she wanted to go into it with her eyes wide open. "Commander," she said, "why not just go ask this reporter for the flash drive? Pretend to be federal agents or something and confiscate it before she has a chance to look at the data?"

"Claire's a smart woman," Will informed her, his anger at her seeming to ebb slightly now that he saw she had accepted her mission. "She'll make copies, have backups. And, if Ralston wasn't bullshitting you, she's going to show up at that gala in Boston in two days, prepared for a confrontation."

"And how exactly does this involve me?" Maddie pressed. When his expression grew irritated she held up her hands. "I'm not being difficult. I just want to know what you see as my part in this mission."

Will studied her for a moment; then, apparently realizing she was on the level, he explained, "You have connections in Boston that will make it easier for us to infiltrate the appropriate circles before Claire does." He sent a meaningful glance Jack's way. "And Jack will need to keep her busy while you deal with the congressman."

When her jaw went slack in shock at his implication, Will's expression hardened.

She took a step closer, lowering her voice as she said through clenched teeth, "Is this your way of forcing Jack and me to deal with our issues? Making me watch as he seduces another *woman*?"

Will's brows came together. "I don't give a shit about your issues with Jack as long as they don't interfere with the job that needs to be done. If you can't handle the fact that we sometimes have to do things that are unpleasant, then I think you might want to reconsider that desk job with the Bureau."

"Commander—"

"Let me make one thing very clear to you," he interrupted. "I have made some allowances because you're new to this and are still figuring out that I'm not your *pal*, Ms. Blake. I am your commander. If you can't take orders when

I give them, you and I are going to have a serious problem. Is that clear?"

Maddie realized that his warning was more than that— it was a threat. She was screwing up big-time by questioning him, by expecting special treatment because of who her father was. And wasn't that exactly what she'd told Jack she *didn't* want?

She heard Will heave another sigh, and when she met his gaze she noticed it had softened. His hand was gentle, comforting when he reached out and gripped her upper arm. "I guarantee you, Maddie, if someone gets his hands on that information before we do, what *you* need, what *I* need . . . none of it will matter a damn. And Ian's death will be for nothing. Because if that intel contains the proof that the Illuminati exist, then it no doubt contains the proof that the Alliance does as well. If our existence and influence is proven, all we've built will fall apart. And the oath that our fathers all took, that my and Jack's fathers *died* for, would mean nothing. I need you on this mission. Can I count on you?"

Maddie studied Will Asher for a long moment, truly understanding for the first time how a man his age could rise so quickly to one of the most powerful positions within the Alliance. She lifted her chin a notch and squared her shoulders. "What do you need me to do?"

He gave her a curt nod, a hint of a proud smile tugging at the corner of his mouth. "Finn will send you all the specifics when you get settled in Boston. For now, I just need you to get your asses moving."

With that, he strode back to the H2 where Luke waited, trying to look like he hadn't heard the dressing-down she'd just received. Maddie hung back for a moment and felt Jack come up behind her, the warmth of his presence enveloping her.

"Are you sure you're okay with this?" he asked. "If not, I'll talk to Will. I can go on my own."

She shook her head. "No, he was right." She turned her head, giving him a sidelong glance. "And so were you."

Before he could ask what she meant, she took out her cell phone and dialed a number she never thought she'd call again. It made her stomach churn when she heard the voice on the other end of the line. "Senator Miles! How are you? I'm going to be in Boston for a few days and would love to see you while I'm in town . . ."

When she finished the call she threw her bag into the back of the H2 and turned to where Jack was leaning a hip against the vehicle, arms crossed over his chest as he waited. "Well?"

"Well, thanks to that perv's crush on me, we now have two tickets to the congressman's little shindig. Make sure you bring something pretty to wear."

She heard his chuckle as she climbed into the H2 and had to close her eyes for a moment as the sound made her chest go tight. God . . . even the sound of his laughter made her heart ache. If it was already this bad just being around him as little as she'd managed to be so far, the next few days were going to be sheer torture . . .

"You didn't say a word when I was ripping Maddie a new one."

Jack swung his bag over his shoulder and straightened, not entirely surprised to see Will standing in the doorway to Jack's office, looking conflicted. He knew that scowl well—he'd seen his friend wearing it more and more often lately as he tried to tighten his grip on those under his command, keep the distance that he told himself he was successfully maintaining. But Jack knew for a fact that the safety and well-being of his people weighed heavily under that stoic exterior. And if there'd been any doubt, his reaction to the news of Ian's death had certainly confirmed it.

"She told me in no uncertain terms that I was not to treat her any differently than I would the others," Jack said, searching his closest shelf for another book to read on the flight to Boston. The office he kept in his home in the compound was decidedly old-world compared to the rest of the place. Its sleek exterior was a modern design, but his office—his library—could easily have been transported from the library at his parents' manor in the English countryside. He finally grabbed a tome at random. "I've seen you offer several of our brothers the same reminder at one time or another."

"Was I out of line?" Will asked, running a hand over his hair as he came into the room, his eyes downcast. "I probably *am* asking a lot of both of you . . ."

"Will, my brother," Jack said on a sigh, "I'm sure you didn't come here to ask me about whether or not I thought you were too hard on Maddie. So shall we get to the true reason for your seeking my counsel?"

Will paced the room for a moment, one hand at the back of his neck. "I want you to do what you can to keep Claire out of this, Jack. I don't want her hurt."

And there it was . . .

"She's not going to stop digging," Jack reminded him, wishing he could lie to his friend. "Not while she still believes you're alive."

"If you see her, assure her I'm not," Will pleaded. "I don't want anything happening to this woman."

Jack came forward and clasped Will on the shoulder. "You can't protect everyone, Will. It's the sad reality of what we do."

"But shouldn't we be able to protect the ones who

matter most?" Will demanded. "Shouldn't we be there when it counts?"

Jack knew he wasn't talking just about the fathers they'd both lost. Few knew the tragedy in Will's past that haunted him and made him keep his distance from those under his command. Jack was one of those few. But he also knew that Will couldn't help caring, no matter how hard he tried.

"Then be there," Jack told him. "Stop torturing yourself about what *could* happen to Claire Davenport and do what you must to ensure it doesn't."

By the irritated look on Will's face, Jack knew he'd struck a chord. "Don't you have a plane to catch?"

"Should I save you a place?" Jack asked.

"What—so I can have a front-row seat watching you and Maddie work out whatever the hell it is between you? No thanks."

Jack lifted a shoulder. "Suit yourself."

"Jack."

Jack turned at the doorway and raised his brows. "Yeah?"

"Don't get yourself killed on this one," Will said. "Could be ugly with us getting this close to the Illuminati."

The gravity in his friend's voice gave Jack a moment's pause. They'd been on missions far more dangerous than this one, missions that had a much greater likelihood that one or both of them wouldn't return. The fact that Will was visibly worried made Jack stay a moment longer. Then he forced an unconcerned grin. "Come now, my friend. Do you think I'd leave you in charge of the commandery without me here to keep you in line? Who would run interference with all the beautiful, intrepid reporters obsessed with your sorry ass?"

Will chuckled. "I'm gonna hold you to that."

Chapter Four

"Where are we going?"

Jacob Stone pocketed his phone and turned to see his wife coming toward him, her blond hair loose and hanging over her shoulders, so lovely he momentarily forgot what she was talking about.

"We're not going anywhere, my darling," he informed her. "But according to my source at the airport it appears Jack Grayson and Maddie Blake are heading to Boston."

She arched a fair brow. "Business or pleasure? They were involved once, right?"

Jacob grunted. "Twice—from what Maddie told me when we were still on speaking terms."

"You sound like you miss her," Allison observed, her tone waspish. Not something he was used to. But now that her meek façade had been stripped away, there was quite a lot he was learning about his wife. "Should I be jealous?"

He sent an angry look her way, irritated by her insinuation—mostly because it hit far too close to the truth. There'd been a time when he and Maddie were close—perhaps even might have had a future. But then

Jack Grayson arrived on the scene, suddenly filling the role of confidant and friend. And more.

"Jealous?" he snapped. "You dare even ask such a question? I married you, Allison."

An emotion he might've almost called sorrow briefly twisted her beautiful features. But then she donned her perfect smile—the one that she had worn every day while pretending to be the doting administrative assistant who secretly pined for him. He'd trusted that smile once, had depended upon it. Now he had to wonder what thoughts and schemes it masked.

"That you did, my love," she said, extending a hand for him to pull her to him. "I'm sorry."

He pressed a kiss to her forehead and held her close. "The Faithful in Boston are among my most loyal. They will handle this, and soon Jack Grayson will no longer be an issue."

Allison pulled back from his embrace, her expression wary. "What do you mean by that?"

"My old friend is not without his enemies." A faint tug at the center of his chest made him pause, but he shoved aside the hint of remorse he felt. "I'm sure they'll be delighted to finally discover his whereabouts after all this time."

Allison's lips twisted into a hungry smile. "And Maddie Blake? What will happen to her?"

He would not order Maddie's murder—no way in hell. For all his protestations to Allison, Maddie still meant far too much to him to order her death. But he couldn't be responsible if she was foolish enough to put herself in harm's way. "If she insists on playing at being the heroine in this little drama, then that's her choice. I can't be responsible for what happens as a result."

* * *

"You're certain being in separate hotel rooms is a good idea?"

Maddie realized how her question sounded the moment she saw the wickedly handsome grin curl Jack's lips. "You'd prefer to share?"

She couldn't help but return his smile. *Damn his charm.* As if this wasn't hard enough already, now she had to be reminded how much she adored that sexy grin that made her pulse kick up a notch—every, single, freaking time.

"You know what I mean," she said, sending Jack a wry look as she swiped her key card and shoved open the hotel room door with a sweep of her hip. He leaned in behind her and held the door open as she rolled her Gucci overnight bag inside.

"Allow me," he murmured near her ear. "We're back among the champagne crowd."

She rolled her eyes, hardly needing the reminder. She'd grown up in prim and proper political circles, constantly having to be "on," always dressed for show, an ornament to her father's public image. It'd been a relief when she'd gone to college and then to Quantico, where she could be herself without having to constantly be on display. And so having to ditch her jeans and T-shirts and favorite, well-worn jacket in order to once more don her designer clothing and uncomfortably pointy-toed heels was a special kind of torture.

But not for Jack. The man lived in designer clothing, was as comfortable (and undeniably sexy) in silk shirts and handmade slacks as in his fatigues and combat boots. If the author of the James Bond novels were still alive, she had no doubt that Fleming could've easily created a rival for his famous British agent, using Jack as the model.

Jack had never talked much with her about his past— only once letting the words *manor* and *estate* slip out when discussing his childhood. But she knew he'd been born into the Alliance and that his family's legacy stretched back almost to the beginning of the Order. So she would've been surprised *not* to see the evidence that the man had grown up with the proverbial silver spoon in his mouth. But it wasn't wealth alone that had shaped the man who'd stolen her heart on the very first day they'd met . . .

She still remembered the day so many years ago when Jack had been assigned to guard her father, Senator Hal Blake. Jack's slow, suave stroll as he'd sauntered into the senator's study had immediately set him apart from the others who'd been part of his security detail. His easy smile had caused her heart to thunder in her chest when he shook her hand, his intense gaze—green flecked with brown and gold—searching hers, sizing her up, so warm she thought she'd melt right there on the Persian rug in her father's office.

And when it was announced a few months later that he would be replacing her security officer at the university when she returned to finish her senior year, she'd already fallen for the man's devastating charm. It was hardly surprising that things had soon gone far beyond just a working relationship between them. She just wished she'd known the truth before it had driven them apart. It was the one big "if only" that still kept her up nights.

She'd thought it was odd that her father's new security specialist had a British accent, but it was explained away as easily as all the other anomalies that Maddie had questioned throughout her childhood, never realizing they all were a means to cover her father's involvement in the Dark Alliance—a new order of Knights Templar. They'd secretly formed after the Order's dissolution in the Middle Ages, to help guard the freedoms and liberties that the Templars had been sworn to protect. And now that Maddie had insisted upon becoming an initiate into the Alliance to continue her father's legacy, it was an oath she'd taken as well.

Which was what had taken her to Mexico City in search of Jacob Stone, the traitorous son of a bitch who'd been like a brother to Maddie growing up, someone she'd trusted without question.

His betrayal had been devastating to them all—especially her father.

Maddie shook her head slightly, banishing the image of her father's shocked, crestfallen expression when he'd learned the truth about Jacob. If Maddie had had any doubts about her decision to join the Alliance as their first female member, her father's expression would've removed it.

But being around Jack was turning out to be a lot harder than she'd expected.

When she'd joined the Alliance as an initiate, she'd asked their commander not to team her up with Jack. Until now, Commander Asher had honored her request, putting her together with other members of the Chicago commandery while she was in training. But after eight months, he apparently thought it was time for her and Jack to move on.

Fair enough.

"Penny for your thoughts," Jack drawled from where he leaned against the wall, framed by the soft white light in the foyer of her suite.

"It'll cost you more than that." She kicked off her black leather pumps and wiggled her toes on the plush carpet before heading toward the bedroom to unpack. But she came to an abrupt halt when she stepped inside.

The room easily accommodated the luxurious king-size bed, a bureau, and a breakfast table situated in front of French doors that opened onto a balcony. Nearly everything was stark white except for the occasional splash of color, and yet the room was surprisingly warm and inviting. On the table was a vase full of yellow roses, their scent drifting to her even from across the room. If she hadn't been on a mission, it would've been nice to snuggle up under the down duvet and forget the world outside these four walls.

Oh, yeah . . . definitely the champagne crowd . . .

It sure beat the hell out of the living quarters back at the Chicago compound. Unlike some of her brethren who'd served the Alliance longer and had earned a house in the exclusive gated community, Maddie was confined to living in a small apartment and training in the network of rooms in the compound's underground bunker until she'd proven herself.

"And what's the going rate for the thoughts of a beautiful woman?"

Maddie started, her hand reflexively going toward the hidden gun in the holster built into her jacket. "Jesus, Jack! You scared the crap out of me."

He strolled into the bedroom, hands in the pockets of his iron-gray slacks, slowly taking in the room before leveling his gaze on her. "This reminds me of—"

When his words abruptly broke off, she frowned. "Jack?"

He offered her a sad smile. "I was just thinking of when we spent that weekend in Vancouver. Reminds me of our suite."

Heat lanced through Maddie's body at the mention of that weekend. It'd been a secret romantic getaway for her birthday—the first of several trips they'd taken to sneak away from her father's watchful eye. And each of the trysts had been incredible, breathtaking—in so many ways. But the Vancouver trip . . . well, that had been when she'd realized just how much pleasure a woman could stand.

Unsure of how to respond and not trusting her voice just then, she turned her back on him and tried to focus on unpacking. But she could feel the weight of his gaze, the heaviness in the air between them as if he wanted to say more but knew he shouldn't.

Finally, she heard him clear his throat, breaking the silence. "I suppose I should go to my room and see where Finn is on procuring our evening wear for the gala." He grinned. "Have to look dapper if I'm going to distract our reporter friend, and I'm not entirely sure I trust Finn's sense of fashion."

The heat Maddie had felt a moment ago faded in an instant, and a stone-cold dose of reality nailed her right in the gut. She'd almost forgotten what Jack's role was supposed to be on the following evening.

"Oh. Yeah. Probably a good idea." She forced a smile and turned back to her unpacking, her movements jerky and angry as she snatched her belongings out of her suitcase and tossed them on the bed to sort through later. "Although, I can't say I trust my sense of fashion any more than Finn's. It's been quite a while since I had to attend one of Dad's political events. I'm sure my girlie skills are a bit rusty."

"Don't worry," he assured her. "You'd be beautiful dressed in rags."

She shook her head. "This was *such* a freaking mistake. I don't know what the hell Will was thinking . . ." She was reaching in for the last of the ammunition for her Glock when Jack leaned in from behind her, taking hold of her hand.

"Maddie," he whispered, his breath warm against her neck, bringing goose bumps to her skin. When she hesitated, he added, "Please look at me. I'm not the enemy."

She swallowed hard, trying to control her breathing and not give away how having him standing so close affected her, how having his body crowding hers, his grasp on her hand loose as his thumb smoothed against her skin, made her head spin with deliciously decadent thoughts.

She turned to face him, immediately realizing that was

a mistake when she averted her gaze only to find herself staring at his lips. "Jack, we just need to get through this mission. Then we'll figure things out, some way to work together without . . ."

He lifted her chin with the edge of his hand, his attempt at his usual sexy, crooked grin now tinged with sorrow. "Without dredging up old memories? Not possible."

"Then what the hell are we supposed to do?" she demanded, her frustration and confusion nosing toward max capacity. "We can't ignore the past, but we have to move forward, Jack. Period."

Jack nodded solemnly. "You're right. I think we just need to get something out of the way." Before she could ask what he meant, he took her face in his hands and pressed a hard kiss to her mouth. She was so startled by the suddenness of it that every muscle in her body went stiff. Then the blissful warmth she'd always experienced with Jack flooded her veins, and she melted into him, her hands drifting up to rest against his chest, where she could feel his heart pounding in time with her own.

But the moment his lips softened and he sank into the kiss, he broke away, setting her at arm's length. "There," he said, his voice gruff. "Awkward moments of *not* talking about the colossally large elephant in the room are over. *Now* we can move on."

She heard the doubt in his voice that was no doubt reflected in her weak, "Yep."

He studied her for a moment longer, his brows coming together briefly in a troubled frown before he regained his composure and strolled toward the door of the bedroom, every step dignified and purposeful. The man commanded a room even when there wasn't really an audience.

"You should read over the file on Claire Davenport," he called over his shoulder, breaking into her thoughts. "Get a sense of this woman before we pay her a visit at her apartment this evening."

She watched him go, then as soon as she heard the suite door close, sank down onto the edge of the bed, her head spinning.

What the hell just happened?

If Jack had meant his kiss to put their past behind them and allow them to move on, he'd miscalculated big-time. If anything, it was a reminder of how much she loved the taste of him, how just the sweep of his mouth over hers was enough to make her want to pull him down onto the bed and lose herself in the desire that had always simmered between them . . .

Maddie closed her eyes and took a deep breath, exhaling slowly to calm her pulse. Oh, yeah, totally not behind her. She needed a distraction hella fast.

Taking Jack's advice, she snatched up the manila folder she'd tossed aside in her furious dismantling of her suitcase and opened it up to see the photo of a very pretty woman with honey-blond hair.

"Well, hello, Claire . . ."

Jack didn't realize he was scowling until he passed by the mirror in his adjoining suite and caught a glimpse of himself. Ah, the Brooding Brit was making an appearance.

That's how Will had referred to him in a rare show of humor in front of his men when Jack had first joined the Chicago team, trying to put Jack at ease and make him part of his new family in spite of the dire circumstance that had brought him there.

Aside from Will, none of the others knew that Jack had been on the run from men who'd put a price on his head. And none of them had learned of it since. They knew he had enemies—hell, which of them didn't?—but had they known who it was that wanted retribution for the blood Jack had shed, and why, they might not have been so welcoming.

Fortunately, his entire life had been allocated to the dark files—buried in the Alliance's archives behind layers of security to which only a very privileged few had access. Now that he was "Jack Grayson," all anyone knew was that he was from an old Order family whose commander in the UK had sent him to the States for reasons no one bothered to ask about or explain. That's just the way it was done.

When they'd experienced a security breach almost a year ago, Jack had been concerned that his past might come tumbling out of the abyss, laid bare for all to see. But it seemed all was still secure. And if Finn had stumbled onto anything when he was digging around to find information on the assassin sent after Luke and Sarah, he wasn't saying anything.

But sometimes he thought it might've been a relief if the truth *had* come out. Keeping it buried for so long, with only Will knowing, was an ever-present weight on his conscience. He and his friend had spoken of things only once or twice before—and after a lot of scotch had been consumed. So that old nagging guilt, that heaviness in the center of Jack's gut, still weighed on him when he thought about the truth he was keeping from those he cared about.

Especially Maddie.

He knew that was really why he'd walked away before. He loved the way she looked at him, wanted to be the person she believed him to be. And having to reveal the man he truly was and see the disappointment in her eyes was a pain he didn't ever want to experience.

He raked his hands through his hair, pulling the wavy locks tight against his head for a moment before releasing them on a frustrated sigh.

Speaking of pain . . .

What the hell had he been thinking by kissing her? He'd said they just needed to get it out of the way and had even believed that—until he'd tasted her lips again. They were as soft and delectable as he'd remembered. He'd kissed other women since her, of course. He'd hardly been living like the Templars of old. But no one else had been able to supplant the memories of every touch, every kiss he'd shared with Maddie.

Even now the memory of the first time he kissed her tortured him. She'd come to him to talk, as she often did, unsure whether she was making the right decisions about her career path, certain her father wouldn't approve and unsure how to tell him she was entering law enforcement—and not politics, as he'd hoped.

Jack had suggested just getting away for a while and clearing her head. He drove her out to the secluded beach that bordered her father's estate and they'd strolled along in silence under the moonlight as ocean waves crashed upon the shore, each lost in thought. At some point, Maddie had slipped her hand into his as if it was the most natural thing in the world. And when he'd pulled her into his embrace to hold her close against him, and her arms circled his waist, it was as if he'd always held her that way.

And when she eventually turned her face up to his, her beautiful face so young and hopeful as her gaze searched his, he'd brushed a kiss over her lips before he'd even realized what he was doing. But, to his amazement, she'd returned his kiss with her own, unhurried and tender, curious even. And he knew he was lost.

His love affair with Maddie had been precious and sweet—two words that had never entered his vocabulary before then. He thought perhaps the allure had been because she was younger than he by six years, but he'd soon realized that their time together had left such an indelible impression upon his heart because he loved her. Loved her with an unguarded abandon that he'd never thought possible.

But he'd been fooling himself. Relationships were always difficult for members of the Alliance. He was happy for Luke and Maddie's sister, Sarah, for the life that they were beginning together without Luke's having to walk away from the Alliance as he'd intended. But their relationship worked because Luke and Sarah were able to maintain some semblance of normalcy separate from the Alliance, from the missions that would call any of them away at a moment's notice.

But there was no "normal" for Jack. There couldn't be. Not when he would forever be looking over his shoulder. Jack had allowed himself to form friendships among his brothers, sure. But *they* all knew the score. After all, none of them really expected to retire to a quiet life in the country. But when it came to romantic relationships, he'd kept his distance from everyone since Maddie, knowing that one day his enemies would find him and that anyone he was close to would pay the price.

And now here they were, thrown together by circumstances. A volatile situation that had all the earmarks of a giant clusterfuck. That had become damned clear when he'd kissed Maddie and felt desire slam into him. He wanted her with just as much intensity and urgency as ever. And that need was intensified by the fact that he knew he couldn't have her.

He'd meant the kiss to be a reminder of that fact, a taste of what he'd once enjoyed, to satiate his appetite for her and allow them both to move on with the business at hand. But that taste had only served to increase his hunger.

A gentle rapping on the door to his suite snapped Jack out of his tortured thoughts. He drew his gun and strode toward the entrance, taking a moment to peer through the peephole before disengaging the lock. A woman in a hotel staff uniform with elegantly arranged pale blond hair and wide blue eyes offered him a friendly smile. Behind her was a bored-looking bellhop carrying several shopping bags.

"Hello, Mr. Smith," she greeted, her tone refreshingly cheerful. "I'm Meghan from the front desk. We have a delivery for you." When his brows came together slightly in a frown, she held up both arms, drawing his attention to the hangers draped in black suit bags. "From a Mr."—she paused, her eyes lifting toward the ceiling in thought for a moment—"*Chumbawamba*. He said you'd be expecting us."

Jack resisted the urge to roll his eyes. Finn was the only Templar he knew who took such delight in coming up with completely absurd cover names. "Yes, thank you. I'll take those."

When he reached for the bag, the woman evaded his grasp and dodged around him to enter the room. "Oh, it's no problem. We don't mind."

The bellhop followed dutifully behind with a nod of greeting even though he looked very much like *he* minded. "Your car's here too." At this the guy's eyes brightened slightly. "Happy to bring that around for ya when you're ready."

"What's your name?" Jack asked.

The guy dropped his load of shopping bags near the white sofa in the center of the sitting area. "Manny."

Jack retrieved a money clip from his pocket and selected a bill, slipping it to Manny. "Well, Manny, I'd like the car out front in an hour. If you're on time, I'll have another hundred for you."

Manny's brows lifted as he took the C-note and quickly pocketed it. "You got it." He gave Jack a nod and a hint of a grin before leaving.

The blonde eyed him rather pointedly. "And is there anything *I* can do for you, Mr. Smith?"

He offered her one of his practiced smiles. "As a matter of fact, Meghan, I *do* have need of you."

Her cheeks flushed very prettily as she gave him a coy look from under lowered lashes. "And what is it you'd like me to do, Mr. Smith?"

At another time in his life he might've eagerly indulged in what the woman was offering. But those days had ended during a moonlit walk on the beach several years before. "Nothing that would compromise your self-respect, I assure you, Meghan," he told her gently. "But I *am* in need of a favor of another sort . . ."

Chapter Five

Maddie wasn't surprised to see a black Jaguar parked outside the hotel, Jack leaning casually against the side. God, the man exuded sex appeal without even trying. *Damn it.*

He offered her a lopsided grin as she approached, and then opened the passenger door. "Your chariot . . . and all that."

She shook her head, pausing to drape her arm over the top edge of the door. "Well, this should be inconspicuous. Nice choice."

He chuckled, leaning toward her, close enough that she could see the flecks of brown and gold in his green eyes. "Not my choice—although I can certainly appreciate the fine engineering of this little dish. More of a Porsche man myself—as you know."

Maddie fought the flush that rose to her cheeks when she saw the twinkle of mischief in his eyes, and settled into the passenger seat. Oh, yes, she knew. One sultry summer evening he'd taught her evasive driving maneuvers in his seductively sleek, silver 911—along with a few *other* maneuvers . . .

"Ms. Davenport lives in a townhome in Beacon Hill,"

he continued, a grin tugging at a corner of his mouth as he started the car and pulled away from the hotel. "It would've been more conspicuous to drive up in a nondescript sedan."

Maddie had to concede that one. She'd been surprised when she saw Claire Davenport's address in her dossier. How exactly did an investigative journalist who made a decent but not extravagant salary, live in one of the most sought-after neighborhoods in Boston?

Tragically, it was the result of her parents having been killed in a collision with an eighteen-wheeler whose driver had fallen asleep at the wheel and didn't notice when he drifted across two lanes of traffic until he nailed the car stranded on the shoulder. Claire's dad had been changing a tire, his wife sitting in the car waiting for him to finish. That's all. Wrong place, wrong time. Shitty luck.

But, apparently, with Claire's inheritance came the brownstone in Beacon Hill—the home her parents had bought so that they could be near their only daughter while she was away at Harvard. And, coupled with the settlement Claire had received from the trucking company, she was set up.

That said, after what she'd read about Claire—her tireless determination to expose those who wronged the innocent—she had a feeling that the woman probably would've given every cent just to have her parents back for one day. Maddie could relate. She'd nearly lost her father almost a year ago. And she'd made a lot of decisions that day as she sat there in the hospital while he clung to life. The biggest one being that she'd make the assholes who'd shot him pay. Not just the actual shooter—who knew what merc the Illuminati had hired for the job?—but the people behind it. *Those* bastards were going to pay.

"Maddie, love."

She started and turned guiltily toward Jack. "Sorry, what?"

He reached over and gently took her hand, smoothing his thumb over her skin until her clenched fist relaxed. "Are you all right?"

Maddie turned her hand over. Tiny crescent-shaped marks marred her palm where her nails had dug into her skin. When she was younger she'd had a bad habit of clenching her fists when she was upset or angry, until her nails drew blood. It'd begun when her mom ran off, abandoning her husband and young daughters, and had returned when Maddie lost her job with the FBI a year ago after blowing the whistle on a guy who'd been selling information on top-secret technology that the government had been developing. Apparently, doing the right thing only mattered when the other guy didn't have your bosses in his pocket.

"I'm fine," she said, rubbing her palms against her thighs. "Just thinking over Claire's dossier. Most of her projects have involved human rights violations, corporate negligence, government waste . . . How did she become obsessed with the Alliance? With Will?"

Jack shifted slightly in his seat as if he was stalling before answering her question. "It's a long story. But the short version is that he saved her life a few years ago."

Maddie's brows came together. "Okay . . . And that turned her into a stalker?"

Jack slid a sidelong glance her way. "I think there's more to their story than even I know. They were in the Nigerian jungle together for several days, fighting for their lives. I imagine that has a way of bringing two people together. And then Will vanished without a trace, letting Claire think he was dead. I think her reporter's instincts tipped her off to the fact that there was more to Will than what he'd let on."

"And now in her quest for answers, she's in deeper than she realizes," Maddie mused. "Been there."

A few moments later, Jack turned onto a tree-lined street and parked in front of a series of brownstones at the bottom of a steep hill. The street leading up the hill was paved in cobblestones, the narrow sidewalks composed of uneven bricks that had settled over time. An American flag—a replica of a colonial design—hung from a flagpole a few houses up. And red, white, and blue blooms for Fourth of July celebrations filled the flower boxes everywhere she looked. The neighborhood seemed frozen in time. Maddie half expected to see the ghosts of long-dead patriots walking along the street as she and Jack began the two-block walk to Claire's residence.

"And how do we know Claire isn't home?" Maddie asked as they came to a narrow pathway that ran behind the row of brownstones where Claire lived, allowing access to stone patios and garden space for the residents on either side.

"I took care of it," Jack told her.

Maddie narrowed her eyes at him. "And how exactly did you do that?"

"She got a tip that Congressman Hale knows she received the flash drive from Tad Ralston and that she is in danger."

"So . . . you told her the truth," Maddie said. "How does that ensure she's away from home?"

"A guardian angel arranged for a room at our hotel under an assumed name until such time that the matter could be handled. She also received a stern warning to give up on this particular pursuit before she got hurt—which, of course, she will ignore."

"You set her up at *our* hotel?" Maddie exclaimed as they reached a wrought iron enclosure that surrounded a very pretty flower garden.

"How better to keep an eye on her? And it should give me the opportunity to bump into her before the gala tomorrow evening." He opened the gate and ushered her inside.

Maddie grunted. *I'll bet.*

She glanced around as she climbed the stone steps to the back door and reached into her jacket pocket, pulling out her lock-pick case. Jack hovered near her, blocking her activities from view.

"They teach you that at the Bureau?" he asked conversationally.

"Nope." The deadbolt lock clicked, and she bent slightly to work on the lock in the doorknob, trying to ignore the little jolt of electricity that shot straight to her gut when her hip brushed against Jack. Fortunately, the lock disengaged almost immediately. "Used to practice on my dad's liquor cabinet when I was in high school. Not for any of the liquor—just to see if I could do it." She grasped the doorknob, and turned her eyes up to his. "Did Finn give you the alarm code?"

Jack gave her a terse nod before glancing around to make sure they were still unobserved.

Maddie swung open the door and slipped inside, greeted by the shrill beeping of the alarm. Jack went straight to the panel on the wall, punching in the code, mercifully putting an end to the alarm's warning.

"Upstairs or down?" Maddie said, not wasting any time. She didn't want to be there any longer than necessary.

Jack gestured toward the open door that led to the stairway. "Up."

As Jack climbed the stairs to the second floor, Maddie took in the living room of the house in a glance. It was cozy, decorated with furniture that was obviously expensive but comfortable and meant to be enjoyed. There were little antiques on side tables and the fireplace mantel, Colonial-era art and décor on the walls.

As Maddie walked the room, checking every surface, every drawer for anything that might be of interest, she got the feeling that she and Claire would've been friends under different circumstances.

The kitchen was just as inviting and warm, a place that would be perfect for baking gingerbread cookies and making eggnog for the friends who would be by later for dinner and to sing Christmas carols around the aged upright piano she'd seen in the sitting room.

Maddie suddenly straightened and gave herself a mental shake. What the hell was she doing, thinking about Christmas? It was July, for crying out loud! And yet a wave of nostalgia for a childhood experience she'd never had, for the quiet, loving family life she'd always wanted, hit her again. Not that she hadn't had a father who doted on her and her sister, who'd given them everything they could possibly want. But it wasn't exactly the wholesome Rockwellian experience she'd always hoped for.

She sighed as she continued her search of the kitchen, her fingers skimming across the wooden countertop marked with decades of use, before she finally turned her attention to going through the drawers and cabinets.

She certainly wasn't going to have that kind of life now, not with the path she'd chosen. Her sister, Sarah, might be able to pull off happily ever after. But Maddie had made her choice. And it wasn't exactly like Jack was the kind of guy to settle down with a wife and kids . . .

Whoa. Jack?

She needed to put an end to that line of thinking ASAP. As nice as it might've been to fantasize about having a happily-ever-after with him back when she was a naïve twenty-something who'd been swept off her feet, she was too jaded now to ever indulge in such a ridiculous idea.

Finding nothing of value in the kitchen, she went back

to the sitting room and took out the little box of listening devices Finn had provided before they left Chicago, searching out a couple of locations where the savvy Claire might not think to look.

Footsteps on the stairs brought her head around. The stairway was fully enclosed, so she didn't actually see Jack until he emerged from the last step. "Did you find her computer?"

Jack shook his head. "There's an Ethernet cable in her office, but it looks like she only had a laptop, which I'm sure she took with her—no servers or other storage devices that I could find. Finn will be able to tap into her main email accounts to see if she sent anything out electronically. When we're back at the hotel, I'll slip into her suite at some point and see what I can do about the laptop."

Maddie eyed him cautiously. She could tell by the way his brows came together that he was holding something back. "Okay . . . So what *did* you find?"

He shook his head, his expression one of disbelief—and concern. "You need to see for yourself."

When they reached the top of the narrow stairs, Jack gestured toward the door to Claire's office. Maddie gasped when she entered the room and saw the walls lined with articles and documents and photos. There was a bulletin board with Post-it notes pinned to it and red yarn indicating connections between the random words and phrases she'd jotted down.

"My God . . ." she breathed. "She's lost her mind."

Jack shook his head and gestured toward the board. "Quite the opposite. She's brilliant. These are all code names for several of the Alliance's ops from the past thirty years." He pointed at one—*Cold Water*. "This one was my father's. I recognize the name from his file." He tapped another—*Evergreen*. "This one was where I crossed paths with Luke and recruited him to the Alliance."

She studied the board for several moments, following the connections Claire had drawn. "Do you think she put all this together since getting the flash drive?"

He shook his head. "Doubtful. She wouldn't have had time to do something this elaborate."

Maddie now understood Jack's reaction. This wasn't intel—this was research. He leaned toward the board and pulled the pin from one of the notes.

"Wait," Maddie cried, covering his hand with hers. When he turned his head to meet her gaze, the air suddenly seemed too close, too thick for breath. Her hand dropped away and she took a step back. "We need to get this to Finn, see if he can analyze the connections, determine if they're accurate or if she just got lucky with some of these code names."

She grabbed her phone from her back pocket and systematically snapped photos of the bulletin board, one of the entire board and then several close-up shots of different sections, ensuring they had a record of all the connections Claire had made.

Then, satisfied she had recorded everything, she began removing the yarn. "I almost feel bad having to do this. Can you imagine the amount of time it took to put this together?"

"Years," Jack muttered. "But it would take seconds for her to bring us down."

When they'd finished, Maddie glanced around until she spotted a stack of empty manila folders on top of a filing cabinet. She snatched one up and put all the scraps of paper inside. "Let's go."

They'd just hit the bottom couple of steps, when Jack's arm suddenly went out in front of her, bringing her to an abrupt halt and damned near clotheslining her.

When she opened her mouth to ask *What the hell*, he

held a finger to his lips and drew his gun with the other hand. "Someone's here."

Jack's body went taut with tension as he listened for movement. They were fish in a fucking barrel standing there in the stairwell. There was nowhere to go but back upstairs if someone came at them. Provided they could even reach the top of the stairs before they each took a round or two to the back.

They had no choice but to get the hell out of the stairway and into the open. And yet he didn't move, his concern for Maddie keeping him where he was, his body shielding hers. If she'd had any idea what was going through his head, his instinct to protect the woman he loved outweighing all his training, all his experience, she no doubt would've pistol-whipped him and taken charge—and probably with a few choice words in the process.

As it was, he felt her tension, her own senses on high alert as she waited for him to take the lead. Her fingertips lightly touched his arms, silently asking a question. At that moment, floorboards creaked in the distance.

"Kitchen," Maddie whispered near his ear.

He repressed a shiver at the warmth of her breath on his skin and brought up his weapon, swinging out from the stairs and clearing the room in a glance. He heard a clatter in the kitchen. Someone else was searching the house, probably looking for the flash drive just as they were. He gestured toward the front door.

They were just going to have to risk being seen by Claire's neighbors. There was no way in hell he wanted to get into a gunfight with the unknown intruder. These old brownstones were sturdy and well built, but he wasn't about to take the risk of a stray bullet going through the wall and hitting an innocent victim.

Maddie sprinted toward the front door, her footsteps nearly silent on the hardwood. Jack covered her, his gun trained on the entrance of the kitchen until he heard the front door's deadbolt disengage. Unfortunately, it seemed their intruder heard it too. The movement in the kitchen came to an abrupt halt.

Shit.

Jack waved Maddie out the door, backing toward her with a whispered, "Go, go!"

He was half a step away from the open doorway when a man in a black suit stepped out of the kitchen. Jack felt the shock of recognition a split second before the man brought up his gun and leveled it at Jack's chest. Jack darted forward, swinging the heavy front door closed behind him just as the intruder's bullet hit the door frame, splintering the wood and sending jagged pieces of wood flying.

Jack flinched, bringing up his arm to block the worst of the shrapnel. Maddie was already running down the front steps toward the brick sidewalk, but as Jack caught up to her, he grabbed her hand and pulled her with him as they bolted down the hill to where they'd left the car.

"Shit," Maddie muttered, glancing over her shoulder. "Company."

Jack searched frantically for a safe place to duck out of sight. If it was who he thought it was—and if the son of a bitch still worked for the same bastards—the intruder wouldn't think twice about firing into a crowd to put a bullet in Jack's skull.

He threw a glance over his shoulder as well, not surprised to see the guy gaining ground. Coming to a cross street, Jack jerked Maddie with him as he suddenly turned down the street and broke into a sprint.

"We're going the wrong way," Maddie told him, trying to pull him to a stop.

But Jack darted down another street without a word,

emerging onto Charles Street. Without pausing, he crossed into traffic, earning blaring horns and shouted curses. He almost grinned, remembering their adventure in Mexico City. Until he realized that Maddie was one of the people cursing at him.

"Are you fucking crazy?" she snapped as soon as they were safely across the street and rushing toward an antique shop.

Jack ushered her inside as he cast a look around. The man who'd followed them was standing at the corner of the intersection, scanning the crowd. Jack entered the store and dragged Maddie away from the windows.

"Just had to put a little distance between us," Jack murmured, scanning the store for another exit.

"May I help you?"

Jack immediately stilled, steadying his breath and plastering on his casual smile before turning to offer the proprietor a nod in greeting. "Just browsing. Thank you."

The woman eyed them suspiciously over her cat's-eye glasses. "London?"

Jack's brows lifted. "Sorry?"

"Are you from London?" she asked.

It was then Jack noticed the woman had a slight accent. "Sometimes," he admitted, cautious. "But I spent summers in Derbyshire."

Her pale blue eyes twinkled. "The back door is through there," she said, gesturing toward a door marked Employees Only. "Anyone I should steer away should they come looking?"

Jack chuckled. "Tall chap in a dark suit."

The woman cast a glance toward Maddie. "Hmm. I understand. I was young once too, you know. But best hurry, love. Don't want your lady friend's husband finding you, do you now?"

Jack suppressed a grin when he heard Maddie choke. *"Husband?"*

"Come, darling," he said, taking her hand and pulling her along. "We don't want him finding us together again, do we? It was so embarrassing last time—what with your ankles over your ears . . ."

Maddie shot him a glare that would've made a lesser man cringe. But he couldn't wipe the grin from his lips when he heard the proprietor's giggle.

"Nice," Maddie hissed when they emerged into an alley behind the store. "What the hell was that?"

"Just making sure our new friend had sufficient reason not to give us up should that asshole come in looking for us," he assured her. He didn't add that the image of her lying naked on the bed, her skin flushed with passion, had come to mind the moment he'd said it and had been another reason for them to make a hasty retreat.

"You recognized him," she said, far too perceptive.

When he didn't immediately answer, she pulled him to a stop. He glanced down at their linked hands, surprised to see her fingers still clasped firmly in his.

"Who is it, Jack?" she pressed. "Illuminati?"

He smoothed his thumb over her skin, finding the silky softness of her hand comforting. "Someone from my past—from before I was part of Will's team. We'd suspected them of being connected to the Illuminati but weren't able to prove it."

When he dared meet her gaze, she was looking at him expectantly, but he wasn't ready to talk. Not about *this* part of his story.

He forced a smile. "Come on, love. Let's put a little more distance behind us and then I'll call for a ride. We'll come back for the car later when our friend has given up searching for us."

"*Will* he give up?" Maddie pressed as they made their way toward the river. "He was looking for something in Claire's house. I think running into you was just a coincidence."

Jack's brows came together in a frown, not quite so sure about that. How in the hell would they have gotten wind of the information on the flash drive so quickly? He'd expected some of Stone's people to show up and try to intercept the information. But who the bloody hell had tipped off the *other* bastards who were still looking for him? The reason Jack was sideways with *them* was personal. There was nothing "business" about it.

"Hey. You still with me?"

Jack's grasp on her hand tightened, suddenly feeling like it was the only tether he had keeping him rooted in the present. "Yeah," he told her. "Yeah, I'm with you."

Chapter Six

Jacob Stone ground his teeth together when he saw the number on his phone's display. It took him a moment to work up the ability to fake a smile in his voice before he answered. "Grandfather. What a pleasant surprise."

"What the hell kind of game are you and that little bitch of yours playing at?"

The old man hadn't bothered even trying to fake civility.

"I'm sorry," Jacob drawled. "I have no idea what you mean. Allison and I are on our honeymoon—as you know."

"Don't play coy with me, you sniveling little coward. You've been interfering with our operations since the *incident* in the fall."

"I'm no longer in the inner circle," Jacob reminded him. "How exactly would I interfere with anything, Grandfather?"

The man grunted. "The only reason you're still alive is because you're my grandson—"

Yeah, right.

"—and because you might still have some use. Your 'Faithful,' as you call them, have been quite persistent in lobbying for your return to the Illuminati's good graces."

Jacob was silent, waiting to hear if there was more to

his grandfather's statement. Most of Jacob's Faithful were lost souls, misguided criminals who would blindly follow anyone who gave them hope of something better—in Jacob's case, hope that he would one day ascend to his rightful position of power as the One True Master, and lead them in creating a world without crippling diplomacy and political correctness, a world where the weak were crushed without mercy to make way for those who were unafraid to take what was theirs.

But his plan wasn't really so different from his grandfather's. The man had once turned his back on the Alliance, frustrated with their stubborn persistence in trying to guide and protect humankind, and had secretly pledged his allegiance to the Illuminati, working as a spy and providing them intelligence that had nearly brought the Alliance to its knees. Until he was discovered and the war of attrition between the two groups cost both sides many of their best.

Those who'd remained loyal to the Illuminati's agenda retreated to lick their wounds and bide their time. But that time had come. And he'd be damned if he was going to let that sadistic bastard claim all the glory.

Finally, when his grandfather said nothing more on the matter, Jacob sighed. "Was there anything else?"

"Stay out of our business, Jacob," his grandfather warned. "The future of the Illuminati is no longer your concern."

As soon as the line disconnected, Jacob released a roar of rage and frustration that brought Allison running into the room, their security guards at her heels.

"Jacob! What is it?" she panted. "What's happened?"

"Not my business?" he raged. "Not my fucking *business*?" He closed the gap between them with a few furious strides. "That son of a bitch will pay for shutting me out. He has no idea what I'm capable of."

Allison's eyes glittered with delight. "There it is," she

whispered. "There is the passion I fell in love with." She turned to the guards. "Get out."

Without a word, they both hurried from the room, shutting the double doors to the sitting room behind them.

As soon as they'd gone, Allison took Jacob's face in her hands. "Your grandfather will be sorry he ever doubted you," she assured him. She pulled him down to press a long, sultry kiss to his lips that immediately soothed his temper. "I will drive a dagger into his heart myself, if you ask it, Jacob." She slid her hand down between them, and his cock sprang to life, eager for her touch. He squeezed his eyes shut as she leaned into him and pressed a kiss to the side of his neck.

"And I want you to be there when I do. I want him to plead for his life, beg you for mercy. I want you to see the fear in his eyes when he realizes you are the One True Master—the man who will lead this world into its glory."

He opened his eyes when she released him to slide down to her knees before him. He gazed down at her hungrily as she freed him and took him into her mouth, her gaze locking with his as her tongue caressed him.

Intoxicated with pleasure and the power that was within his grasp, he let his head fall back on his shoulders and raised his arms to his sides, as he let out a cry of triumph.

"I'm pretty sure that picture hasn't changed since you looked at it five minutes ago."

Will Asher dragged his gaze away from the photo of Claire Davenport on the flatscreen that hung on his office wall. "Thank you for that keen observation, Finn. Remind me why you're still here?"

Finn leaned back in Will's chair and propped his feet up on the desk, then raised a single brow at him. "Offering up my keen insights and dazzling intellect for the betterment of humankind?"

"More like being a pain in my ass," Will muttered. "Did you get into Claire's email?"

Finn gave him a wry look. "*Please.* Email at home, work, secret account used for corresponding with confidential sources . . . Want to know what she's got on the secretary of the treasury?"

"Probably nothing we don't already know," Will said with a shrug. "All I care about is what she has on us and the Illuminati."

"Well, I have to give the gal credit—she's good. Had pretty decent passwords," Finn said, dropping his feet back to the floor and leaning in to type on his laptop. "Actually took me about twenty minutes to crack one of them."

"And the others?" Will prompted.

Finn gave him that *look* again. "Seriously, brah? It's me you're talkin' to. I said she was *good*. But, alas, she is a mere mortal after all . . ."

Will heaved a sigh and crossed his arms over his chest. "Finn. The data?"

"Sorry, boss-man. Nothing sent out via email. She contacted a few colleagues, making some vague inquiries, but didn't mention anything specific about what she had. I guess it's always possible that she sent something via snail mail, but I didn't find any transactions at USPS outlets on her bank or credit cards. Could've paid cash, but, seriously, do people still do that?"

"When was the package delivered?" Will asked. "Is it possible she hasn't gone through it yet? Is she just taking it straight to Hale?"

Finn frowned at this. "Can't believe that. She's too smart to just waltz in there and confront a politician about his association with a secret organization that took out hits on high-ranking members of *another* secret organization—

information that has already resulted in the death of the good congressman's aide—without having some kind of insurance. Someone somewhere has a copy of the info on that flash drive."

Will massaged the back of his neck as he paced his office. "Keep looking. I don't want her to have a shred of information left after Jack and Maddie get the flash drive."

"That's the plan," Finn assured him. "The listening devices that Jack and Maddie placed in her house earlier today will give us ears if she goes back home. And Jack's going to try to get to her laptop at the hotel so that I can do a little more exploring. I've also deployed our COW—"

Finn's words ended abruptly at Will's confused frown. "Dude. C'mon. Hop into the twenty-first century with me for a minute."

"I don't need to understand what you do, Finn," Will drawled. "That's why I pay you."

Finn sighed. "Like I said—I've deployed our *cell on wheels*, courtesy of our brothers in the Boston commandery, so I can also listen in on any calls she makes. And my buddy Peanut—don't ask; it's a college thing—who works for her cell phone company, is sending me data reports every hour. So we should have her pretty well covered."

Will nodded, mulling over everything they had in place. "And her hotel room?"

"Within spitting distance of Jack's," Finn said. "Not sure if that's a good thing, considering what you have him up to, where the lovely Ms. Davenport is concerned."

Will shot him an irritated look. "I don't care what Jack has to do as long as he keeps Claire safe and we get that flash drive."

A slow smirk curved Finn's lips. "Huh."

"What?" Will snapped.

Finn shook his head as he got to his feet and gathered

his things. "Nothin'. Just think it's interesting what order you put those goals in. That's all."

Will's scowl deepened. "What the hell is that supposed to mean?"

Finn strolled toward the door but paused before leaving the room and sent a knowing look his commander's way. "Just not used to you putting anything or any*one* ahead of the Alliance."

Will stood in his office staring at the empty doorway for several minutes after Finn left, considering his observation. So they'd spent a few days together running for their lives. It wasn't like he really knew Claire or had any feelings about her one way or another. He'd saved her life and had damned near gotten himself killed in the process. He just wanted to make sure his efforts weren't for nothing. That was all.

With a harsh sigh, he went to his desk and pulled out the leather-bound journal he kept in the top drawer. Half an hour later, he'd detailed the most recent updates to the situation, including his personal musings. It was an old habit—as evidenced by the number of old journals on his shelf and the dozens more that were in his personal library at his safe house. Old-school, sure. But if someone was going to look for confidential information, they'd be searching his computer, his email, his phone . . . No one would think that the man who ran the North American arm of the Alliance would still keep a daily journal.

And he'd kept them all, a record of his life since he was a stupid kid still trying to figure out what path he wanted to take in life. There was only one journal missing from his collection—the one that detailed his time in Nigeria, the atrocities he'd witnessed, the horrors he'd experienced. It had burned in the same fire that had destroyed the village he was supposed to have saved. It was for the best. He didn't want to remember those days—or how that horrific time had brought Claire into his life.

He was still trying to convince himself of that when his laptop started beeping. He glanced down at it, surprised to see a notification of an incoming video conference call. He closed his journal and stowed it in the drawer, then tapped his mouse pad. A moment later the window popped up. "Jack? We weren't scheduled to debrief until later tonight."

"They've found me," Jack said without preamble.

There was no need for further explanation. Will knew exactly whom Jack was talking about. "How do you know?"

Jack tugged at his eyebrow. "It was Kozlov."

Will's eyes went wide. "He's still alive?" he asked before he stopped to consider his words. That dark day in Jack's history was largely off-limits, even between the two of them. They'd rarely spoken of it and for good reason. Will knew that day haunted his friend. And if anybody could understand what it was like to be haunted by the past, it was Will. So he never pushed Jack to fill in the blanks. But the fact that Kozlov was alive was a damned big one.

"Kozlov surrendered when he saw what had happened to his comrades during the Russia op, so I let him live." Jack chuckled bitterly, then raked his hands through his hair, pulling it taut against his scalp for a moment before releasing it—one of the few tells Jack had that he was upset. "Once again fucked over by my sense of honor."

"I'm pulling you out," Will told him. "I'll personally sub in with Maddie until we figure out how the hell they found you."

Jack lifted a brow. "That could make it difficult to avoid the lovely Ms. Davenport, Will."

Will's jaw tightened reflexively before he could check his reaction. "If it means keeping you alive, then I'll take my chances. Come back to Chicago, lie low for a while until they lose your trail again."

Jack shook his head, his expression growing more serious. "No. I made a mistake letting Kozlov live that day. God knows how many lives have suffered for it. I'll handle this."

"And if he gets the drop on you instead?" Will prompted.

Jack leveled his gaze at Will. "Make sure Maddie doesn't learn the truth."

Will shook his head. "Jack, don't you think she should know why you really bolted?"

"I won't have her remember me that way," Jack insisted. "Please, Will. I want your word."

Will considered his friend's request for a long moment. There wasn't a single Templar who didn't have regrets. God—he was probably right there on the leader board when it came to shit he wasn't exactly proud of. Abandoning a certain woman at a Nigerian hospital when she needed someone most and then letting her believe he was dead, telling himself it was to *protect* her, when he knew damned well it was himself he was protecting, was probably chief on his list of things he would change if he could. The other one involved failing the people he loved most in the world. So, yeah, Will could relate to Jack not wanting Maddie to find out his deepest, darkest secret from someone else.

"You have my word that Maddie won't hear anything from me," Will vowed. "But you need to tell her, Jack. Do you really want it to come from someone like Antonovich or Kozlov?"

Chapter Seven

Jack slipped out of his hotel room and into the hallway, the device Finn had provided them in his pocket as he strolled down the hall. Meghan—his little friend at the front desk—had informed him when they'd returned to the hotel that Claire Davenport was staying in a room two floors below his. Now he just needed some way to draw Claire out of her room so that he could pop in and attach the device to her laptop . . .

He nodded in greeting to a member of the housekeeping staff as he passed her in the hall, grinning to himself when he remembered Maddie in her too-tight uniform shirt and short shorts. The woman looked stunning no matter what she wore—and in nothing at all.

That happy thought made him groan before he could check it.

Stay on task, Jack.

He forced his mind back to the matter at hand and away from a favorite memory of Maddie—naked in his bed, the sheets pooled around her waist as she lay sleeping on her stomach, her dark curls a tangle around her shoulders.

At that moment, a door at the end of the hallway opened

up and Manny emerged, pushing a cart with serving trays. The man smiled at Jack and raised a hand in greeting.

Jack jerked his head at the cart as they came to a halt in front of the elevators. "Anything good on the menu?"

Manny shrugged. "A whole lotta fancy shit that only rich people eat." He sent a glance Jack's way. "No offense."

Jack chuckled. "None taken. But I'm curious—does your key get you into every room? What happens if you arrive with all this food and no one's in the room to accept it?"

"Oh, yeah," Manny assured him, patting the pocket of his jacket. "We can just drop it off. No problem. You need somethin'?"

"Perhaps later," Jack told him. "I was thinking strawberries and champagne. Or is that too cliché?"

Manny grinned, nodding in appreciation. "You got a bae coming up later—that it?"

Jack wasn't quite sure what to say . . .

Because what the hell is a bae?

Fortunately, the elevator arrived at that moment, saving Jack from admitting that even though he was still hanging on to his thirties—barely—he was tragically unhip. He started to step into the elevator as the doors slid open, but halted, instead motioning for Manny to enter the elevator first. When the wheel on Manny's cart caught on the track, Jack leaned over and grabbed the cart handle. "Here, allow me."

Guiding the cart with one hand, he slipped the other into Manny's jacket pocket, grabbing the key card and stowing it in the pocket of his own slacks without Manny's noticing. Never let it be said that he didn't learn a thing or two during his days running the streets of London with the sort of people who would scandalize his parents.

They chatted about nothing in particular on the short trip to the first floor; then Jack sent a departing nod Manny's way before striding toward where Meghan stood behind the front desk, her pretty smile currently bestowed upon an elderly gentleman. But when she saw him, she quickly wrapped up the transaction, then beamed at Jack.

"Well?" she asked, her excitement impossible to contain. "What's next?"

He hushed her good-naturedly and leaned his forearms upon the counter. "I need a distraction. Do you think you could manage it?"

Her eyes widened briefly with excitement. "What kind of distraction?"

He reached across the counter to take a notepad near her computer and scrawled a quick note before tearing the paper off the pad and folding it in half. He slid the note across the counter to Meghan. "In five minutes, please call Ms. Davenport's room and let her know that a gentleman left her a note at the front desk."

Her expression sank a little. "That's all?"

"Actually, no," he said. "There is one other thing you can do for me . . ."

Five minutes later, on the nose, Jack saw Claire leave her hotel room in a hurry. As soon as she was out of sight, he strode to her door and used Manny's key to slip inside. He took in the details of the room at a glance. It was considerably smaller than his and Maddie's rooms, so there were only so many places one could stash a laptop. He finally located it on the floor of the closet, inside a backpack.

Jack snatched the laptop out of its hiding place and flipped it upside down onto the bed. He grabbed a brown leather pouch from his pocket and hastily removed a tiny screwdriver to open the case. A moment later, the device was installed. He put the laptop back into its hiding place and darted back into the hallway, shutting the door quietly behind him.

And not a moment too soon, it turned out.

He'd taken only a few steps away from Claire's door

when the woman came around the corner, her steps swift in spite of the height of her espadrille wedges. Her honey-blond hair was pinned up in a messy twist that allowed random locks to spill out around her face and shoulders. Her well-worn jeans and mint green T-shirt hugged her curves perfectly, a loosely knitted summer scarf draped decoratively around her neck to add a bohemian nonchalance that belied the intensity of her expression.

Jack gave her a casual smile when he met her crystalline blue gaze and nodded in greeting as he passed. He felt rather than saw her do a double take, but kept going, not wanting her to recognize him until the moment was right.

"Excuse me," Claire called. "Do I know you?"

So much for that plan

He donned a confused expression and turned back to face her. "I'm sorry?"

She narrowed her eyes at him and tilted her head to one side. "It's just . . . You look familiar."

He flashed his most charming grin. In truth, he'd been the one who'd managed to find Will and Claire at the extraction point in Nigeria and had evacuated them to the hospital where Will had reluctantly left Claire so he could return to his duties. Fortunately for Jack, she'd been delirious with fever the one time she'd seen him, so any remembrance would be hazy at best.

"I'm afraid I haven't had the pleasure of meeting you before," he lied, extending his hand. "But I'd certainly welcome the opportunity to remedy that. Jack Smith."

She glanced down at his hand as if not trusting it was clean but then accepted his handshake. "Claire," she said, her stiffness easing slightly. "Claire Johnson."

So she'd taken an alias as well . . .

Well done, Claire. Well done.

His smile widened in appreciation. "Delighted. What brings you to Boston, Ms. Johnson?"

"Research." Her tone was friendly, easy. But her eyes still bored into his, searching no doubt for a tell, some give-away that he wasn't what he seemed. Wary, untrusting . . . Oh, yes, this woman was made for his dear friend Will. "I'm a . . . historian."

He lifted his brows. "Ah, is that so? Fascinating."

"What about you?" she prompted.

"I'm attending a Fourth of July celebration hosted by an old friend," he admitted. He noticed her hand reflexively clutch the note he'd left. When his gaze dropped at the sound of the crumpling paper, she slid the note into the pocket of her jeans.

"Well, I'm sure it'll be quite a production," she said, forcing a smile. "We tend to take the Fourth of July pretty seriously in Boston." She flushed slightly and took a step back. "Anyway, it was nice meeting you."

He watched as she retreated toward her room, lifting a hand in farewell when she glanced his way. "It was nice to meet you, Claire. I hope we cross paths again."

The moment she was inside her room, he strode toward the elevators, texting Finn as he walked, letting him know the device was in place. Unfortunately, in his cursory search of Claire's hotel room, he'd not found the flash drive. He just had to hope that he could persuade her to give it to him at the gala before Hale got his hands on it—or before Claire Davenport wound up dead.

"How are you holding up?"

Maddie flopped back onto the bed with a groan, covering her eyes with one hand, the other holding her phone to her ear. "I don't know, Sarah. I honestly don't."

She heard her sister's sympathetic sigh. "Tell Jack you still have feelings for him."

Maddie pinched the bridge of her nose and squeezed her eyes against the headache she felt coming on. "But I'm not sure that I do. I mean, I'm still attracted to him—the guy's sexy as hell. But that doesn't necessarily mean things would work out for us if we gave it another go. I don't want to do that to him, Sarah. It wouldn't be fair. That's even if he still has feelings for me. I know he cares—but . . ."

"Talk to him, Mads. You have to—for your own peace of mind if nothing else."

Maddie sighed. "Because that wouldn't make things awkward at all."

Sarah laughed. "And it's easy between you two *now*?"

"He kissed me, Sare," Maddie confessed. "Said it would help us get it out of the way so we could move on."

There was a beat of silence—then, "And . . . ?"

Maddie took a deep breath and let it out on a frustrated sigh. "Then he bolted. And when we met up later it was like nothing had happened."

"Oh."

"Yeah, 'oh,'" Maddie echoed. "He couldn't get out of here fast enough."

"Maybe he felt more than he'd expected to," Sarah suggested. "The first time Luke kissed me it was part of our cover when I was hiding out with him. I don't think he expected it to affect him the way it did."

Maddie couldn't help but smile at the love-struck quality of her sister's voice. She adored her baby sister, had hated seeing her widowed so young with a small child to raise on her own. Sarah had denied herself happiness for years, focusing all her attention on her son, Eli, and her job as an elementary schoolteacher. Seeing Sarah so happy now with Luke, finally enjoying the love and devotion she deserved, made Maddie's eyes sting.

She pressed the heel of her palm to her eyes, sniffing to clear away the tears. "Maybe. But, I'm not sure—" Her words halted abruptly at the sound of a hard knock on her hotel room door. "Hey, Sare, someone's at the door. I'll call you later. Kiss Eli for me."

She hung up and pocketed her phone before snatching up her gun from the bedside table. She kept it low at her side as she approached the door and peered through the peephole. A man in hotel uniform stood in the hallway with a food cart.

She opened the door as much as the safety latch would allow. "May I help you?"

"Room service," he said, giving her a mischievous grin.

What the hell?

"I didn't order room service."

"This is from Mr. Smith," he said in a rush. "He asked me to bring it to your room."

Maddie frowned. *Mr. Smith? Who the—Jack.*

She'd momentarily forgotten all about his alias. Admittedly curious, she tucked her gun into the small of her back, making sure her shirt covered it before opening the door and allowing the young man in.

He unpacked three silver trays, setting them on the small dining table. Then he added two champagne glasses and reached beneath the cart to bring out a bottle of champagne on ice, all the while sending knowing glances her way. God knew what he thought was going on. Hell, *she* had no idea what was going on.

Although, the moment he lifted the lid from the first tray to reveal chocolate-dipped strawberries, she began to understand.

"I'm assured they're quite delicious."

She spun around toward the door to see Jack leaning against the door frame, his arms crossed and that damnably impish smile gracing his full lips—lips she'd been longing to feel on hers again since that searing kiss earlier in the day.

"Enjoy," the young man said, sending another grin her way. Then she saw him wink at Jack. "I'll have your car retrieved as soon as possible, Mr. Smith."

Jack shook his hand as he passed and slipped money—and what looked like a key card—into the man's pocket. "Thank you, Manny. And please give my compliments to Meghan for her assistance. This is perfect."

Jack came to the table to stand near her, his eyes never leaving hers until he turned his attention to the serving trays. Jack lifted the lid of one of the remaining serving dishes to reveal other delectable treats—all the same or at least nearly the same as what they had enjoyed together during their trip to Vancouver.

"Well, I *assume* these are perfect," he said, his gaze capturing hers. "But I require your opinion."

Maddie's chest tightened with a mixture of pleasure, excitement, and . . . sorrow. Not exactly the response that Jack was going for, if she had to hazard a guess. And that made her feel like the biggest bitch ever. Here he was trying to do something nice, something special and meaningful for her, and all she wanted to do was bend over double and hyperventilate in a full-blown panic attack. "What are you doing, Jack?"

He looked away again before she could catch the full extent of his expression, but there was something wistful and fleeting that she *could* see in his profile. *Nostalgia.* That's what she would've said if she'd had to put a name to it.

"Talking about Vancouver earlier reminded me of the day we spent holed up in our room, lying in bed and just talking . . . among other things." He laughed. "Until we were starving and had to take a break. Do you remember? As I recall, you particularly enjoyed the strawberries we shared." He selected a plump, dark berry and lifted it to her lips. "Care to try one?"

At least, that's what she thought he said. Her heart was pounding too hard in her ears to be certain. Did she remember? Good God—how could she *forget*? She'd never been with anyone like Jack—so gentle and kind, so concerned for her feelings and opinions and desires. He'd touched her with such tenderness and reverence—as if she was a precious, fragile thing that he must not break—that she'd felt treasured and safe in ways she'd never realized had been missing from her life.

She covered his hand with both of hers and brought the strawberry to her lips, his sharp intake of breath telling her he'd tucked away a few memories of his own. Keeping her eyes locked with his, she closed her lips around the tip of the berry and bit into it. The burst of flavor on her tongue made her shudder. That and the intensity of Jack's gaze.

Slowly, she licked the juice from her lips, loving the way his eyes sparked with desire, wishing she had the nerve to act on it. "Delicious."

She saw him swallow hard, and then something in his expression changed and his hand came up to slowly caress the skin near her collarbone. Her eyes fluttered shut at the gentleness of his touch. Damn her pulse for how it was pounding as his fingertips drifted down to the center of her chest.

"You still have it," he murmured.

Her eyes snapped open and she remembered to breathe again. For a few seconds she wasn't quite sure what he was talking about. Then she realized it hadn't been her skin he was caressing but the silver chain she wore around her neck. Resting against her chest just above the valley between her breasts was a red Templar-cross pendant. But the knowledge that it had been the necklace that captivated him at that moment did little to still her hammering pulse or the heat that flooded her cheeks at his touch.

"Of course, I have it," she said, her voice just above a whisper. "You gave it to me—the first present you ever gave me. I didn't realize the significance then."

He lifted the pendant, smoothing it gently between his thumb and forefinger for a moment before his gaze shifted to capture hers. "There was far more significance in this gift than you probably even now realize."

Maddie wanted to ask him what he meant, but she couldn't find her voice at that moment. Or perhaps the rapid, shallow rising and falling of her chest as Jack's eyes held hers as his free hand came to rest at the small of her back drove the words away. She stepped closer, giving in to the gentle pressure of his hand and allowing him to pull her to him. And when his head lowered toward hers, she cupped his jaw, urging him on.

His lips swept over hers, slowly, tentatively, asking a question she didn't know how to answer. At least, not with words. But her body apparently was willing to shout the answer loud and clear. Her arm slid around his neck, drawing him in closer as his kiss became more certain but still so tender she felt tears stinging the corners of her eyes.

He released her pendant to wrap her tighter in his arms, and the kiss deepened, making Maddie shiver with desire when his tongue swept across the seam of her lips. But apparently mistaking her shiver for apprehension, he suddenly broke off the kiss, leaving them both panting as he pressed his forehead to hers.

"I should apologize," he told her softly.

She shook her head. "Jack—"

"I should," he repeated, "but I won't. I can't. I have never regretted anything that's ever happened between us, Maddie. My only regret is letting it all fall apart."

The words broke the spell over her, forcing her to set

aside her wants and desires—her *needs*. "I can't do this again, Jack."

His hold on her loosened and he pulled back to peer down at her. "Not now or not ever?"

God, how in the hell was she supposed to answer that? She loved him. There it was. The answer she'd been searching for. She had to be honest with herself, had to listen to what her heart was telling her. Loved him with an intensity that defied time and distance and left a hollow ache in the center of her chest when she lay awake at night wishing for his arms around her.

But if she told him that now, what would it get them? Additional heartache. She'd made a choice to join the Alliance. And although romantic attachments certainly weren't forbidden, they were discouraged as a distraction that the Templars should avoid if they were to focus on their mission. And if there was one thing she'd come to realize, it was that Jack was nothing if not distracting.

"I don't know," she admitted. Her fingertips skimmed the line of his jaw, her heart skipping a beat when his dark lashes lowered at her touch. "I want to. *My God*, I want to. But every time we find ourselves here, one of us ends up with a broken heart to show for it."

He covered her hand with his and turned his face into her palm, pressing a kiss to her skin. Then he sighed and lifted his lids to capture her gaze once more. "Walking away from you was the hardest thing I've ever done. I don't know that I could do it again without doing irreparable damage to this battered heart of mine. But I won't push. And I won't kiss you again until you ask me to."

As if to make good on his word, he took a step back and held his arms up to his sides, gesturing vaguely toward the table. "I'm sorry if my rare moment of wistful romanticism was too forward and made you uncomfortable." He laid his hand on his chest and offered a slight bow. "My heartfelt apologies."

Great. Now she really *was* the biggest bitch on the planet. Who shuns a romantic gesture—especially when there's chocolate and champagne involved, for crying out loud? Had she really grown that jaded that she couldn't just accept a little kindness, a little affection from a man she truly loved with all her heart?

Maddie reached out and took his hand. "C'mon," she said, jerking her head toward the table and offering him a smile. "Turns out a little wistful romanticism from an old friend is just what I was looking for today."

He pulled out a chair for her and bent as if to press a kiss to the side of her neck, which had been his habit when they were lovers, just a little brush of his lips against her skin as if he couldn't help himself. When he pulled back, true to his word not to kiss her again until she asked, she tried not to let her disappointment show and instead reached for the bottle of champagne.

Chapter Eight

Jacob Stone was seriously fucking pissed. It was rare that he let his temper get the better of him. After spending almost all of his career as a politician, he was nothing if not restrained and polished. He'd had one of the best mentors possible in Hal Blake—the senator who had treated him like the son he'd never had. He felt a twinge of guilt at how things had played out there. He'd hated betraying the man, but it was all for a greater good.

The world was struggling, slowly destroying itself with infighting and posturing among the superpowers, which would continue until one of them called another's bluff and blew them all to hell. Terrorism—domestic and abroad—was at an all-time high, making the citizenry feel that there was nowhere they were safe. And divisiveness over pretty much every issue imaginable was becoming increasingly hostile and confrontational. The vitriolic rhetoric coming from those who were supposed to be leading their people was merely feeding the flames of hatred and acrimony.

The Alliance was determined to work from within, to guide the world out of this present darkness and usher in the kind of accord that would eventually heal the wounds that had battered the world and left it bleeding, curled up in a little ball, whimpering on the floor. They weren't willing to take control and eliminate any who disagreed with them. Oh, no. They were all about empowerment and diplomacy and using violence as a last resort.

Fucking pussies.

Jacob had thought the Illuminati were on the right path, that they were determined to assert their authority and drag the various world powers out of their ineffectual stupor, kicking and screaming if necessary, and forcing them to quit acting like petulant children and accept the rule of those who knew better and could enforce peace with a firm hand. And if any serpent reared its head in retaliation against the Illuminati? Then that head would be severed.

How wrong Jacob had been.

The Illuminati—his grandfather chief among them—had no idea what it was going to take to rescue the world from itself. They were just as cowardly and ineffective as the Alliance when it came down to it. There needed to be one man, One True Master, who would force the world to see that he knew what was best for them. There would be resistance, certainly. But eventually they would welcome Jacob as their savior, accept him as their benevolent ruler.

The Faithful already understood this. They were willing to die for him, for their cause. And it was these true servants that he called upon now. They would not abandon him when he needed their loyalty most.

The man who'd been notified of Jack's presence in Boston had failed to take him out. He no doubt would continue pursuing his vendetta, but Jacob wasn't going to take any chances. He'd already missed the opportunity to obtain the data that bastard Antonovich had offered up to the highest bidder, but he wasn't going to make that mistake again. Even if Kozlov took out Jack, there were others in the Alliance who would come up behind him, take his place like good little soldiers and try to fuck Jacob over again.

He couldn't take that chance. Not now when his own future hung in the balance. The Illuminati leadership had abandoned him. He would have to persevere on his own with the resources available to him.

Unfortunately, he'd reached the end of those resources and was now forced to call in the help he'd dreaded. Brothers Demetrius and Stefan Shepherd were two of the Illuminati's most feared assets, called in only for missions that required a certain . . . skill set. And, luckily for Jacob, the brothers were willing to offer their loyalty to whomever paid the best—if it suited their own agenda.

The man before him was as deadly as anyone Jacob had ever known and had the added benefit of lacking a conscience. That said, Jacob didn't entirely trust him. The way Stefan's eyes glittered with delight at the prospect of killing made Jacob realize the man was barely hanging on to his sanity. But most only saw the polished veneer and charisma that Stefan presented to his flock—idiots so desperate for hope they hung on his every word, making him a superstar on the dark web. He believed himself to be some kind of modern day messiah who would usher in a new era.

Jacob grunted inwardly. He seriously doubted that if there was a second coming it would be kicked off by a delusional serial killer with a God complex. But Stefan served his purpose. He was useful, a means to an end. And when Jacob reached that end, the Stefan problem would be eliminated. It wasn't Jacob's fault the man was too much of an idiot to recognize he was expendable.

Stefan's brother Demetrius was an entirely different matter. He couldn't have been more different from his elder brother. Stefan's long dark hair and dark eyes made him look like some kind of rock star—perhaps that was by design. From what Jacob had heard, the man was like sexual catnip to members of all genders. But Demetrius's hair was pale blond, cut short and styled to make him look like he was meant for the silver screen. He was an enigma to Jacob—and probably to most everyone else he met.

Demetrius was shrewd, intelligent, and *sane*. He clearly had ambitions of his own, which made him dangerous. But Jacob trusted him far more than Stefan. Demetrius played along with his brother's little game, but Jacob could see that the man was only feeding his brother's delusions, biding his time. But for what, Jacob couldn't discern.

They were quite the triumvirate, the three of them. And Jacob knew that when it came down to it, they would each turn on the others without a second thought. Their only bond was a common enemy. And once that enemy was removed . . .

Well, Jacob would deal with that when it came to pass. For now, they were his allies.

"What can we do for you, Mr. Stone?" Demetrius asked, his voice smooth, cultured. "I assume you didn't ask us here to contribute to your campaign, seeing as how your political ambitions have . . . *stalled*."

Jacob forced a smile. "I assure you, Mr. Shepherd, my ambition is the same as it ever was. I have merely adjusted my goals to suit my present circumstances."

Demetrius offered a smile that bordered on mocking. "Of course. And how do my brother and I factor into your plans?"

"I need to make a statement," Jacob explained. "An old friend is trying to obtain data that I need to threaten the Alliance and force the Illuminati to recognize my abilities."

Stefan narrowed his eyes, his lips twitching with amusement. "Don't we seem a bit *overqualified* for pilfering data?"

Jacob leaned back in his chair, careful to keep his voice even and his manner unconcerned. He wasn't about to let the brothers rattle him. They were just pawns in this little game. "One of our Illuminati brethren from Russia will no doubt eliminate my friend Jack Grayson—they have a long-standing debt of their own to settle. However, there's a woman named Claire Davenport who's currently in possession of a flash drive with said data. I want the data retrieved and Ms. Davenport eliminated."

Demetrius lifted a pale brow. "You have called my brother and me here merely for a *hit*, Mr. Stone? You could hire any garden variety hitman to handle something of that nature. As a matter of fact, it sounds like you already have. That Russian you mentioned is the assassin who survived Jack Grayson's rampage, yes? Kozlov, is it?"

"Kozlov serves his purpose," Jacob replied, trying to hide his surprise at the depth of the man's knowledge. Was there anything Demetrius Shepherd *didn't* know? Well, he could wear his smug superiority like a crown, but Jacob wasn't about to be intimidated by the golden-haired bastard.

"Seems a bit like overkill—if you'll pardon the pun," Demetrius drawled.

"A recent endeavor of mine didn't go quite as I'd planned," Jacob admitted, figuring Demetrius already knew all about his failure to steal the Templars' treasure. "Failure is not an option this time, Mr. Shepherd. So, please don't be offended by the fact that I am taking a multipronged approach."

Demetrius gestured with his hand with a bored shrug. "I have no interest in your schemes, Mr. Stone—as long as they don't interfere with our own. So if you'd like our assistance with this little matter of yours, we will send someone to handle it."

Jacob inclined his head with a smile. "I'd like Ms. Davenport's death to send a message, if possible. And if she's not the only casualty, so be it. I'm certain Jack will be hovering somewhere nearby. If you get to him before the Russians, then my problem is resolved either way."

"Collateral damage beyond that?" Stefan pressed, that insane glimmer in his eyes growing brighter.

Jacob shrugged a shoulder. "Outsiders to the cause need to be reminded that there are dangers at every turn, that they need someone to deliver them from our present crisis."

"And you are that man, I presume?" Demetrius guessed.

Jacob inclined his head.

"And so you're asking us to put on some kind of . . . *display*?" Stefan asked.

Jacob offered him a tight grin. "What I'm asking for, Mr. Shepherd, is chaos."

At this, Stefan leaned forward, his dark eyes practically glowing. "I think we can manage a little chaos," he said, his voice low and sinister.

Demetrius sent a warning look toward his brother. "Stefan "

"Just tell us where and when," Stefan interrupted.

Demetrius opened his mouth to protest, but it snapped shut again when Jacob's office door opened and Allison strolled in. Her hair was pinned loosely at the crown of her head and her tight, pale green skirt hugged her curves so deliciously that Jacob's mouth began to water. "Allison," he greeted, standing and extending a hand to her. "I believe you remember Stefan and Demetrius Shepherd."

She smiled at each of the men in turn, her eyes lingering on Stefan for a little longer than Jacob would've liked. "Of course. Welcome, gentlemen. Please make yourselves comfortable while you're here. And if there's anything you need, please let me know."

Jacob stiffened at the hungry look in Stefan's eyes. "Unfortunately, my darling, they will have to leave almost immediately if they want to make it to Boston in time for Congressman Hale's gala."

Apparently picking up on Jacob's tone, Demetrius stepped forward to shake his hand. "Thank you for your hospitality, Mrs. Stone," he said, turning to Allison and taking her hand. He pressed a kiss to her fingertips. "But as your husband says, we must leave immediately." He then turned his attention back to Jacob. "We accept your offer and will do what we can to ensure Congressman Hale's gala is one people will remember for years to come."

Stefan shook their hands as well, kissing Allison's hand as his brother had done, his lips lingering against her skin far longer. Then he sent a glance Jacob's way. If Jacob hadn't known any better, he would've called it taunting.

Fucking psycho.

As soon as they'd gone, Allison slipped out from under Jacob's arm and sauntered to the other side of his desk, her fingertips seductively trailing along the edge. "What do you think they have planned?"

"I couldn't even guess," Jacob told her. "But if they betray me, it'll be the last mistake they make."

"You have to trust them, Jacob."

"A little distrust in situations like these is healthy," he assured her. "They're both far too interested in their own power to be trusted, Allie. Besides, I only need them for this job; then they'll be eliminated."

"Is that wise?" she asked. "Won't that discourage others from trusting you?"

Jacob came to her and took her hand, leading her over to the settee along one wall, where he pulled her down onto his lap. "What it will show is that I will not tolerate anyone whose loyalty is in question."

"Jacob, I wouldn't double-cross these men," she warned, genuinely concerned. "Their followers—they're *fanatics* beyond anything you have with the Faithful, and that's saying a lot. And they follow the *old ways* of the Illuminati."

Jacob laughed. "Oh, come on, Allie. You don't believe that occult bullshit, do you? We've distanced ourselves from all of that over the centuries."

"You believe in God," she reminded him. "Is it so hard for you to believe that there are negative forces as well? Belief gives even the most ridiculous superstitions power, Jacob."

"If they want to be superstitious idiots, that's their business," Jacob told her, curious at his normally pragmatic wife's sudden fear. "I assure you, I make deals with the devil every day—that was especially true when I was a politician—but those devils are flesh and blood men and women. There's nothing supernatural about them, trust me. When the Shepherd brothers have been eliminated, I will spread word among the Faithful that they went against me. That will prevent others from trying to do the same. Even Stefan and Demetrius's followers would be wise to pledge their loyalty to me—unless they, too, wish to meet the fate of their masters."

Her lips curved into a smile. "I love to see you embrace your destiny, Jacob. When I see the measure of your strength I can't help but envision you lording over all these cowards who sit in positions of power around the world."

He kissed her briefly, then leaned back against the back of the settee as she pressed kisses along his jaw, the curve of his neck. And when her hand slid down between them he groaned in appreciation. "Thank God I don't question your loyalty, my darling. It would be a shame to have to do without you . . ."

Her hand paused and her head slowly lifted from where she'd just pressed a kiss to his chest. "I hope I've never given you reason to doubt me."

His fingertips caressed her cheek and down along her jaw until he reached her neck. In one swift motion, his fingers tightened and he slammed her down against the cushions, his face close to hers when he hissed, "I saw how you looked at that fucking psycho Stefan. Do you want to fuck him? Is that it? Because I can arrange it if you want to be his whore. But be warned, Allison, most of the bitches he beds end up dead. I hear he likes to carve them up—like an artist sculpting his masterpiece."

"Jacob!" she gasped, clawing at his hand. "I'm your wife!"

He leaned closer. "Then don't fucking forget it."

The moment he released her and sat up, she scrambled to her feet. Far from being frightened of him in his jealous rage, she merely looked furious. That was confirmed when her open palm struck his cheek.

"Don't you ever accuse me of anything again," she spat. "Or it won't be Stefan that you have to worry about, Jacob."

He merely chuckled. "Oh, darling. I do love you. But don't think for an instant that I wouldn't smother you in your sleep if it suited my purposes." When her eyes widened, he merely smiled. "How's that for a show of strength?"

When he saw her swallow hard in a rare show of apprehension, his dick went rock hard.

"Now," he said, standing and unfastening his belt, "take off that skirt. If you want someone to fuck you, it's going to be me."

Her eyes now glistened with desire instead of fear. Within seconds, she had stripped out of her clothes and got on her knees, presenting her naked ass to him. He knelt behind her, smoothing his hands over her back and hips and then sliding his fingers along her cleft. He wasn't a bit surprised to find her hot and wet for him.

And when he thrust into her hard, savagely, over and over, she moaned with pleasure.

"Is this want you wanted?" he demanded. "Is this what you wanted Stefan to do to you?"

She ground her hips against him with a wordless moan. And when she screamed with ecstasy a few moments later, he shouted his own release. After his final shudder left him, he withdrew and cast her aside before standing and zipping his trousers.

Then he strode from the room, leaving her lying there panting on the floor. He slammed the door behind him and made his way to his bedroom to shower, knowing she'd most likely follow. There were two things he knew well about his wife: Ruthlessness and power turned her on. And he couldn't trust her a damn.

Chapter Nine

Jack sat on Maddie's bed, his back against the headboard, typing on his laptop and stealing a glance at her now and then as she paced the room. "You'll be fine. As you've reminded me, it's not as if you haven't done this before."

She waved away his words, her nose scrunching up adorably in her frustration. "I know. But I'm going to have to ditch that perv Senator Miles before I can move into position to intercept Hale. And won't that look wonderful? Flirting with one old man to get into the hotel room of another?"

Jack grunted and lifted a brow at her. "Careful. Congressman Hale is only a few years older than I am."

Maddie halted her pacing and turned an apologetic look on him. "You'll always be young to me, Jack—no matter what your age."

"And handsome too?" he asked, offering her an over-the-top "sexy" look, playfully wagging his brows at her. "Tell me the women will never notice my gray hair and age spots when I'm old and decrepit, because they'll be too enraptured by my stunning good looks."

She laughed and rolled her eyes. He could see the tension easing in her shoulders but could've used a little something to ease the tension he felt creeping into his muscles when she flashed him a playful smile and ran toward the bed, leaping at the last moment and landing beside him with a laugh. He tried not to notice how her full breasts bounced invitingly beneath her T-shirt.

If she saw the look in his eyes, she pretended not to notice as she rolled over and looked up at him, still grinning. "Yes, handsome too," she said. "You'll be the sexiest geriatric Templar ever."

He shook his head and begrudgingly dragged his gaze back to his laptop, looking over the building plans that Finn had sent them. "Here," he said, pointing to a stairwell on the east side of the ballroom. "This looks like a good route for ditching perverted elected officials if he corners you before you head upstairs."

She scooted up until she was sitting next to him and leaned in to see the screen, her breasts pressing into his upper arm. He tried to focus on the screen. He failed. Miserably.

"Yeah, that should work," she said with a terse nod. "The bar is in this little alcove, so I can pretend to be getting us a drink and then slip out to the stairs. And you're sure Congressman Hale will be in his hotel room at that point? He wouldn't be at the party?"

Jack shook his head. "According to the itinerary Finn was able to find, the congressman won't be entering the party until around eight o'clock. Apparently, he likes to make an entrance after everyone else has arrived."

She nodded again. "Okay. And what should I tell Hale about why I'm there? Presumably you will have intercepted Claire before then."

"All you need to do is keep him busy until I can secure the flash drive from Claire and prevent her from making a scene at the party."

Maddie lifted her face and gave him a wry look. "And

how exactly am I supposed to do that? I imagine he's going to be a little put off by me suddenly cornering him in his room."

Jack tried to focus on her eyes and not the soft lips so close to his own at that moment. "Be honest. Tell him you know about his involvement in Ralston's death and that even now evidence is being sent to the authorities."

"And you think that'll keep him busy?" Maddie asked, her nose scrunching up in doubt. "I'd be surprised if he didn't have his security detail throw my ass out."

Jack turned his mouth down briefly in the equivalent of a shrug. "True. But it's also possible that he'll try to talk himself out of trouble or implicate someone else, giving us another lead. Finn and his people will be listening in and recording the conversation, so just roll with it."

She drew back slightly, eying him warily. "And how do you intend to persuade Ms. Davenport to hand over the flash drive? She doesn't have any dirt you can use as leverage."

Jack thought he caught a note of jealousy in her voice. "I don't. It doesn't take much to find something like a flash drive concealed on a woman's body. And she and I met earlier in the hallway, so—"

"You *what*?" Maddie interrupted. "Why didn't you tell me?"

Good question . . .

"I didn't think it was pertinent," he said.

"Is she as pretty in person as she is in the dossier photo?"

He suppressed a grin, pleased more than he liked to admit that she was fishing for information. "She is beautiful," he admitted. "I can see why Will is so taken with her."

Maddie leaned back against the headboard and picked at the hem of her T-shirt. "Well, at least seducing her won't be completely horrible."

"I've seduced women who were less attractive, certainly,"

he said with a shrug. When she snorted derisively, he grinned and closed his laptop, setting it on the bedside table before turning back toward her. "But seeing as how I have no intention of seducing her . . ."

"That's what Will was asking you to do, though, wasn't it?" Maddie blushed, making the freckles on her nose seem darker in contrast.

He nodded. "Probably. But I think that was more for his own benefit than a real directive on how to handle this situation." When her brows came together, he explained, "I think it was Will's way of trying to convince himself that he has forgotten about Ms. Davenport, that he's not interested in her except as a pain-in-the-ass reporter he keeps having to deal with every time she gets too close, and now as someone who needs our protection."

"And you think that's total bullshit," she surmised.

"I know it is."

"So what do you plan to do to get the flash drive, then?"

He took a deep breath and let it out slowly. "I plan to offer her something else she wants in return."

Maddie frowned. "What?"

Jack's conscience made him avert his gaze. "The flash drive holds information about the Alliance and the Illuminati—but that's not what she's interested in. Not really."

She slowly sat up until she was at eye level with him. "You plan to give her information on Will."

"I know what it's like to need answers and be frustrated at every turn," Jack told her. "I think it's far less harmful— to her and to the Alliance—to have her on the right track than floundering around in the dark, uncovering the truth haphazardly."

"You have no right, Jack," Maddie warned. "That's for Will to deal with."

Jack took a deep breath and let it out on a long sigh

before responding. "Perhaps not, but it's my duty to protect the Alliance and act in the Order's best interest. This has been Will's issue to deal with for quite a while, Mads, but his unwillingness to do so has put us all in jeopardy."

He saw disappointment in her eyes when she shook her head at his words. "So you'd risk damaging one of the most important relationships in your life?"

He casually rose to his feet and picked up the laptop, tucking the device under his arm. "Will is a brother to me. I have no doubt he will understand."

She rose up on her knees and moved to the edge of the bed so that she was a few inches from him, and took his face in her hands. "I hope you're right, Jack. There's only so much damage a relationship can take before it's beyond repair."

He searched her gaze, sensing that she wasn't just offering him a warning about his friendship with Will. So when she drew him down to brush her lips against his, he savored the warmth of her kiss, let it envelop him as his free arm came around her waist, pulling her closer. He couldn't suppress a groan when her tongue lightly teased against his.

And when she sank back on the bed, pulling him with her, he tossed his laptop onto the mattress so both his hands were free to tangle in her dark curls as their kiss became more frenzied.

He groaned again when she shifted beneath him so that he was cradled between her thighs, arching into him in the process and sending a shot of need through him that was so powerful he shuddered. She felt too damned good beneath him, her curves fitting perfectly against him in a manner far too enticing.

She pulled at his shirt, untucking it to slip her hands beneath the material. Her fingertips skimmed lightly against his skin, bringing goose bumps to his flesh as he left her mouth to trail kisses along the side of her throat.

"I should go," he murmured against her skin as he kissed his way to the valley between her breasts, contradicting his own words. Her fingers speared into his hair when his teeth grazed her hardened nipple through her T-shirt. He kissed his way back to her lips, claiming them once more until she clawed at his shirt, pulling it over his head and tossing it aside.

"Stay," she rasped.

"Why?" he panted, moving to her other breast, feeling like a fucking moron the moment he uttered the word. The *why* was pulsing in his dick like a homing beacon. But he wanted her to say the words, wanted her confirmation of where things were headed so that he wasn't assuming that her desires aligned with his.

She moaned, grinding her hips against his. "I want you."

He cupped her cheek, his gaze traveling over her face, taking in every beloved curve. "Are you sure about this?"

Unfortunately, his question seemed to flip a switch. "Damn it." She closed her eyes and brought one hand to her eyes as she pressed the other against his chest, holding him back. "You're right. This is a bad idea."

His brows came together. "Sorry?"

She opened her eyes at this and allowed her hands to smooth tenderly over his bare skin, over his shoulders, across his chest. "I want you, Jack," she told him. "My *God*, I want you. But I don't want to just fall back into bed with you. It's far too easy to slide into our old pattern. It's not fair to use you just to satisfy my libido."

He caressed her cheek with the back of his fingers. "Really? That would be such a terrible thing?"

She shook her head. "No. It would be beautiful and thrilling and amazing—just like it was before. But, ultimately, heartbreaking. At least, that's my fear. That seems to be our track record."

"I can't promise you that we'd live happily ever after,

Maddie," he admitted even as he realized that's exactly what he wanted. He could easily picture them growing old together. And never once in his life had he thought of himself as a father, but when he looked at Maddie, he could imagine a future that included the kind of happiness he'd never dared to dream of. But that was *his* dream. He wasn't sure if it was hers. And he sure as hell wasn't going to allow himself to hope for anything beyond the moment.

As difficult as it was to leave the warmth of Maddie's arms, Jack eased off of her and pulled on his shirt. He grabbed his laptop and turned back toward the bed to see Maddie still lying on her back, the heels of her palms pressed against her eyes. It pained him to leave her, but she clearly had reservations about going further, and he knew if he stayed, they'd be right back where they'd left off. And the thought of her regretting being with him was far more painful than the raging hard-on he was sporting.

He headed toward the bedroom door but paused. "I honestly don't know what the future holds," he told her. "But I know I will always want you, Maddie. *Always.*"

At this she moved her hands away from her face and gave him a pointed look. "I want you too, Jack. But *wanting* and *loving* are two very different things."

Maddie finished pinning her curls in place and peered at her reflection in the mirror. She was surprised she remembered how to do anything with her hair beyond throwing it up in a ponytail or messy knot. But apparently all those formal events growing up had stuck with her.

She slipped into the little black dress Finn had sent, and added the diamond earrings and necklace that complemented the low-cut neckline perfectly. She smoothed her hands down her sides where the material hugged her curves and found herself wishing that she was spending the evening with Jack instead of heading to a sting operation with a skeezy politician.

And that thought, of course, led to other, more deliciously naughty thoughts about how a night out with Jack might end. She'd so desperately wanted to give in earlier, to make love to him with the reckless abandon she once had. She shouldn't have kissed him, shouldn't have pulled him down onto the bed with her. Not when she kept pushing him away.

But, damn it! Everything had felt so *right*, so *perfect*. She'd been ripping his shirt off before she'd even realized what she was doing. And once she'd caught a glimpse of the lean, sculpted muscle she'd so often fantasized about, it was *on*.

And if he hadn't put the brakes on . . .

Her breath left her on a gasp as her nipples tightened and everything womanly began to ache with need. She grasped the edge of the countertop, reliving every kiss, every touch, as the ache increased and her muscles began to clench . . .

If she hadn't been dressed, her hair already in place, she would've hiked up her skirt and given herself a little relief, but even the thought of pleasuring herself had her panting as she remembered how much Jack used to like to watch her touch herself while they made love.

Dear God . . .

What the hell was wrong with her? Even the thought of being with Jack was enough to get her hot and bothered. Well, that and the fact that it'd been almost two years since she'd been with a man. But regardless, there was the plain and simple fact that the only man she wanted to be with was Jack.

Her cell phone rang on the vanity next to her. She snatched it up and answered it without looking at the number first. "Blake."

"Are you all right?" Jack's voice caressed her senses as if he'd been standing there in the room with her, his finger-tips smoothing her skin.

"Yeah, I'm fine," she said in a rush, as if worried he might somehow guess that thoughts of him had been tor-menting her just moments before.

There was a slight pause before he said, "I just wanted to let you know that I'm leaving for the gala. I'll see you there, and Finn will link us on the comms once you're on-site."

"Okay, then," Maddie said, still sounding far more breathless than she'd like. "I'll see you there."

"Maddie."

She cleared her throat and then forced a cheerful tone as she said, "Yeah?"

"Be careful, love," he said so tenderly tears stung her eyes.

She swallowed the emotion that rose up in her before answering, "You, too."

She hung up before he could say anything else, and grabbed her small evening bag, stowing her phone inside along with the cloned key card for the congressman's hotel room that Finn had sent by courier shortly after Jack's visit.

A few minutes later she was seated in the black Lincoln that had been sent by the car service and was in front of Boston's Liberty hotel far sooner than she would've liked. "Okay, Jack," she murmured as the driver came around to hand her out. "I'm going in. You with me?"

She could hear the smile in his voice as he replied, "Always."

She plastered on the bright, inviting smile she'd per-fected growing up as a senator's daughter and entered the throng of social elite and other celebrities who were slowly making their way along the red carpet that led inside to the evening's black-tie political fund-raiser.

"Ms. Blake! Ms. Blake! Look over here!"

Maddie paused and turned toward the paparazzo calling out to her, offering him a bright smile and turning slightly with her hand on her hip to pose for a photo.

She heard Jack mutter a soft curse over the comm device in her ear. "Who was that? And how in the hell did he recognize you?"

Maddie offered the photographer a parting wave, then pretended to adjust her diamond earring to cover the slight movement of her lips as she answered. "That was Todd Marx. He used to cover my father's press events before going to the dark side of the tabloids."

She made her way into the rotunda of the hotel that had once served as the Charles Street Jail. The amber light cast too many shadows, making it hard to make out faces. But there was one face she couldn't mistake. Jack stood at the bar, looking heart-stoppingly debonair in his black tuxedo. It took more than a little effort to drag her gaze away and focus on the others milling about the rotunda.

"Do you have eyes on any of our companions for the evening?" Jack asked as Maddie nodded in greeting as she passed by an actor she recognized but whose name she didn't recall.

The actor didn't hide the fact that he was looking her up and down, but when he started walking toward her as if to engage in conversation, Maddie turned on her stiletto heel and headed in the opposite direction.

"Negative," she told him. "You?" When Jack didn't immediately respond, her gaze drifted back toward the bar and locked with his from across the distance. "Jack, do you copy?"

Jack took another sip of his wine, trying to disguise the fact that the sight of Maddie had made him momentarily speechless. She was lovely beyond compare—her thick dark hair swept off her neck into an elegant arrangement, long curls having slipped out to rest against the delicate curve of her throat. The little black dress she wore accentuated the curves he'd often enjoyed tracing gently with his fingertips. His fingers tingled at the remembrance of the nights they'd shared together and of how close he'd come earlier in the day to being able to caress her in the way he so longed to.

If he hadn't questioned her certainty about where things were going earlier that afternoon, there was no question how far things would've gone. But he was determined not to push her into "falling into bed" with him again, as she'd put it. They'd rushed toward satiating their yearning for one another far too quickly before, and Maddie had bolted. He wasn't about to make that mistake again.

So why did he feel like he'd fucked up by bringing everything to a screeching halt just as they were revving up?

"I'm here, Mads," Jack murmured, a familiar ache in the center of his chest.

Regret. Ah, yes, he knew it all too well . . .

He forced a grin and raised his glass in salute. "Care to join me for a drink?"

She smothered a smile and turned away to resume her casual stroll through the crowd. "Another time."

"I'll hold you to that," he assured her. "Remember where you're going?"

"I'm good," she assured him. "It doesn't look like Senator Miles is here yet, so I'm going up to Hale's room as soon as our favorite surfer-dude decides to grace us with his presence."

"Sounds like that's my cue," Finn suddenly chimed in through their comms. "We've got you both online, so you need anything, just hollah. Safe word today is *shitstorm*."

"Isn't that two words, Finn?" Maddie teased.

Jack grinned and strolled away from the bar to do his own mingling among the crowd. "Perhaps it's hyphenated?"

"What, you guys are correcting my grammar now?" Finn replied. "By the way, happy Independence Day, Maddie. And, Jack—condolences on our having to kick your compatriots' collective asses back in the day."

Jack chuckled. "Thank you, brother. But I think we got over losing to a bunch of uppity colonists quite a while ago. Probably a blessing in disguise, really, considering how much mischief you Americans get up to."

"Ouch!" Finn shot back.

"Sorry to interrupt, gentlemen," Maddie interjected, "but I'm entering the elevator."

"Copy that, Maddie," Finn replied. "Stay safe."

Jack tried not to think too hard about the potential danger Maddie could be walking into as he wound his way through the rotunda, heading toward the ballroom, where the congressman would later be making his speech. He wanted to see if Ms. Davenport had perhaps come through another entrance and made it to the ballroom without his spotting her.

The room was already crowded with partygoers in formal attire, their conversations an indistinct mass of noise as they all attempted to be heard over the music. The scene reminded Jack far too much of the parties his parents had often hosted at their home in the city. He'd much preferred the quiet peacefulness of the manor house in the country. It was an escape from the breakneck pace of London, and the one place where he and his family were most likely to actually be in the same room together without being interrupted by his parents' work.

Maybe someday he'd be able to take Maddie there, let her meet the staff who still maintained the place, their salaries paid by a benefactor whose name they didn't even recognize . . .

Jack was so caught up in his thoughts, he didn't see the familiar face leering at him from among the throng of partygoers until they were within a few yards of each other. A cold chill passed through him as he casually shifted his trajectory and moved toward a more heavily populated area of the ballroom to shield his movements.

"Maddie, how much longer do you think you'll be?" he murmured.

"Almost at Hale's room," she said, her voice barely audible and cutting out. "Why?"

Jack slipped out of the ballroom and back into the rotunda. "We have a problem. Kozlov is here."

He heard both Maddie and Finn curse in response to the happy news. But it was Maddie who spoke first. "How the hell did he know you were going to be at the event?"

"No fucking clue," Jack replied, handing his wineglass off to a waiter and adjusting his tuxedo jacket slightly to have better access to his weapon. "I'm going to need to lead him away from here. The man doesn't give a shit about collateral damage. The last thing we need is for him to take a shot at me in a crowded political event."

"What about Claire Davenport?" Finn demanded. "We've got to get that flash drive, Jack."

Jack sent a nonchalant glance around the room and saw Kozlov entering the rotunda. The man hadn't yet spotted him, but the crowd was thinner here, so it was only a matter of time. "I haven't seen her yet. Maddie, abort mission and meet me at the west exit of the hotel. I'll get the car and pick you up there."

"Negative," Maddie insisted. "Kozlov's after you, not me. I'll handle things here."

"Not leaving you without backup," Jack insisted. "We'll find another way. This is not up for discussion."

"Oh, is that right?" Maddie shot back. "Well, I seem to remember another discussion that took place just the other day, Jack. If you don't recall, I'd be happy—"

"Uh, guys," Finn interrupted. "We have another problem. The sensors I had the Boston *confreres* put in place are going apeshit."

Christ.

"What does that mean?" Maddie demanded, her voice sounding like she was on the move.

Jack halted abruptly and turned once more to survey the crowd. "It means there's a bomb somewhere in this hotel."

Chapter Ten

"I think this qualifies as a shitstorm, gang," Finn said, his normally chill voice edged with tension. "I'm scrambling the Boston team that was on standby."

Maddie strode back toward the elevator as quickly as she could in stiletto heels, but not quickly enough for her liking. Within a few feet of the elevator, she kicked off the damned torture devices and snatched them up, now racing barefoot toward the elevator doors. She was within a few feet when the doors suddenly slid open and two men, followed by a small detail of guys in dark suits, stepped out, laughing at some inside joke.

One of them came to an abrupt halt when he saw her. "Well, Maddie Blake! There you are!"

Maddie forced a smile at the man with carefully styled gray hair and a too-white grin. "Senator Miles! So good to see you. I was wondering when I would run into you."

"Get out," Finn warned in her ear, his voice breaking up, allowing her to catch only a few words. "—notified . . . evacuate . . . building."

"Have you met my good friend, Congressman Hale?" the senator asked.

Congressman Hale's gaze, which had been lingering at

her cleavage, slowly wandered upward to her face, his cold blue eyes sparking with lust he didn't even bother trying to disguise. "You didn't tell me you were bringing this tasty little morsel with you tonight, Miles." He took Maddie's hand and brought it to his lips, kissing her fingertips. "Where are you running off to, sweetheart?"

Maddie suppressed a shudder. The man was devilishly handsome—dark and swarthy with strikingly blue eyes, but *devilish* was precisely the word for him. There was something fiendish in his eyes, something sinister and soulless. It reminded Maddie of the pictures she'd seen of serial killers—difficult to see behind the veneer of polished charm and respectability, but obvious once the truth came out. "It's wonderful to meet you, Congressman. But I'm afraid there's something I must urgently attend to." She moved to slip around the men blocking her path. "If you'll excuse me—"

"Nonsense!" Miles interrupted, stepping in front of her. "I heard that you'd left the FBI, so what could be more important than catching up with an old friend?"

Her answering smile was tight and felt grotesque as she glanced at the elevator doors, which had already closed behind them. "I wish I could, Senator. But I really must—"

Congressman Hale grabbed her arm as she once more started to pass. "You're not going anywhere, Ms. Blake."

Maddie lifted her brows. "I beg your pardon?"

At that moment, the men in black suits rushed forward as if to take her into custody, but Maddie spun into the congressman's hold, sucker punching him. Instantly he released his grip. She pivoted, using the stiletto heel in her hand to catch one of the guards in the face. He stumbled back just as another of the guards made a grab for her. She took hold of his arm, dropping down and spinning, sweeping the leg of the third guard before flipping the one in her grasp onto his back and punching him in the throat. The guard she'd caught with her shoe came back at her, earning a jab to the solar plexus for his efforts. When he staggered, she grabbed his arm and slammed him into the wall and then onto the ground.

"Stay down, asshole," she hissed.

Ignoring Jack's and Finn's garbled words in her ear, she ducked a punch. "I'm on my way," she grunted, nailing one of the guy's pressure points so his knees crumpled, hoping they could hear her better than she could hear them.

She caught the senator's look of surprise a split second before she heard a click and felt the pressure of a gun at the back of her head.

"You're just full of surprises, Ms. Blake," Hale drawled.

"What the hell are you doing, Hale?" Miles cried. "Have you lost your mind?"

"Let's go to my room for a little chat, shall we?" Hale said, grabbing Maddie's arm and shifting the gun to her side. He jerked his chin at the guards, who were picking themselves off the floor. "Bring the senator as well."

Maddie heard Jack saying something in her ear. She couldn't make it out because of the interference with the comm device, but she thought she'd heard Claire Davenport's name. Perfect. *Now* the woman decides to show up?

A shitstorm indeed . . .

As the authorities began to quickly but discreetly move people out of the hotel rotunda, Jack was rushing toward the stairs when he overheard what sounded like fighting coming over the comm.

He cursed roundly under his breath. "Finn, we need that backup ASAP."

"I'm on it, brah. They're already on the premises searching for the bomb," Finn assured him. "Just concentrate on getting Maddie out of there. The feed is breaking up on Maddie's comm, but from what I can catch, it sounds like all hell's breaking loose upstairs."

He'd just reached the door to the nearest stairwell when he caught a glimpse of Claire Davenport in the crowd of people being forced toward the exits. After a few steps, she ducked out of the horde near the stairs on the opposite side of the rotunda and pulled open the door.

"Damn it!" Jack ground out. "Claire's here. And she just went upstairs."

When he received only static in response, he tapped the device in his ear. "Finn, do you copy?"

The level of interference increased, a high-pitched electronic screech making him cry out and snatch the device from his ear. Someone was interfering with their transmission. Which meant whoever it was had known they were coming.

Shit.

He was just going to have to go it alone.

Jack dropped the comm device into his pocket bolted up the stairs, drawing his gun as he went. H it to the third floor just as another stairwell door at the end of the hallway and Claire emerge one of the waitstaff for the party.

The moment she saw him rushin frowned. But then her gaze dropped was held by his thigh and her eye

She instantly pivoted, ready

"Ms. Davenport!" he ye you."

The use of her real for a moment bef well. Fortunate time to gain the secon

"Don't make me shoot!" he said. She halted immediately and raised her hands before turning to face him. He hurried down the remaining steps, keeping his gun trained on her chest.

"Are you trying to kill me too?" she demanded.

"I'm not the enemy, Claire," Jack assured her. "But they *are* here. And they *are* looking for you. We need to get you out of this building. You're in danger. We all are."

She gave him a wary look. "Right. You mean the bomb threat? Nice distraction."

"It's not a distraction," Jack told her. "It's for real. And I don't know who the hell is responsible for that one, but I do know I'd rather not die today." He holstered his gun underneath his jacket and held out his hand. "What do you say?"

She drew back, her wari̶ ̶ ̶ ̶ ̶ ̶ ̶ ̶ ̶ ̶ ̶ some-
̶ ̶ ̶ ̶ ̶ ̶ now I

and
̶ ̶ made
̶ opened up
̶, dressed as

̶ toward her, she
̶ down to where his gun
̶ went wide.

̶ to bolt back down the stairs.
̶d. "Claire! I'm here to help

̶ name brought her up short, but only
̶ she disappeared back into the stair-
̶, her brief hesitation gave Jack enough
̶ome ground. Just as she made the landing on
̶ floor, he raised his gun.

rn for
aking
from
w, he

t?"
"Be-
d of

t his

uch
on't

him

suspiciously. But her voice trembled with excitement when she asked, "How do you know about him? Is he alive?"

"Will you come with me if I promise to tell you more?" Jack asked. "We have to evacuate this building, Claire."

As if on cue, the door to the stairwell opened and a SWAT officer appeared in full gear. "Gonna need you folks to exit immediately. Anyone else in your room?"

Claire shook her head, sending a glance toward Jack. "No."

The officer nodded and then headed to the first room in the hall and knocked on the door.

"They're clearing the hotel, Claire," Jack told her. "Please, come with me and we'll talk some more as promised."

She gave him a wary look, but then nodded and allowed him to lead her quickly down the stairs. Within moments, more footsteps joined theirs as other guests were evacuated.

Jack's concern for Maddie increased with every step he took away from her. Desperate for an update on what the hell was going on, he fished his earpiece out of his pocket as he and Claire reached the final landing.

"Finn, do you copy?" he said in a rush.

"Where *the fuck* have you been?" Finn demanded. "Do you have Maddie?"

"Negative. But I do have Claire Davenport." Jack's hold on Claire's arm tightened as they entered a throng of people pushing their way out of the narrow hallway toward the exits. He could feel the tension as they elbowed and cursed at one another. Officers at the doorway were trying to keep people moving and calm, but they were one hysterical guest away from full-blown panic. "Any word on the emergency situation? Do we have an ID?"

"Nothing yet," Finn told him. "Local LEOs have the dogs on the scent, though. Your bomber is still on premises."

Jack steered Claire out of the crowd. "What was Maddie's twenty at last transmission?"

"Still headed toward the congressman's room in the presidential suite when I heard from her last."

Shit.

"I have to go back in," Jack muttered. "She's in trouble."

"Not advisable, Jack," Finn warned. "Will would have my ass if I let you go back in when there's a bomb threat. I can't lose two Templars in one day, brah."

"I'm not leaving her." Jack glanced around, looking for a safe place to leave Claire. "Guess you're just going to have to say you tried to talk me out of it, brother."

He snatched the comm from his ear and dropped it back in his pocket, knowing he was going to get an earful from the normally Zen tech specialist. "Claire, I have to go back for my . . . colleague. I want you to stay here with the rest of the guests. Blend in. And don't go with anyone else but me. I don't care who it is."

She nodded, looking a little uncertain about his plan. He turned to go but pivoted back to her and held out his hand. "And I'll take that flash drive, if you please."

She blinked at him in surprise and then pressed her lips together in a stubborn line. "I need that information."

"You promised to trust me, Claire," he reminded her. "Trust me on this—what you're looking for isn't on that flash drive."

She crossed her arms with a huff. "But—"

"Will's alive, Claire," Jack interrupted, impatient to get the hell upstairs and find Maddie. "He's alive and he's in Chicago. That's all I'm going to tell you until you give me the damned flash drive. When I get back, I'll fill in some more blanks for you, but I have to have that device or you'll put all of us at risk—Will included."

She hesitated for a brief moment and then reached into the pocket of her black slacks and handed Jack the flash drive.

He grabbed it and spun back toward the hotel, slipping around to the service entrance he remembered from the maps he'd studied with Maddie. The darkness hid his movements, but he still couldn't shake the feeling that he was being watched. He reached into his tuxedo jacket's inside pocket and took out the key card Finn had created for him and slid it into the slot on the door. The green light on the lock came on and the door clicked.

Jack sent one last glance around the darkness, but seeing no one, he slipped inside and raced down the hallway until he found another stairwell that would take him to the top floor. He took the stairs two at a time, hoping to God he wasn't too late.

Chapter Eleven

Maddie sat in the chair Congressman Hale had pulled out for her and kept her expression bland as one of his guards, pissed off at being taken down by a woman, tied her wrists to the arm of the chair with a couple of the congressman's neckties.

"What the hell are you doing?" Senator Miles demanded, hands raised in response to the gun pointed at the center of his chest. "This woman's father is a senator, for chrissake!"

The congressman gave Miles a tight smile. "You believe that my loyalties are to the government? That just because we are all elected officials, I owe you some measure of fidelity?" He shared an amused glance with his guards. "You poor, naïve fool . . ."

"Hale's Illuminati," Maddie spat. "His only loyalty is to those assholes."

"Illuminati?" Miles laughed. "This is bullshit. I'm leaving."

Miles waved away the man with the gun on him and strode toward the door. Maddie's adrenaline spiked as a wave of fear washed over her. "Senator!"

But she'd barely gotten the word out before one of the

guards swung his arm, nailing the senator in the back of the head with his gun. When the senator stumbled and fell face-first on the floor, the same guard snatched up a pillow and kneeled to put it over the senator's head. Maddie cried out when the guard fired through the pillow. The senator's body twitched once, then went still.

"Now," Hale drawled, completely unaffected by the murder of his supposed friend, "where were we, Ms. Blake?"

She glared at him. "I was about to use one of your guards as a human shield while I shot the other two. Then I was planning to take you out." She turned toward the guard who had shot Senator Miles. "I think you'll go first, dickhead."

Hale chuckled. "Is that so? Well, thank you for the warning." He sent an amused grin toward the guard nearest Maddie. "Perhaps we'd better tie her legs as well so we can have a civil conversation, eh?"

The guard loosened his tie and slid it from around his neck with a snap, leering at Maddie through the swollen eye and split lip she'd given him earlier.

"So," Hale said, strolling toward the wet bar as the guard stalked toward her, "why don't you start with what you know about the missing flash drive my colleague Mr. Ralston was supposed to deliver?"

Maddie sent a glance around the room, getting the position of each of the guards at that moment. A familiar calm settled over her, and she exhaled slowly as the guard with the necktie bent to tie her ankles. Time seemed to slow to a crawl. She brought her knee up hard, connecting with the guard's jaw, sending him staggering. In one fluid motion, she slipped her wrists from the restraints she'd been loosening from the moment they'd tied them and shoved her hand into the guard's jacket, snatching his gun from its holster.

In the next instant, she was on her feet, wrenching the guard up by the front of his shirt to block her as the other two guards opened fire. The man in her grasp jerked with the bullets' impact as she fired off two rounds, nailing each of the remaining guards in the center of his chest.

She pivoted toward Congressman Hale in time to see him bring up his own weapon, but anticipating his move, she fired off a shot, hitting his shoulder. His gun dropped from his grasp as he fell back against the minibar. He blinked at her in stunned silence.

Maddie shoved her shield's body away and strode toward Hale, sweeping his gun out of reach with her foot. She saw him glance toward where his gun lay, obviously contemplating making a move. "Go ahead. Make a grab for it if you think you can get to it before I put another bullet in you."

"What do you want?" Hale gasped.

"Tell me who you're working for," she demanded. "Who's your contact in the Illuminati? Is it Jacob Stone?"

Hale chuckled, wincing at the pain in his shoulder. "Stone? He's a puppet. Just one of many. He thinks he'll rule the world someday, but he's a delusional little prick. But then we all have a role to play."

"And what was Ralston's role?" she demanded. "What were you after on that flash drive? Information on the Alliance? Was it worth killing Ralston over?"

"Ralston was expendable," Hale wheezed. "He double-crossed the wrong people and he paid the price."

"Get up," Maddie ordered, gesturing with her gun. "I'm turning you over to the authorities. This place is crawling with them, thanks to your little bomb-threat distraction. I assume your operative is waiting for your signal? What, not enough fireworks in Boston tonight?"

Hale's brows came together. "Bomb threat? Do you think I'm a fucking idiot? Why in the hell would I want to risk blowing myself up?"

In her flurry of thoughts, Maddie had thought maybe Hale had set up the bomb threat to generate publicity, tout himself as some hero—the government official who was being attacked for his politics but couldn't be intimidated. She'd seen it happen more times than she could count while growing up in political circles. So much of the bull-shit controversies were staged, generating sympathy and outrage that helped a politician's ranking, especially in an election year.

But if Hale wasn't behind the bomb threat, who the hell was?

She tapped her earpiece, trying to raise Finn or Jack, but all she received in response was hissing static. Inter-ference.

"Get up," she ordered, motioning with her gun. "Now. We have to get the hell out of here."

A long beep and a soft click sounded behind her as someone slid a key card into the suite's door. She pivoted, gun raised as the door swung open. Jack charged inside, his weapon at the ready. She instantly dropped her gun to her side when she saw his beloved face, and heaved a sigh so heavy her shoulders rounded.

Jack's gaze swept the room, taking in her handiwork at a glance. He rushed toward her, gun trained on Hale. His eyes darted toward her. "You okay?"

She nodded and grabbed Hale by his good arm, hauling him to his feet. "I'm fine. But Hale's not behind the bomb. Did you find Claire?"

"Yeah," Jack said, clearly winded from his mad dash to get to her. "Let's go."

Maddie followed him at a jog, dragging Hale along with them as they made their way down the hall to the stairwell. Jack opened the door and cleared it before they entered and scrambled down the stairs.

They were about halfway down when Maddie suddenly heard Finn's voice in her ear. She stopped short, pressing her fingertips to the device to try to hear better.

"Jack, hold on," she called. "Did you catch that?"

He shook his head, frowning as he pressed his ear, straining to catch Finn's garbled transmissions. "Keep moving."

A few minutes later they hit the final landing, but just as they slipped out of the stairwell toward the exit, Jack suddenly slid to a halt, throwing out his arm and nearly clotheslining Maddie and Hale.

He held a finger to his lips and jerked his chin. Maddie frowned and turned her attention to the open area of the rotunda. Standing to one side of the escalator that went down to the lower level, a group of perhaps a dozen people stood in a tightly spaced cluster, facing outward. Maddie could see some of them were crying, others looked terrified and on the verge of bolting in fear, but something was keeping them there.

Then Maddie noticed the SWAT officers spaced out behind furniture, a couple of them on the balconies overlooking the floor below. A bald man in a ballistics vest slowly inched toward the group. He was talking, but Maddie couldn't quite make out what he was saying at that distance. But the reality of the situation was clear.

"Oh, shit," she breathed. Apparently, she wasn't the only one using human shields that night. The son of a bitch who'd brought a bomb to the party was surrounded by innocent victims.

"Behold the power of the One True Master!" the bomber yelled, his voice echoing in the eerie silence.

Shit, shit, shit . . .

"Get me outta here," Hale whimpered.

"Shut up," Maddie spat with a disgusted glance. She then sent a pointed look toward Jack. "We gotta go, Jack."

"Tremble at his vengeance!"

"No one has a clear shot," Jack muttered, his gaze darting toward the various SWAT officers and their hostage negotiator. "They're all going to die. He's going to detonate."

Maddie laid a hand on his arm. "We can't help them, Jack. We have to deal with Hale and Claire. Let the locals handle this one."

"Behold his righteous glory!"

But Jack was still searching for an opening, some way to neutralize the situation.

"Jack," she said in an urgent whisper. "You don't know what kind of detonator the guy has. You shoot him, the bomb could go."

He cursed, knowing she was right, and sent a tortured look her way. Maddie could hear the negotiator, trying to reason with the bomber. But there was no reasoning with a fanatic intent on becoming a martyr and taking out half a city block with him.

"I offer up my soul, Master! I give my all to you!"

"Jack!" Maddie cried.

This time, he turned on his heel, shoving Maddie and Hale ahead of him, racing toward the exit at the end of the hall. They'd just cleared the glass doors when Maddie heard a deafening roar, felt the ground tremble, heard glass shatter. The concussion from the blast threw them forward, the heat at her back searing her skin. She landed hard, sliding across the pavement for a few feet before rolling over with a groan.

She couldn't hear anything except the muffled sounds of first responders rushing toward the site of the explosion. Thank God the blast seemed to have been largely contained within the hotel, but as Maddie surveyed the scene, she saw dazed and bloodied people wandering the street, injured by flying debris.

She glanced around frantically for Jack and saw him already on his feet, hurrying toward her. Then her gaze lighted on Hale, who lay on his stomach near the curb, unmoving. She managed to crawl over to him and rolled him over to reveal a huge gash across his forehead, white bone poking through. He must've nailed his head on the edge of the sidewalk when they'd been knocked off their feet, cracking his skull.

"Damn it!" she spat as Jack reached her side and dropped down to check Hale's neck for a pulse.

Apparently finding none, Jack wiped his forehead with his forearm and sank back on his heels for a moment before rising to his feet and extending a hand to Maddie to help her up.

She stood but hesitated before taking a step, searching for a path that wasn't covered with shards of glass. Jack glanced down at her bare feet and without missing a beat, swept her up into his arms, carrying her away from the devastated hotel toward the police barricades, where dozens of bystanders looked on in startled disbelief. One of the faces in the crowd was familiar—a lovely woman with blond hair and crystalline blue eyes.

The woman shoved through the onlookers, meeting up with them as Jack cleared the crowd.

"Is she okay?" the woman asked. "Is there anything I can do?"

"Just stay close," she heard Jack reply. Her head began to swim and her vision went blurry as her head lolled against Jack's shoulder. As darkness rose up to claim her, Maddie heard Jack's frantic words. "Finn? Finn, do you copy? We need an evac!"

Jack sat next to the bed where Maddie lay, still unconscious. The doctor had said she had a concussion, but that it wasn't too serious. So why the hell hadn't she woken up yet? He bent forward in his chair, resting his forehead on his clasped hands and closed his eyes, trying to bring his emotions back under control.

"I'm sure she'll be fine."

He lifted his head at the sound of Claire Davenport's voice. He'd almost forgotten that she was sitting in the corner of the hospital room, curled up in the only other chair in the tiny space. The hospital had been flooded with injuries as a result of the blast that had apparently left twenty people dead and nearly a hundred injured, several critically.

When he looked away without responding, Claire added softly, "This is my fault, isn't it? None of this would've happened if Tad hadn't sent me that flash drive."

He shook his head. "No. This isn't your fault, Claire. These people are ruthless, shameless. They don't care who they hurt, how many lives they ruin."

"Why did they want the flash drive?" she asked. "Don't they already know what's on it?"

He shook his head again. "It contains proof of who we are, what we do. At least, that's what we think it is. We won't know for certain until I get this back to headquarters and have our tech people take a look at it. But we can't risk exposure—that's why everyone is after it. I'm sorry, but we couldn't let you confront Hale about it and risk letting it fall into his hands."

"I only wanted to find Will," she said so softly he almost didn't hear her. "I needed to know that I hadn't dreamed what happened in Nigeria, that there was this guardian angel who'd saved my life. I just wanted to know that he was still alive, that there were . . . that there were still people out there who gave a damn and made a difference. After all I'd seen in that town, the carnage . . . I needed something to believe in again."

Jack turned back to her, studying her for a long moment. "You have to give up this search, Claire. It's too dangerous for you. That's why Will has stayed away."

She swiped at her cheeks, where silent tears streaked her skin. "How exactly am I supposed to do that? There are things I've seen, things I've experienced that I *can't* forget. I owe it to the people who've died, to remember."

"We'll relocate you," Jack promised, "give you a new identity, make sure that the men who've been after you won't be able to find you. You'll be safe."

What he didn't say was that she'd have no choice in the matter.

She offered him a tremulous smile. "I don't even know your name. Not your real name."

"Not many people do," Jack told her. "Not even the woman lying in this bed. And I love her more than life."

"Does she know that?" Claire asked.

Jack's brows lifted. "She did once. I don't know if she does now."

Claire sniffed and wiped her cheeks again. "It seems to me life's too short to keep that kind of thing to yourself."

"It's complicated," he muttered.

Claire gave him a sympathetic smile through her tears. "When *isn't* love complicated?"

Maddie moaned softly, drawing his attention back to the

hospital bed. He gripped her hand, smoothing her skin lightly. "How are you, love?"

She opened her eyes, squinting against the dim light in the room. "I feel like shit. How are you?"

He chuckled, relieved that her sense of humor was still intact. "Doing better than you are."

Maddie's eyes went wide. "Where's Claire? Do you have the flash drive?"

Claire was at the bedside in an instant, offering Maddie a shy smile. "I'm here. Thanks to you and Jack. And he has the flash drive."

"So what now?" Maddie asked, her lids heavy.

"You rest," Jack told her, smoothing her curls away from her face. "Then we'll head back to our hotel to grab our gear before leaving for Chicago. Finn's eager to get to work on this intel."

She nodded. "Sounds good. What about Claire?"

Jack traded a glance with the woman in question. "She'll be fine. After all, she has a guardian angel watching over her."

When they left the hospital several hours later, it was with a full escort from the local commandery. Jack wasn't about to take any chances of getting attacked again with Maddie still reeling from the effects of her concussion and Claire still out in the open. He'd been texting with Will to apprise him of the situation and how the local team was planning to spin events at the hotel, but he'd held off calling him, not wanting to be on the phone with his friend, in Claire's presence—it just seemed like an unnecessary torture for both of them.

When they reached the hotel to gather their things, he escorted Claire to her room and waited just inside the door as she gathered them up. She kept sending glances his way as if she wanted to say something, but didn't speak a word.

Finally, he sighed. "What is it, Claire?"

She slung a well-worn leather satchel over her shoulder and straightened to her full height. "This is bullshit. You know that, right?"

Here we go . . .

"Not my call," he told her. "You're going to be in danger as long as our enemies think you know something."

She huffed and put her hand on her hip, her cheeks flushed with indignation. "So protect me. That's what you guys do, right?"

Jack inclined his head slightly. "Yes, that is what we do. But we can only protect you if you follow instructions. Think of it as a witness protection program. Relocating you is necessary to keep you safe. Perhaps at some point you can resume your identity."

"So will I be able to retrieve any of my things from Beacon Hill?" she snapped. "Those are the only memories of my parents that I have. You can't just waltz in here and uproot my entire life without giving me *something* here."

Jack nodded. "Of course. I'll see to it personally. All of your belongings will be sent to you wherever you're placed."

"What will I tell my friends? My boss?" she pressed. "They'll wonder what happened to me."

Jack shoved his hands into his pockets, trying not to be irritated that he was the one having this conversation with Claire. Will should've been there. He should've been the one explaining everything to her. "There will be an accident. Something plausible. But they won't recover a body. Your friends will have a lovely memorial service for you, I'm sure."

She pressed her lips together and shook her head. "So my life dies today."

"Well, you do," Jack corrected. "But this is only so that

you can go on to live a normal, happy life as someone else."

They stood in silence for several long moments before Claire spoke again. "Could you do me a favor after I go wherever it is you're sending me?"

He nodded. "Of course."

"Tell Will he's a goddamned coward," she spat. Then she shook her head again. "C'mon. Let's just get this over with. You have your own issues to deal with. You certainly don't need to be worrying about mine."

Jack opened the door and held it as she stormed past him. Maddie was waiting for them in the hallway, looking tired and pale but otherwise okay.

She offered Claire a sympathetic look. "They're waiting for us downstairs."

The three of them rode the elevator in tense silence—or at least that was Jack's take on things. Maybe he was just projecting his own sense of guilt. He'd never had any second thoughts about an order before now, so why did it bother him so much that they were planning to deliver the vibrant, intelligent reporter to a trusted associate who was planning to interrogate her to find out everything she knew about the Alliance before they made good on the promise of relocation?

He hadn't been lying when he'd said it was for her own protection. When the Alliance took someone off grid, they did a damned thorough job of it. And yet Jack couldn't help grinding his teeth in anger as they stepped off the elevator—because Claire had been right about one thing. Will should've had the balls to break the news to her personally.

"Hello, Mr. Smith." Meghan greeted him cheerfully when he approached the front desk. "We're sorry to see you go!" She glanced at Maddie and Claire as if she felt much different about the two women with him.

"Thank you for all of your assistance, Meghan," he told her sincerely, shaking her hand and slipping several hundred dollar bills into her palm. He offered her a wink that made her blush. "Truly, you were a trusted ally."

"My pleasure," she assured him. "Please visit us again."

He gave her a nod and glanced around the foyer. "Is Manny available? I'd like to thank him again before I go."

Her grin widened. "Oh, yes, he's working today. In fact, I believe he was pulling your car around for you."

Jack's brows twitched together. "My car? My car was in the parking garage of the Liberty last night when the explosion occurred. Some of my local colleagues were going to take care of it for me after the police finished at the crime scene."

Meghan frowned. "I don't know what to tell you, Mr. Smith. I guess they released it early. A gentleman came by earlier this morning and dropped it off. He left the key with the valet attendants and told them it was for you."

Apprehension made Jack's muscles tighten, his fight or flight response kicking into overdrive. "How did you know the car was for me? Did he use my name?"

"Jack, what is it?" Maddie interjected.

"Did he use my name, Meghan?" Jack pressed.

She shook her head. "No, I don't think so. He just said it was for his good friend Jack. Yours is the only black Jaguar we've had in the last couple of days, so we all knew it was for you."

"What did this man look like?" Jack demanded.

Meghan shook her head, obviously flustered by the flurry of questions. "Uh, um . . . tall, dark hair, black suit. And he had an accent. Russian, I think."

Jack heard Maddie take a sharp breath. "Oh, God."

"Does Manny have a radio? Phone? Some way to contact him right away?" Jack asked in a rush. "He needs to get out of the car immediately."

Meghan nodded and picked up the phone, punching in a number. "Where's Manny? Did he get the black Jag yet?"

She hung up and snatched up her cell phone, searching rapidly through her contacts, then dialing. "Manny, where are you? You need to get out of the Jag right now."

Jack hung on to every word, gripping the edge of the counter until his knuckles were white.

She glanced up at him. "He's already bringing it around. He'll be out front any second now."

Jack's head snapped toward the front of the hotel and the wall of glass doors. The Jag pulled up to the curb in front of the hotel where other cars and cabs for guests checking out were lined up.

"Tell him to get out now!" Jack cried as he raced toward the doors. He waved his arm, motioning for Manny to get out. The man flashed him his wide grin and waved back, revving the engine playfully.

But then he must've seen the look of fear on Jack's face and frowned, tilting his head down to hear what Meghan was telling him over the phone. He nodded and opened the door to step out of the car.

The second Manny stood, Jack realized his mistake. Flames instantly tumbled out from beneath the car in a rush, engulfing Manny in fire as it lifted the Jag into the air and pitched it over on its side, hurling Manny several feet onto the circular drive in front of the hotel.

Jack slid to a halt and instinctively ducked, bringing up his arms to block flying debris. But in the next moment, he was racing out the door toward where Manny's body lay, barking out orders to the hotel employees rushing forward to assist, snatching their jackets from their hands and trying to smother the flames.

"Someone call 911!" Jack bellowed to the individuals who'd gathered around, their faces frozen in shock. "Don't just stand there, goddammit!"

But even as he batted away the hands that tried to grab his shoulders and pull him away, Jack knew the man was dead.

"Jack! It's too late!"

Maddie's voice finally broke through his frantic efforts, and when she put her arm over his shoulder and pulled him back, he stumbled several feet before ass-planting on the cobblestones. He didn't resist when Maddie pulled him into her arms, cradling him against her, rocking him and smoothing his hair as he clung to her, bone-deep sobs shaking him to the core in his sorrow and guilt.

A young man lay dead on the pavement, taken by the death that was meant for *him*.

Chapter Twelve

Will Asher sat at his desk, his hands hanging limp over the arms of his chair. He felt defeated, deflated. The mission had essentially been a success. They'd apprehended Claire Davenport before she'd confronted Congressman Hale. Claire was safe. Hale was dead. The flash drive was in hand and headed back to Chicago for Finn to decrypt. And Jack and Maddie got out of it with their lives.

But there'd been collateral damage.

Will closed his eyes on a heavy sigh. Innocent blood had been spilled. Again. And for what purpose? To make a statement? That's what it appeared. A little research on the bomber revealed he was most likely one of the Faithful that Jacob Stone was so fond of dispensing as needed to do his dirty work.

But, far more disturbing, it hadn't been Stone spotted in the security footage Finn had obtained after the bombing. It was the Russian assassin—Kozlov. The same man who'd delivered the car bomb meant for Jack and Maddie that instead ended the life of a young man with a promising future. The kid had been working his way through college, supporting his mother, and a younger sister with medical issues and special needs.

Will reached up and pinched the bridge of his nose, trying to squeeze away the headache that was beginning to build behind his eyes.

The Alliance would take care of Manny's family, ensure that his mother and sister wanted for nothing for the rest of their lives. It was the least they could do. They sure as hell couldn't give Mrs. Velázquez her son back.

Will tried to keep at bay the memories of having to call his own mother to tell her the news that she'd lost a son. Will's older brother—a doctor, changing the world for the better in his own way, irrespective of the Alliance—had been brutally murdered, along with his wife and children. He could still hear his mother's screams, her sobs of grief. First her husband, then her favorite son. Her heart was broken beyond repair. And two years later, her damaged heart finally gave out and death claimed her as well.

A quiet knock on his office door brought his head up. "Enter."

Adam Watanabe came in as commanded and stood at attention on the opposite side of Will's desk. "Jack and Maddie will be arriving within the hour. We'll take a car to pick them up."

Will nodded. "And Claire?"

Adam's chin dipped slightly, something like sympathy passing over his normally impossible-to-read face. "She is in the care of our colleague."

"It's for the best," Will murmured. It was supposed to be a statement, but when the words came out, they almost sounded like a question.

Adam didn't respond.

His silence drew Will's gaze. "Do you think I should've handled things differently with her?"

Adam's brows lifted slightly as if he was surprised that Will sought his opinion. He seemed to consider the question for a moment before answering. "I think you've done what you thought was in her best interest. However, I'm not so sure it's in yours."

Will drew back a little at the assessment. "You barely know me, Watanabe."

Adam dipped his head, conceding the point. "True. But I don't need to know you well to see that your past torments you. There are ghosts in your eyes, Commander."

"We all have a past," Will assured him. "I don't know that there are any of us who have memories we wouldn't like locked away in some cerebral vault. Claire was delirious during most of our time in Nigeria. Seeing me again might dredge up memories it'd be better to leave alone. I've been kinder to Claire than I've been to myself."

"Hmm."

Will frowned. "What's that supposed to mean?"

Adam bowed slightly. "I mean no disrespect, Commander."

Will motioned with his hand for Adam to continue. "Say what you have to say."

Adam paused, seeming to consider his next words carefully. Finally, he said, "If you are being so kind to Ms. Davenport, why do you punish yourself? The story I have heard is that you rescued her from the Boko Haram. If I may ask—what is the rest of the story? What did you do that you fear she will remember? What has persuaded you to cower here at headquarters in order to assuage your own guilt instead of facing the woman you insist upon protecting from afar?"

Will leaned back in his chair, stunned by the man's perceptiveness. Even Jack hadn't heard the entire story. He knew more than anyone about what had happened in Nigeria. But there was one crucial piece of information that Will had kept to himself.

"It was my fault she was captured in the first place," Will said, his voice coming out as a harsh rasp now that he was putting it into words. "I fucked up. And she paid the price. I swore that I'd never again let anything happen to her."

"Hmm."

"What now?" Will snapped.

"It's just that you made a foolish promise," Adam mused. "You cannot possibly keep it."

With that, Adam bowed and strode from the room, shutting the door behind him.

Will clenched his jaw, angry at the man's words. Adam Watanabe had been with the Chicago commandery for only a year, for chrissakes. What the hell did he know about anything where Will was concerned? Who the hell did he think he was, lecturing his commander about his past when Watanabe was clearly running from his own ghosts?

But even as he fumed over Adam's assessment, Will had to admit that the most infuriating part of it was that the man was right.

Jacob sat alone in the back of the limousine, peering out the window as the scenery flashed by in a blur. But his mind wasn't really on the rolling hills or the breeze off the ocean. He'd been summoned. And had been instructed to come alone.

That couldn't possibly be good.

His grandfather was in a rage, foaming at the mouth like a rabid dog since news of the explosion in Boston had hit the media, and audio from the local police caught the bomber proclaiming to be a follower of the One True Master before martyring himself.

He'd have to have a lovely little chat with Stefan and Demetrius about their lack of discretion in their choice of sacrifices and their blatant implication of Jacob in the crime. Really, they couldn't have just scooped up one of their own nutjob fanatics to take up the banner? When you've somehow convinced people that you're the freaking anti-Christ, you're bound to get some believers who are willing to do whatever they're asked, to become martyrs as an act of faith and loyalty just to feel like they've played a role in helping your destiny. Power was the ultimate aphrodisiac. Hell, Jacob had his own version of that going on with his wife. He had no delusions whatsoever about whether or not she'd stay with him if he gave up his ambitions.

When Jacob finally arrived at the abandoned observatory that served as the meeting place for the Illuminati, he took a deep breath and let it out slowly, forcing his pulse to slow and assuming the aloof demeanor that had failed him once eight months ago, giving his grandfather the mistaken impression that he was insignificant.

How quickly the man's opinion had changed in recent months. The old geezer had long outlived his usefulness. Soon Jacob would remove him permanently from his position of power, proclaiming himself as One True Master. His Faithful already believed him to fulfill that role. He just needed to make it official.

Jacob nodded politely to the driver before buttoning his suit jacket and strolling into the observatory as if he owned the place. They might as well start getting used to the idea now.

The last time he was here, he'd been broken, defeated. His attempt to locate and appropriate the Templar treasure for the Illuminati had failed miserably. And his grandfather had seen his failure as just another reason that Jacob was a disgrace to the family name, not fit to assume his rightful place among them. So, instead of storming in triumphant, to demand the respect and deference he deserved, Jacob had come crawling on hands and knees to beg forgiveness.

But never again. Never again would Jacob get on his knees for anyone.

He struggled to suppress a grin as he jogged down the stone steps that led into the bowels of the building. The cold, dank rooms belowground were perfect for these meetings. So secretive . . .

Antiquated.

When he took over, he'd make sure the entire place was renovated and restored. He wasn't going to lurk in the shadows. Jacob wasn't meant to be hidden away in some dark corner. He would take the world by storm—a bright beacon of hope that would bring order to chaos.

"You're late."

Angus Stone's voice echoed like a cannon, bouncing off the walls.

Jacob tsk-tsked dismissively. "You summoned me at a moment's notice from my honeymoon. I had a few things to finish before I could tear myself away." He smirked at the old man. "After all, a good lover always leaves his woman satisfied."

"I don't give a damn who you were fucking," his grandfather ground out, leaning forward from his perch in the shadows to reveal his furious expression. "All I want is an explanation regarding the explosion in Boston. Do you know how many of our trusted allies died in that incident?"

Jacob scoffed. "Really? You're going to mourn the loss of that bastard Hale and his cronies?"

"Hale served a purpose, Jacob."

"Oh, yes," Jacob agreed. "He was very good at taking money from us and banging hookers and trusting naïve up-and-comers whose own ambitions turned out to be problematic. That was a problem, by the way, that *I* solved. You're welcome."

"I didn't ask you to have Tad Ralston murdered," Angus spat. "There are better ways to handle things."

Jacob gave him a tight smile. "Well, we'll have to agree to disagree on that one."

"Jacob, you have always been a spoiled, petulant child. I blame your mother for pampering you and filling your head with grandiose ideas of your own importance."

Jacob clenched his fists at his sides at the mention of his mother. She'd died when he was still a young man. Poisoned. He had his suspicions that it hadn't been one of his father's enemies behind her death as the official Alliance investigation claimed. He'd always suspected his grandfather's hand in it. The man had never liked her, had always seen her as a distraction to Jacob's father.

"We didn't come here to talk about my mother," Jacob said, forcing his tone to remain civil. "You summoned me here to discuss Boston."

"Very well then, here it is. You will make no further moves against the Alliance without my permission," Angus Stone ordered, his bushy white eyebrows knitting together in a livid frown, his face flushed, verging on purple in his outrage. "I thought I had made that *abundantly* clear. But in case there was any doubt, I am telling you plainly, your days of running your own rogue operations are over. If you weren't my grandson, your insubordination would've already cost you your life."

Jacob laid his hand across his heart. "Your compassion and mercy are touching. Truly."

"Is this a *joke* to you?" Angus Stone roared, the sound deafening in the small chamber. "I assure you, this is nothing to be taken lightly. My influence only goes so far, Jacob. There are others who believe I have been too lenient. Others who wield far more power within our organization than I do. They are watching."

Angus Stone had been placed in charge of the Illuminati in its newest iteration, but there was someone else pulling his strings, someone his grandfather actually feared. And as soon as Jacob discovered who that was, he'd begin the final stages of his plan to completely remove the geezers in power and install himself over all. But he needed to tread carefully, ensure his allies were in place before he made his move. If there's one thing his political career had taught him, it was that this sort of maneuvering had to be managed with precision, or it could go to hell in an instant.

Jacob blinked his eyes slowly, bored with his grandfather's ceaseless bellowing. "Is there anything else?"

"As a matter of fact"—his grandfather leaned back, his face now partially veiled in shadow—"you will call off those fanatical brothers, Stefan and Demetrius Shepherd. They're impossible to control. I don't want them anywhere near you or our operations."

Before he could check his reaction, Jacob flinched in surprise at his grandfather's knowledge of his affairs. "How did you know about the Shepherds? You have a *mole* in my security detail?"

"Did you expect anything less after the debacle last year over the treasure?" he countered. "I also know that you've been in contact with the Russians regarding Jack Grayson. Do you really want to make an enemy of him, Jacob?"

Jacob felt that damnable sinking in the center of his gut at the reminder of his betrayal. "I'm afraid I've already done so, Grandfather. The moment he learned of my involvement in trying to steal the treasure, there was no hope of things ever being the same between us. I guess we have to allow old emotional encumbrances to fall away if we're to truly succeed in achieving our goals. But then you'd know all about that, wouldn't you? Family . . . friends. What do they matter if they impede your ascension to greatness? Am I right?"

Now it was the old man's turn to look nonplussed. "Tread carefully, Jacob. Your ambition is admirable but dangerous. One day it'll control *you*."

Jacob flashed his grandfather his practiced politician's grin. "Well, I guess the apple doesn't fall far and all that." He then raised his brows expectantly. "Will that be all? I have a beautiful wife waiting naked in my bed, so if you have nothing further . . ."

Angus Stone shook his head. "Yes, go. Go before I regret my decision not to punish you."

Jacob inclined his head and offered a mocking salute before turning on his heel and striding from the chamber, his footsteps echoing in the silence.

Chapter Thirteen

Maddie had given Jack his space after Manny's death at the hotel and for most of the flight back to Chicago. Jack had seemed to be struggling with Will's orders to leave Claire in the custody of the Boston commandery, and looked like he was on the verge of revolting, so Maddie had stepped in to take care of it. As much as it sucked for Claire, the woman seemed resigned to her fate. Perhaps getting a firsthand glimpse of the kind of danger she was in had made her realize she was better off far away from Will Asher and his team.

Or maybe just knowing he was alive was enough for her and now that she had the answers she needed, she was at peace.

Maddie liked to hope that *that* was the reason for Claire's lack of protest when they'd handed her over. She liked the feisty reporter. They'd talked a little on the way to the Boston commandery's headquarters, small talk mostly. Being an only child and orphaned by an accident when she was a teenager, Claire was mostly interested in hearing about Maddie and her sister, Sarah. By the time they'd arrived at the Boston compound, Maddie found herself wishing there'd been another way, that maybe they could've become friends. As it was, if all went well with Claire's relocation, odds were good that their paths would never cross again.

Maddie sighed and pushed up from her seat, restless and tired of having only her own thoughts for companionship. Though it was only her and Jack on the flight home, she had intentionally sat apart from him, giving him some space. But he'd been so quiet, she began to worry. She walked up the narrow aisle to where Jack sat, his head resting against the cream-colored leather, eyes closed. Seeing he was asleep, she turned to go back to her seat, but before she could take a step, he grasped her hand, keeping her at his side.

"Stay."

It was the same directive she'd given him the previous day in her hotel room when they'd been on the verge of slaking some of the desire that was making things so damned uncomfortable between them. She peered down at him, trying to determine whether he was aware of the connection to their make-out session the day before. But when he began to caress her skin with his thumb, she took it as a sign that he really *did* want her there.

Without a word, she slipped into the row with him, taking the seat on his other side, by the window. "You're not reading."

Eyes still closed, he shook his head. "Couldn't concentrate."

She waited in silence for a long moment before linking her arm with his and resting her head on his shoulder. "Anything I can do to help?"

He seemed to consider her question for a moment before finally opening his eyes and turning his face toward her. "Just being here is enough."

She placed her hand upon his cheek, her heart aching for the pain he was feeling. He blamed himself for Manny's death. He hadn't told her so, but she'd felt it in the sobs that had wracked his body outside the hotel, had heard it in his voice when he'd spoken to Finn on the phone right after they'd boarded the plane, could see it now in his eyes.

"I'm not going anywhere, Jack."

"You should," he told her, slowly reaching up to grasp her hand and pull it away. "You'd be safer if you weren't with me."

"You sound like Will." When he frowned, she offered him a hint of a grin. "But, unless you have a parachute handy, looks like I'm at least with you until we get to Chicago."

"And then what?" he asked, his dark brows drawing together, the flecks of gold in his eyes seeming brighter than ever before.

"Then . . ." She shook her head, not knowing how to answer his question. "I have no idea."

He lifted his hand as if to caress her cheek, but stopped just short of making contact. Before his hand could drop away, Maddie grasped it and kissed his fingers, then drew his hand in close and clasped it against her chest. Her heart began to thunder as his gaze grew more intense.

"Maddie," he breathed, his voice choked. "I want you far too much for you to be looking at me like that."

"Then close your eyes," she whispered.

When his lids lowered, she leaned in and brushed a kiss against his cheek, loving the way the coarse stubble at his jaw scraped lightly against her lips. When she pulled back, his hungry gaze met hers, the intensity she saw there making every muscle in her body go tight with anticipation and longing.

She wasn't sure who leaned in first, but her mouth found his in a slow, sensual kiss. His lips clung to hers, taking all she gave. She took her time, savoring the moment between them, no longer holding back. When his tongue teased against her lips, she shuddered as a wave of desire claimed her. A soft moan escaped her before she could stop it. She wanted more, needed more. Desperate to be close to him, to feel his hands on her, she lifted the seat arm that separated the two plush seats and shifted, straddling his lap.

His hands settled at her hips, his fingers gripping her tightly as she took his face into her hands and deepened their kiss, not able to get enough of him. Her mouth sought his again and again, their kisses growing more frenzied. Jack's arms slid around her, pulling her closer, his hands tangling in her hair.

The jet suddenly rose and dropped, hitting a pocket of turbulence. Maddie was lifted an inch or two above his lap, then crashed back down, eliciting a deep groan from Jack and a muttered curse.

"Oh, God—I'm so sorry." She winced, pressing kisses to his jaw, the side of his neck.

In answer, he brought his lips back to hers in a savage kiss that left her panting when that amazing mouth began to explore again. He nipped at her shoulder through her T-shirt, then at the sensitive spot where neck and shoulder met. She gasped at the sudden pleasure and guided his face back to hers to capture his mouth again.

He pulled at her T-shirt, untucking it, and slipped his hands beneath the hem to roam over her skin. She shivered at the contact, breaking their kiss as she let her head fall back. Apparently taking that as an invitation, Jack trailed a sultry line of kisses along the curve of her neck to her clavicle. As his lips trailed lower, he eased her back just enough to capture one of her nipples through her shirt, grazing it with his teeth.

Maddie cried out as an orgasm unexpectedly rocked through her. Then Jack was suddenly on his feet, lifting her with him and switching places with her, setting her in the seat and getting on his knees before her. He looked up at her, his chest heaving, his eyes asking a silent question.

In answer, Maddie grabbed the edges of her shirt and pulled it over her head, tossing it aside. Jack leaned in, his mouth slowly exploring the sensitive skin on her belly. Every graze of his lips, every breath, hot against her skin, set her mind spinning. And when he slipped one of her bra straps from her shoulder and kissed where it had been, she reached behind her and unfastened the clasp, allowing him to slide the other strap down and remove the satiny garment.

Her nipples grew instantly harder when the cool air hit them, aching for his touch, but he paused, taking her in with silent reverence. His hands slid lightly up along her torso until he reached the edge of her breasts. She gasped when his thumbs brushed over her skin. Every inch of her tingled with electricity.

"My God, Maddie," he whispered, lifting his eyes to her. "You're even more beautiful than I remembered."

He bent and took one of her nipples in his mouth, his tongue flicking and rolling, until she began to writhe and moan, desperate for relief. He pulled back slowly, his teeth grazing her skin, drawing out her pleasure. She groaned when he switched to the other breast, the ache in the center of her almost more than she could bear.

"Jack," she panted, finally pulling his head up when the intensity became too much. There was a tense pause as they stared at one another, their ragged breathing the only sound over the constant hum of the jet engines. She wanted to say something, anything. Wanted to tell him that she loved him, that she'd never stopped loving him, but the moment seemed so tenuous and fragile, she was afraid to utter a word.

When she didn't speak, Jack sat back on his heels, his breath gradually slowing. His gaze took her in, his visual exploration so sensual, he didn't even need to touch her to bring a flush of desire to her skin, to make her burn even hotter for him. Finally, though, he did reach out, tenderly caressing her skin with the backs of his fingers, his touch bringing goose bumps to her flesh.

"I want you, Maddie," he told her. "I don't think there's any secret there." He chuckled, a strangled, tortured sound. "My God, 'want' isn't even adequate. My need for you is as vital as air. But I won't go any further unless you ask it of me."

Her gaze holding his, she scooted to the edge of the seat and pulled him back to his knees to place a tender kiss upon his forehead, the sculpted edge of his cheek, his lips. When she deepened the kiss, he must've taken it as the encouragement he sought.

Jack wrapped his arms around her and gently urged her from the seat, rolling them out into the aisle. He now took the lead, his kiss so achingly sensual, Maddie could've gone on kissing him forever. His hand splayed across her lower back, pressing her into him as they lay side by side. But when he rolled her onto her back, his hand smoothing over her belly, sliding lower until it slipped beneath the waistband of her jeans, Maddie cried out, arching against him. But instead of delivering her from the sweet agony of her desire, his touch inflamed her more.

He cursed under his breath as he slid his hand even lower. "My God, I've missed touching you."

She arched her hips against his touch, meeting every stroke, every caress, her chest heaving as her breath sawed in and out of her lungs, her head thrashing amidst wordless mews of pleasure.

And when he thrust a finger inside her, caressing the elusive spot of pleasure there, she arched her back off the ground as heat and light engulfed her, crying out as her orgasm overtook her. She vaguely thought she heard the cockpit door click, as if someone had peeked out to discover the source of the cry, but then Jack's caresses increased, driving her toward another release and she grasped the front of his shirt, dragging him down to receive her kiss.

When the last shudder shook her, she collapsed for a moment, trying to catch her breath, but Jack's caress continued, slowly, deliberately, offering her no time to recover before her hips began to writhe against him again.

Needing to feel his skin upon hers, to feel him inside her, Maddie grasped his shirt, tearing it open and scattering the buttons. She shoved the shirt off his shoulders, helping him shrug out of it. Her hands roamed over his sculpted chest, taking in the sight of him. The hard, athletic body she'd been so familiar with hadn't changed in the years since they'd last been together. If anything, he was even more gorgeous than she'd remembered in the fantasies she'd indulged too many times to count.

Never one to shy away from getting what she wanted, Maddie reached down between them, palming the hard length pressing into her thigh. He groaned, squeezing his eyes shut. "I've missed touching you, too," she whispered.

He cursed softly, then captured her mouth again, his kiss savage, hungry. But when she began to fumble with the button of his slacks, he broke the kiss, pressing his forehead to hers for a moment, his breath ragged. "Maddie—"

"Make love to me," she whispered. "I need you inside me, Jack."

He shifted, allowing her to slide his slacks over his hips, pausing to snatch his wallet out of his back pocket. Then she was shedding the last of her clothes, kicking off her shoes to allow him to remove her jeans. And when he pulled her against him so that they were skin to skin and draped her leg over his hips, she ground her hips against his. His hand smoothed along her thigh, around to her bottom, his fingers entering her again at a different angle this time. But he caressed her only for a moment before grabbing a condom from his wallet and slipping it on. A few seconds later, the head of him pressed in, just the tip, teasing and playing.

She moved her hips, trying to take him deeper, but he held back, building her anticipation, stoking the desire that burned for him, until she felt as if she would burst into flames. Then without warning, he thrust deep.

She dug her nails into his back, clinging to him with each powerful thrust, her head spinning. "Oh, God, Jack," she gasped. "I've missed you."

Jack was an idiot. A total goddamned idiot.

He had no business making love to Maddie there in the middle of the Alliance's private jet. Hell, the copilot had already stuck his head out to see what all the commotion was. He should've had more respect for her than to make love in such a public way.

And yet he didn't have the willpower to stop, to pull out and wait until their first time after so long apart could be special, romantic—what Maddie deserved.

He felt her muscles begin to tighten again, squeezing him and increasing his pleasure. Considering he was drunk with desire, he wasn't quite sure how his pleasure could *be* any greater than it already was; he was on the verge of having a goddamned out-of-body experience.

Then she was arching into him, her body shuddering, the intensity of her orgasm transferring to him like an arc of electricity. And he was coming with her, shouting his release and digging his fingertips into her skin as he clung to her.

When they finally collapsed together in a tangle of limbs, they could only drag in breath after ragged breath. After several moments, he rolled her onto her back and brushed a kiss to lips that were red and swollen. Then he buried his face in her shoulder, still struggling to catch his breath, needing a moment away from that tender, forest-green gaze.

She smoothed his hair, pressed kisses to the top of his head. When he finally pulled back to peer down at her, the look in her eyes was just as loving as he'd feared. And yet, he didn't withdraw, didn't extract himself from her embrace. Being in her arms had, for a few moments, allowed him to escape the memories that haunted him.

They lay there for some time, kissing and caressing one another without a word, until finally Jack withdrew with a groan and strode to the lavatory to dispose of the condom. When he returned, he paused to watch her move about the cabin on hands and knees as she gathered up her discarded clothes, the sight of her nakedness a temptation he could barely withstand. God, it would've been sheer bliss to grasp her hips and bury himself balls-deep inside her again, to hear her moaning and panting as they lost themselves once more to their desire.

When she felt his gaze upon her, she sent a knowing glance over her shoulder and gave him a sultry grin. She couldn't read his mind, thank Christ, but based on her smile, she'd sure as hell noticed the massive wood he was sporting.

He dragged his gaze away, forcing himself to look for his own clothes and try to get himself back under control.

"My God," she said, her voice husky, bringing his attention back to her. Her gaze was hungry as it took in every inch of him. "You're even sexier than I remembered."

He didn't bother suppressing a smile as he grasped her hand and pulled her to her feet and into his arms to receive another brief kiss.

She sighed when the kiss ended. "I should probably get dressed."

He kissed the curve of her neck, unable to resist. "Clothing is overrated."

She laughed and slipped out of his hold, slapping him on his bare ass as she ducked behind him. "We're landing soon. You might want to throw some clothes on. And maybe a different shirt. I think I ruined that one."

His brows lifted, but he realized what she meant when he glanced down at the floor to see buttons scattered at his feet. Fortunately, his go-bag was in the cabin and he was able to extract a black T-shirt, pulling it on as the captain came over the intercom to announce their descent.

"Not a moment too soon," Maddie quipped, pulling her long curls up into a ponytail to disguise how disheveled her hair was, thanks to Jack's frenzied hands. Tiny ringlets managed to slip out to frame her face, making her appear almost impish.

Unable to resist, he grasped her around the waist and gathered her close for an all-too-brief kiss. "And here I was thinking it'd been far too long."

She returned his kiss, then snuggled under his arm as he led her back to the seats they'd vacated earlier. He dropped a kiss to the top of her head when she rested against his chest, her arm draped over his waist.

"So . . . should we, uh . . . *talk* about things?" she asked.

His arm around her shoulders tightened. "Not now. I just want to hold you."

She heaved what sounded like a contented sigh and snuggled closer. "Works for me."

All too soon the plane jolted as the tires hit the tarmac and he was forced to let her go, leaving him feeling cold, bereft, without her body pressed against his.

Maddie was a beautiful dream made flesh. And she was

his. At least for now. But at some point they *would* have to talk. It was a moment he dreaded. He didn't want to see the look on her face when he told her the truth of why he'd left her before, without a word, why he hadn't fought harder to keep her when she'd been the one to walk away the second time around. But Will was right. He needed to tell her before she found out some other way. And then what would become of this beautiful dream?

As the plane came to a halt outside the Alliance's private hangar, Jack sighed, wishing like hell that they could have just a few more minutes, stall the inevitable.

He was on the verge of inviting Maddie to run away with him—only half-jokingly—when the door to the cabin opened and Adam Watanabe stuck his head in, sparing them only a glance before looking away.

"Your car is waiting," he announced before discreetly vanishing.

Maddie got to her feet, slinging her go-bag over her shoulder. "I guess it's back to work."

Catching the note of disappointment in her voice made him briefly reconsider his running-away-together scheme, but instead he nodded and reached up to grasp a curl that had escaped from her ponytail. He tugged it playfully and offered her a smile. "Sadly, yes. No rest for the wicked, it seems. But I'd like to propose that we hold our own debrief later, Ms. Blake, if you're available."

Her mouth turned up at one corner and her cheeks reddened at his insinuation. "As it turns out, Mr. Grayson, I have an opening in my schedule. You cook dinner and I'll bring the wine. Then we'll see what we can come up with for dessert . . ."

A few minutes later, they were sliding into the backseat of the black SUV waiting for them. As she settled on the seat beside him, Maddie's fingers brushed over his briefly, sending that familiar surge of desire and need straight to his dick. Jack felt like a teenage boy again, sharing secret touches with a girl in his parents' backseat.

Well, that's what he imagined it would've been like had he been an average teenage boy. He'd never ridden in the backseat when in the car with his parents—they always split the family into different cars for safety reasons. And he'd never had to sneak around with his girlfriends. His father rather encouraged his skills with women, knowing they'd be useful in his work for the Alliance. Turned out he was right. Too right.

"What's up with you guys?" Maddie demanded, bringing Jack out of his thoughts.

It took him a moment to understand why she was asking. Adam sat silently behind the wheel, keeping his eyes straight ahead. The man was reserved and closed off even on a good day, but there was an added reticence to his demeanor that was unusual even for him. Finn, seated in the front passenger seat, wasn't quite so subtle.

He twisted around in his seat, giving them a wide, mischievous grin. "Welcome home, kids."

"Thanks," Maddie said, drawing out the word.

He grinned at them for a beat longer, as if expecting them to fill in the silence. Finally he asked, "You bring me any presents?"

Jack reached into his pocket and handed over the flash drive they'd received from Claire. "A souvenir."

"Sweet!" Finn exclaimed. "Just what I wanted! You know me so well."

He plugged the flash drive into the device on his lap and tapped a few keys before muttering a curse. "Figured as much. I'll have to get this back to the ops center to decrypt it. The software I have on this computer isn't going to do it." He flashed his wide, easy grin at Jack. "Well, guess we *all* couldn't get lucky today . . ."

Jack frowned at him, wondering what the hell that was

supposed to mean. But Finn didn't elaborate and Jack had learned a long time ago that when it came to Finn, sometimes it was better just not to ask. No one said another word as they drove back to the compound, but both men in the front seat sent the occasional glance backward.

"Commander Asher would like to debrief with both of you in an hour," Adam finally said as he pulled through the gates of the compound, but he seemed to hesitate as to which direction to go from there. "Where would you like me to drop you, Maddie?"

She glanced between Adam's studiously bland expression and Finn's shit-eating grin, and then turned to Jack. "My quarters would be fine. Were you thinking of taking me somewhere else?"

"Nope." Finn's grin widened. "Just checking."

Jack had had enough of the odd behavior. "What the hell is your problem, brother?"

Finn cleared his throat and tried to smother his smile. "Just glad you two have finally worked out your issues. That's all, brah."

"And how exactly would you know anything about our issues?" Maddie asked, her cheeks flushing.

But before she even finished asking the question, Jack suddenly realized why they were acting so strangely. "Bloody hell. Who saw us?"

"*Saw* us?" Maddie echoed, her voice shrill.

"The jet has security cameras in the cabin," Jack mumbled, feeling like an asshole of the lowest order for exposing Maddie to her fellow Templars.

Her eyes went wide, her mouth dropping open on a gasp. "Are you fucking *kidding* me?" Then she started smacking Finn on the back of the head, shoulders, anywhere she could make contact. "And you watched us, you little perv?"

"We didn't watch." Finn laughed, holding his hands up in surrender against Maddie's onslaught. "When I saw what was going on, I tanked the footage. But, yeah, Adam and I caught a glimpse. Sorry—ow! Damn, Maddie. It's not like we were expecting you guys to be getting busy in the jet. Shit."

"You're sure the security footage has been erased?" Jack demanded as they reached the building that housed the barracks for the initiates and Templars too new to have earned their own private estates within the exclusive gated community.

"If I'm lyin', I'm dyin'," Finn vowed.

In spite of his assurances, Maddie still pegged them both with an angry glare as she got out of the car. Jack hopped out with her, grabbing her bags from the back of the SUV before carrying them to the door.

"I'm sorry," he told her sincerely. "I didn't even think about the security footage. Please forgive me, Maddie, love—"

Without warning, she grabbed the front of his T-shirt and yanked him to her, laying a hungry kiss on him that left him speechless. She gave him a saucy grin, then sent a wink toward the guys in the SUV.

"Go brag to your boys, you sexy beast," she told him, giving him a swat on the ass. "They *wish* they could be half the lover you are."

He laughed at her playfulness and was shaking his head as he jogged back to the SUV and hopped inside. When Finn and Adam both turned in their seats to give him a questioning look, Jack lifted a single brow.

Adam muttered something in Japanese that Jack didn't quite catch before turning around to continue the drive to Jack's place. But Finn was far more pointed.

"Dude," he said, his voice carrying a note of awe. "*Dude*. You are *so* my hero . . ."

Chapter Fourteen

Will was pacing the situation room, his impatience earning more than a few irritated glances from Finn. "Do you have it yet?"

"No," Finn said, dragging out the word. "And you asking every two minutes isn't helping. Just sayin'."

Will huffed and increased his pacing, rubbing the back of his neck where the familiar knot of tension was growing. "How long will it take? You said it shouldn't take long for you to decrypt the flash drive."

Finn glanced up from his keyboard. "Seriously, brah, not helping."

Will raised his hands. "Sorry."

At that moment, Jack and Maddie entered the room, somehow looking at ease and awkward at the same time. There was a heaviness hanging around Jack, a sorrow that had added a few creases to his brow. But that dark cloud seemed to lift just a little when he glanced Maddie's way, his gaze lingering on her for a few seconds.

And Maddie . . . she seemed self-conscious and kept shifting positions in her chair after she took a seat at the table near Jack.

"Glad to have you two back," Will said, taking the seat

across from them. "Finn's working on the flash drive right now, so we should be in soon. Right, Finn?"

Finn gave him a chastising look. "*Dude* . . ."

"How was Claire when you left her?" Will asked, taking the hint and changing the topic.

"Pissed but resigned," Maddie said, her voice edged with sadness. "For what it's worth, I really liked her."

Will nodded, not sure how to respond. "And she understood why I . . . why *we* have to relocate her?"

"Yes," Jack answered. "But, as you can imagine, she wasn't thrilled with the prospect of being uprooted. I left out the part about the interrogation to find out what else she knows. I figured telling her that she was about to be detained for an indeterminate length of time until she gave up everything she knew might be a bit of a sticking point."

Will didn't miss the note of disapproval in Jack's voice. "I wish it could've been different," Will muttered, rubbing his neck again. "But it's for her own good. We can't protect her unless we know what's at risk."

"We saw with Luke and Sarah what can happen when an innocent has information our enemies want," Jack said. "You don't have to explain to us why we need to detain her. But an explanation to Claire was probably in order."

Will pulled his hands through his hair, holding the back of his head for a moment. He'd done what he'd had to do. It was better for everyone if he stayed out of it. "I could've sent Adam," he defended. "I'm doing her a favor by sending in the examiner instead. He's got a much . . . *gentler* approach."

"Who's the examiner?" Maddie asked, glancing between them. "He's the guy you brought in?"

Will merely nodded, his thoughts on the woman he'd ordered away, too much of a fucking coward to face her again.

"The examiner these days is an experienced psychologist

and interrogator," Jack explained. "Back in the day, he was just . . . Well, let's just say that the former examiners' methods weren't as dignified. Claire's in good hands."

"Well, fuck me," Finn exclaimed, bringing Will to his feet like he had a spring in his ass.

"Are you in?" he demanded.

Finn shook his head. "Past the first one, but there's at least one other layer of encryption. Why don't you guys go grab some dinner or something? This is going to take a while."

Will caught the glance that passed between Jack and Maddie and frowned at them, his attention momentarily diverted from his thoughts of Claire's situation and the intel on the flash drive. "You two have other plans?"

Jack shook his head. "Nothing that can't wait." His response earned a disappointed look from Maddie, but Jack didn't seem to notice as he added gently, "When did you eat last, Will?"

Good question.

Will actually had to stop and think about that one. "Yesterday, I guess."

Finn held out a bag of some kind of granola bullshit that seemed to have magically materialized from the computer bag that appeared to offer an endless supply of sticks and twigs to satisfy Finn's appetite when he was working. "Help yourself, brah."

Will would rather eat cardboard than the shit Finn was always munching, but he politely waved off Finn's offer. "Thanks, but I'll pass."

Jack rose to his feet with that superior, big-brother air he had where Will was concerned and gestured toward the door. "Then you'll be taking dinner with Maddie and me. Shall we?"

Will gave him an irritated look. He'd had an older

brother growing up and had resented David's hovering just as much as he resented Jack's at that moment. Of course, there were days he'd give anything to hear David's nagging just once more, so he nodded. "But only so you two can debrief me on Boston."

An hour later, they sat in Jack's dining room, the filet mignon Jack had prepared making Will's mouth water so much he had to swallow before he asked, "So how long have you two been sleeping together?"

Maddie's fork hesitated halfway to her mouth and her eyes darted toward Jack before dropping her gaze to her vegetables, trying to cover her initial reaction. But she hadn't given away anything he didn't already know. He'd picked up on the sexual tension simmering between Jack and Maddie even before he'd sent them to Boston—hell, that was one of the reasons he'd forced them to team up. They needed to get their shit together and either talk it out or fuck it out—and it seemed he'd correctly guessed which option they'd gone with.

Jack's reaction was far more composed. He leaned back in his chair, wiping the corner of his mouth with the polished manners of the British aristocracy from which he hailed, before offering Will a hint of a smile.

"Only recently." His eyes seemed to spark, as if inviting Will to challenge him.

Jack Grayson was deadly, calculating. He could be one seriously cold son of a bitch when the situation called for it, as it had at various times during the man's career with the Alliance. But Will knew his lifelong friend was also a man who felt deeply—especially when it came to Maddie Blake.

Will turned his attention to his filet and finished off the first insanely delicious bite before he asked, "You sure that's a good idea?"

"I'm sure it's none of your business," Jack countered.

At this, Will brought his gaze back up to lock with Jack's. So, it was going to be like that. "It *is* my goddamned business," Will said, his tone even. "Yeah, I put you two together so you could work out your issues and do your fucking jobs effectively. You got me there. But I'm thinking maybe that was a mistake. Because now I've got two colossal clusterfuck missions to explain to the High Commander. And I can guaran-damn-tee that he'd like to know just how the hell you two managed to allow a bomb to detonate in a crowded Boston hotel, and then allowed *another* bomb to detonate out front of yet *another* hotel."

Jack didn't even flinch at the censure, his gaze steady. But Will could see that his comment cut through Maddie.

"Our objective was to secure the flash drive and to keep Claire Davenport safe," Jack reminded him. "We achieved both."

Will inclined his head in agreement. "Can't argue there. But the collateral damage on this one . . ." He leaned back in his chair and shook his head. "I just need to know whether you two were distracted by what was going on between you and got sloppy. I need to know that I can count on you in the future. If you can't guarantee me that, I'm going to have to put you on a mandatory mental health leave, Jack, and reconsider Maddie's request for a transfer to another commandery."

Jack's carefully stoic expression registered a hint of alarm at this. He glanced Maddie's way before returning his attention to Will, offering him that charming smile that meant he was about to try to wheedle his way out of something. "Will, don't be—"

"It won't be a problem," Maddie interrupted. She cleared her throat and pushed her chair back from the table. "You have my word, Commander Asher. Yes, Jack and I slept together." She sent a look Jack's way that seemed heavy with meaning as she continued. "But now that it's out of the way, we can get back to work. Of course, I respect your decision if you think I'd better serve the Alliance elsewhere."

Will noticed that she didn't glance toward Jack at all when she spoke. His gaze darted toward his friend to see Jack's jaw tighten, the muscle in his cheek twitching, the only visible tell that he was angry. Apparently, he'd seen things between them a little differently.

"Jack," Maddie said, rising to her feet and setting her napkin on the table, "thank you for dinner. I'm sorry I can't stay for dessert as we'd planned."

As she strode from the dining room, Will's phone began to ring. He snatched it up from the table as he watched Jack bolt from his chair and go after Maddie.

Shit.

Maybe he should've played that one differently. Maybe he should've talked to each of them privately rather than confront them together. Maybe he should've just minded his own goddamned business and defended his people to the High Commander as he'd always done. Why the hell was what was going on between Jack and Maddie getting under his skin so badly anyway? Although his concern about them being distracted was valid, there was something more about the situation that was eating away at him . . .

He glanced down at his phone, having forgotten that it was ringing, and rested his forehead in his hand as he answered, "Yeah."

"It's Finn."

Will straightened. "Tell me you're in."

Finn hesitated. "Yeah. I'm in, but . . . well, hell. There's not shit on it, boss-man."

Will's heart began to pound. "What the hell does *that* mean?"

Finn sighed. "Just what I said. There's nothing there. It's blank. Either the data was wiped or this isn't the flash drive. I think she played us."

"We need to know which it is, Finn," Will barked, surging to his feet and striding from the room.

"I'll see if I can try to recover anything that was on the drive," Finn told him, "but the only person who knows for sure is Claire Davenport."

Will's stomach clenched painfully, and for a second he seriously thought he was about to yack on Jack's expensive-ass marble flooring.

"Get me on the phone with Boston," Will barked. "I want to talk to—"

A sudden collision sent Will slamming into the wall, his phone flying from his hand and sliding across the marble. He grunted as his shoulder took the impact, and he turned with a furious frown, ready to take on his attacker. His frown deepened when he saw it was Jack. "What the hell is your problem?"

"I was about to ask you the same thing," Jack shot back. He took an angry stride forward, closing the gap between them, and pressed his forearm against Will's throat. "What the fuck was that all about with Maddie?"

Will shoved him back. "Step off, Jack. I'm only going to warn you once."

"And then what, brother?" Jack demanded. "You think you can take me on? Is that it? Do you want to throw down with *me*? Will that help you get over whatever bullshit is going on with you since Claire Davenport came back into the picture?"

"Leave Claire out of this," Will snapped. "You have no fucking idea—"

Jack laughed, cutting him off. "Don't even finish that

sentence, Will, or I will be forced to fuck you up just for being an idiot. You don't think I know what a guilty conscience feels like? Really?"

Will forced the tension from his muscles, willing his adrenaline to subside. "The flash drive Claire gave you was empty. Looks like you got your wish, Jack—I'm going to have to get my ass to Boston and interrogate her myself."

Jack hissed a curse. "Why would she give us an encrypted flash drive with nothing on it?"

Will was wondering the same thing. Had she played them as Finn suggested, or was she unaware that it contained no information? He massaged the back of his neck, weighing the possibilities. "She was too determined to find out info on the Alliance to wipe the flash drive. And my gut's telling me she wasn't trying to play us." He bent to pick up his cell phone. "I'm thinking the flash drive was blank all along. A decoy."

"Or a double cross," Jack told him.

Will's brows lifted. "You think it was blank when Ralston got it?"

Jack sighed. "I think it was all a ruse, Will. I don't think there ever was anything on *that* flash drive or any other."

Will shook his head. "Why?"

"To draw out the Alliance," Jack told him. "To draw *me* out."

"You think Antonovich is working with Kozlov," Will guessed. "Neither of them is mastermind material. Who are *they* working for? I want to know if this is one of Jacob Stone's schemes or if it's someone else above him controlling the game."

Jack leaned casually against the opposite wall and crossed his arms, resuming the calculated calm Will was used to. "Only one way to know for sure. I'm just going to have to come in from the cold and confront the sons of bitches."

Will eyed him askance. "Don't even think about it. Two attempts on your life in as many days isn't enough for you?"

Jack shrugged. "Let's just say I'd rather enter that particular lion's den on my own terms. Better chance of walking out again that way."

Will wasn't so sure. "Odds are good, you go looking for Antonovich, you won't be coming back, brother."

Jack's answering grin was tinged with sorrow and regret. "It's something I should've done a long time ago, Will. I've been stalling the inevitable and putting other people at risk. I won't have anyone else's blood on my hands because I'm a coward."

"Bullshit," Will spat. He knew for a fact his old friend was the first one to rush in to save a fellow brother, the first to put his own neck on the line to save an innocent. Hell, he'd been on the receiving end of that bravery. A coward he wasn't. "Say that again and I'll clean your clock. If you were a coward I wouldn't be alive. Neither would Claire Davenport."

"I have to do this, Will. I've put off dealing with everything for too long."

Will could relate. He'd said he didn't think Claire had played them, that she was an innocent victim of this deadly game as much as any of them. But he wouldn't know for sure until he got to Boston and assessed the situation.

Will heaved a resigned sigh. "When are you heading out?"

"As soon as Finn can get a lock on Antonovich," Jack said. "I think he and I need to have a little chat."

Will nodded, not letting on just how concerned he was about his friend entering the lion's den he was so determined to go charging into. "Speaking of chats, I need to get Boston on the phone and let them know I'm on my way. I don't want Claire to be too exhausted for our conversation."

"Go on," Jack said with a jerk of his head. "Get out of here. I've got this."

Will leveled his gaze at him. "Do you?"

He could see doubt flash across Jack's face. And fear. But a split second later, Jack resumed his reckless smile. "Of course."

Will took a step closer to the door but hesitated, a heavy mantle of dread descending upon him. Although he wanted to order Jack to take Adam or Luke or any one of the others with him, he knew it'd just turn into an argument, and probably one that Jack would win. Jack was right about needing to settle things himself. He'd never rest again until he did. Will knew that all too well.

He clapped his friend on the back briefly, then walked away, calling over his shoulder, "Make sure you say goodbye to Maddie before you go. You don't want that hanging over you—or haunting *her*."

Jack watched his friend's retreating back, wondering if he'd ever see Will again. He'd never asked for all the details on what had happened between Will and Claire when they were on the run in the Nigerian jungle. He knew that they'd been through hell together while they were captured, and he suspected that the bond they'd forged during their time together was something that shook them both to the core—hell, why else would a beautiful woman with a promising career and a second chance at life spend countless hours searching for Will, determined to believe he was still alive in spite of the carefully planted evidence the Alliance had provided to the contrary?

He knew that whatever it was that had happened haunted Will, tortured him. Will thought he'd failed Claire in some way.

Jack ran his hands through his hair, holding the dark waves tight against his head for a moment before letting go with a sigh. God, he understood that kind of torture. He'd failed every woman he'd ever cared about. And he knew for damned sure that Maddie deserved better than his sorry ass.

That was why he wasn't about to go to her now and tell her good-bye. Besides, she'd made it perfectly clear at dinner that there was no future for them. What had happened between them on the plane was nothing more than satisfying a craving—at least, that's how she'd put it when he'd followed her out of the dining room. The look on her face, the awkwardness when she tried to explain that she'd been an idiot to think things would work out and that she apologized if she'd led him on . . . It shredded his goddamned heart.

Then she'd thanked him. Fucking *thanked* him. As if making love to her had been nothing more than a favor, a way to finally get him out of her system.

Even now as he remembered her words, he balled his fists at his sides. But the hurt, the anger he felt was nothing to the ache that sat like a boulder in the center of his chest, making it momentarily impossible to breathe.

No, it was better for them both if he just walked away without a word and dealt with his bullshit once and for all. He'd assured Will that he wasn't concerned about coming back, but he could see in Will's eyes that his old friend knew Jack's confidence on this one was all for show. In truth, Jack knew how this was going to end. There was only one way it could end. Otherwise Jack would always be hunted, the people he cared about would continue to be in danger.

But Jack knew for damned sure that when he felt the cold steel muzzle at the base of his neck and closed his eyes to accept his fate, it'd be Maddie's face he pictured, the moments they'd shared replaying in his mind before eternal darkness engulfed him.

An hour later, he drove his silver Porsche through the compound gates and opened it up, the scenery zipping by him in a blur. When he was finally on the interstate and heading east, he hit the call button on his control panel.

"Whaddup, brah?" Finn asked, the words followed by the sound of video game explosions in the background. He must've already been hard at work on something, using the games to "warm up" his brain, as he put it. Well, whatever it was, it was going to have to wait.

Jack's eyes narrowed on the road before him and he shifted gears. "I need you to find Sergei Antonovich. I want to know where he is, where he's been, what he's eaten, who he's screwing. You feel me?"

"Already on it," Finn told him

Jack's brows lifted. "Did Will give you a heads-up that I'd be asking?"

"No," Finn said, drawing out the word, his tone cautious. "Will's already on the jet to Boston. Maddie was the one asking for our pal Sergei's location."

Jack hissed a curse under his breath. "Where's she now?"

There was a slight pause. "Probably somewhere in northern Indiana at this point. She was headed east and wanted me to send her hourly updates on Antonovich's movements. I was able to pick up his trail in Boston right away—dude wasn't really covering his tracks, if you know what I mean. It's like he *wanted* us to find him. Airport security footage had him boarding a plane to Detroit around the same time you guys left Boston. Kozlov too, but not together. Not sure what that's all about . . . Think they're trying to keep a low profile? Not let on they're working together?"

"Detroit?" Jack mumbled. "What's in Detroit?"

He could hear Finn typing. "Apparently, Antonovich's granddaughter Eva. She's a college student at University of Detroit Mercy. Studying to be a nurse. She lives in an apartment near campus. Only connection I can find for Kozlov is Antonovich."

Jack's frown deepened. "Send me the address," he demanded, apprehension creeping along his spine. He was liking this mission less and less. And the fact that Maddie had an hour and a half's head start did nothing to diminish his anxiety. "And get me a location on Maddie."

More clacking on the keyboard. "You got it. Texting it to you now."

Jack glanced at the coordinates when they came up before him, projected upon his windshield. He pressed down on the accelerator, shifting smoothly as the Porsche's engine revved. "What's Maddie driving?"

"Hang on," Finn mumbled. "Lemme check the fleet. Oh, *sweet*. Your girl is totally badass, Jack. She's got one of the Harleys."

Jack shifted again, pushing one hundred miles per hour now. "Finn, I'm going to need you to clear a path for me. I need to catch up to her before she reaches Detroit."

"You got it. I'll alert our pals in law enforcement. You won't have any issues." There was another pause. "Hey, brah, I'm sorry about you and Maddie. I figured you were in this together."

Jack's jaw clenched so hard he felt his muscle begin to twitch. Whether Maddie liked it or not, they were sure as shit in it together *now*. She was walking into a trap—a trap clearly meant for him. There was no other explanation for how visible Antonovich's movements were. The man was a master at going dark—he'd been one of the best operatives the KGB had in the field when he was an active agent. This was just another attempt to draw Jack into their snare. And his old enemy wouldn't hesitate for a moment to use Maddie against him to get whatever it was he was after.

But there was no way in hell he was going to let *another* woman he cared about die trying to protect him. If anything happened to her, Antonovich had better pray to whatever god that double-crossing motherfucker worshiped that someone else took him out before Jack got to him. Because if there was one thing Jack was good at, it was making his enemies bleed . . .

Chapter Fifteen

Jacob Stone fastened his diamond cuff links—a wedding gift from one of his Faithful in South Africa—irritated that the current conversation had already gone on so long. "In case the message is unclear, Kozlov, this is my pissed-off voice."

"Forgive me," Kozlov beseeched on the other end of the line. "I had intended the car bomb for our mutual acquaintance. I will not fail you again, Master."

"I expect not," Jacob returned. "I want this business with Antonovich resolved. That son of a bitch has outlived his usefulness. Double-crossing my grandfather was supposed to provide me with all the data Antonovich had pilfered. And I have yet to receive it. I thought bringing you in would rectify that. But I have to say, Kozlov, so far I'm unimpressed."

"I will take care of Antonovich immediately," Kozlov assured him.

Jacob removed the jacket of his charcoal-gray suit from its hanger and shrugged into it, vaguely noting that his tailor was a genius. The fit was perfect. "Good," he said. "Because if the Alliance gets to Antonovich, I will be extremely disappointed. And I'm afraid someone will have to pay the price for my disappointment."

"Understood."

"And what of Jack Grayson?" Jacob prompted. "I gave him up so that you could take your retribution. But I don't want him figuring out your connection to me. He goes to his grave not knowing the truth. Is that clear?"

"Perfectly clear," Kozlov agreed. "I pledged my loyalty to you, Master. I will not betray you. Antonovich will be eliminated and Jack Grayson will be punished for his sins. You have my word."

Jacob grunted, wishing someone's word mattered a damn these days. But he knew how to play the game. "Very well. I will look forward to hearing an update soon."

Jacob hung up and adjusted his tie in the mirror, giving his reflection a self-satisfied smirk. It gratified him to know that he still had loyal support where it counted. Soon loose ends with the Russians would be tied up with a neat little bow and Jack Grayson would cease to be an issue.

He raked his hands through his hair, then turned his head from side to side, taking in the debonair man who stared back at him. The new patches of gray at his temples gave him a distinguished, sophisticated appearance— exactly what was needed for a world leader. He chuckled as he left his dressing room and strode down the hallway that led to his study. He gave his security detail a mock salute as he passed.

"Please give my grandfather my regards," he snarked. Calling over his shoulder, he added, "And by regards, I mean 'tell him to go fuck himself.'"

He threw open the door to his study, his smile instantly fading when he saw he had guests. And that they were already being waited upon by his lovely wife.

Allison sat on the very settee where he'd screwed her

earlier, Stefan Shepherd next to her, his eyes openly devouring her in spite of Jacob's sudden appearance. The son of a bitch didn't even have the decency to disguise the fact that he wanted Jacob's wife, didn't turn away, didn't even remove his hand from where it rested upon her thigh, just below the hem of her skirt.

Allison offered Jacob an overly bright smile, her cheeks flushing—but whether out of embarrassment at being caught allowing another man to feel her up or from her own arousal, Jacob couldn't tell.

"I don't recall requesting your presence," Jacob said, keeping his tone flat, unemotional in spite of his fury.

Demetrius Shepherd, who sat in one of the high-back chairs, slowly dragged his hungry gaze away from his brother and Allison, and rose to his feet, his movements surprisingly elegant and polished. "Perhaps not. But your wife was good enough to show us her hospitality while we waited, so I assure you it was no inconvenience to us whatsoever." He turned a sly smile on the others in the room as if they shared a private joke at Jacob's expense.

"Why are you here?" Jacob demanded. "Surely you didn't come all this way just to molest my wife."

He turned a pointed look on Stefan, who sneered but lifted his hands away from Allison to lean back against the settee with a chuckle. "My apologies, Stone," he said, although the wicked twinkle in his eyes belied his words. "I just couldn't help touching the silky soft skin peeking out at me from the inside of her thigh. It's really too much for any man to resist."

"Shut the fuck up," Jacob ground out, clenching his fists. "I'm warning you—"

"Had you waited another moment," Stefan continued in his lazy drawl, "I would've had to taste it too. But I don't think I could've stopped there." He looked back at Allison, his gaze taking her in slowly. Her eyes were wide as she sent a panicked glance Jacob's way. "Not until I'd buried my face between her legs and—"

Jacob lunged forward, dragging Stefan up by the front of his shirt and slamming him against the wall. "Say another fucking word, Stefan," he growled. "One. Fucking. Word. All I need is a reason to break your goddamned neck."

Stefan merely laughed in his face, not intimidated in the least. It was enough to make Jacob snap the asshole's neck like a twig, but before he could react, he felt the tip of a dagger pressed to the side of his throat.

"I would not advise such a drastic course of action," Demetrius said mildly. "I realize my brother can be a bit forward, Mr. Stone, but I hope you can overlook his bad manners this time for the sake of our business relationship."

Jacob's mind raced, trying to determine what the odds were that he'd be able to disarm Demetrius and kill both brothers before he or Allison suffered injury. But the increased pressure of the dagger against his carotid made him shove Stefan away, pegging the man with a furious glare.

"Brother, would you mind giving us the room for a moment?" Demetrius asked.

Stefan straightened his clothing, his eyes burning with fury as he returned Jacob's glare. "Of course."

Stefan moved toward the door like a good little pawn in his brother's game, but when he turned his gaze on Demetrius, something unspoken passed between them that made Jacob glance from one to the other. And he saw what appeared to be *fear* pass over Demetrius's features, making Jacob wonder exactly which brother was running the show. He'd always thought it was Demetrius—ever polished and polite, the consummate mastermind. But now he wasn't so sure.

The moment Stefan closed the door behind him, Demetrius tucked his dagger into the pocket of his suit jacket and offered Jacob a tight smile. "To your question, Mr. Stone, we came for payment. I assume the display in Boston was to your satisfaction?"

Jacob shook his head, having to stow his anger before he could think clearly enough to understand what Demetrius was talking about. But then his fury flared for another reason. "No, it wasn't to my satisfaction," he spat. "The idiot mentioned the One True Master before he blew himself up. Now the Alliance has proof that I was involved. The last thing I needed was a goddamned neon sign with an arrow pointed at my head!"

Demetrius nodded solemnly. "Unfortunate, indeed. Perhaps we should've scripted his farewell a little better."

"You think?" Jacob snapped. "It was supposed to be a display of chaos. I want people to be afraid, to doubt that those currently in power can protect them."

"So that you can become the world's savior when you rise from the ashes and rescue them from the horrors of our time," Demetrius supplied. "Yes, well, I think your message was still received loudly and clearly by the public, don't you, Mr. Stone? Is it really so horrible that the Alliance and the Illuminati both see what you are capable of? What lengths you will go to in order to achieve your rightful place in the world?"

Jacob's brows twitched together slightly, not trusting Demetrius but intrigued by his understanding of the situation and of Jacob's aspirations.

"Let us make it up to you," Demetrius said, clasping Jacob on the shoulder. Jacob flinched in spite of himself, but if Demetrius noticed, he didn't let on. "Come, shall we strike another bargain?"

"What kind of bargain?" Jacob asked, suddenly feeling like he was on the verge of making a deal with the devil.

Demetrius's answering smile did little to dispel his misgivings. "I looked into the woman you mentioned previously—Claire Davenport. She is quite a talented reporter, her investigatory skills unparalleled for one so young. In fact, thanks to her obsession with the Alliance, she has uncovered some very damaging evidence of their existence—the Illuminati as well. Quite impressive work—and I don't impress easily."

Jacob drew back slightly. "So I hear. That information you're talking about was supposed to be delivered to me, but the little shit who I had as my inside man ended up double-crossing me."

Demetrius chuckled. "Ah, the wily Mr. Ralston. Yes, I looked into him too. He did send Claire *a* flash drive, but not *the* flash drive, it seems. What happened to the actual flash drive of information you seek is still a mystery."

Jacob frowned, his stomach sinking with this surprising news. "What?"

"But fear not—I'm sure your friends in the Alliance will locate it if given time," Demetrius said. "Let them do all the work, and then you can reap the rewards."

Jacob's mind was racing, trying to figure out how the hell he'd been outwitted by that idiot Ralston. And just how *the fuck* Demetrius knew so much about Jacob's affairs yet again. But there was more that he didn't understand. "So . . . what? You want me to share the information on the flash drive with you once I have it?"

Demetrius's smile became more of a smirk. "I have no interest in the flash drive, Mr. Stone. I'll leave that particular game of capture the flag to you and your playmates. I want Claire Davenport."

"Claire Davenport?" Jacob repeated, confused. "What the hell do you want with *her*?"

Demetrius spread his hands. "It seems that while conducting her research on the Alliance she unearthed information that I would very much like to have."

Jacob gave him a wry look. "You'll have to be a *little* more specific, I'm afraid, if you'd like my help. There's no telling what the woman may have come across. How do I know whatever it is you're after won't be damaging to me and my ambitions?"

Demetrius inclined his head. "Fair enough. Let's just say that the information could be mutually beneficial, providing us both with a great deal of leverage."

"Leverage?" Jacob repeated. "Against whom?"

Demetrius took a step back and spread his arms wide. "Why, *everyone*. If we work together on this, Mr. Stone, I guarantee that you will soon be named One True Master, just as you desire. And that kind of recognition would be extremely influential in bringing to power a certain former politician whose talents are *woefully* unappreciated."

Jacob studied Demetrius for a long moment, wondering just what his game was. "And . . . ? What do you want from me in return?"

"I'll be in touch when I need you," Demetrius assured him. "Until then, I simply ask that you trust me and allow me to prove to you that my brother and I are your allies."

Demetrius's smooth smile made Jacob's stomach turn. He didn't trust the man. There was something sinister in the way he grinned that was far more subtle and dangerous than his whack-job of a brother, who at least wore *his* insanity like a frigging badge of honor for all to see.

"I'll think it over," Jacob replied, his tone stiff and even.

"Jacob," Allison said in a harsh whisper, suddenly at his side, gripping his arm with urgency, "I think you should accept his offer. You could use someone in your corner whom the other Illuminati fear."

The look he sent her way must've been beyond furious, for she immediately shrank back a step.

"I will be in touch," Jacob told Demetrius, mimicking his tight smile. "Thank you for coming today."

Demetrius must've realized he was being pointedly dismissed, for he immediately inclined his head in farewell and left the room without another word.

Jacob stood stiffly where he was, his feet rooted to the floor in case the brothers returned. When he believed enough time had passed, he ground out, "Did you like the way that bastard Stefan leered at you, Allison? Should I have left you two alone?"

"What?" she cried. "Jacob, you can't be serious! That man scares the hell out of me. I was afraid to slap his hand away when it was on my leg—Stefan is completely insane! I was actually relieved when you came in."

Remembering how she had flushed and smiled at the other man, Jacob slowly dragged his gaze away from the door to study her face now. She honestly did appear frightened, but he wondered if that fear was more a result of being caught or if she honestly had been terrified to react to Stefan's sexual advances.

He took a deep breath and exhaled slowly, forcing away his doubts, and took Allison's hand, pulling her into his embrace. He pressed a kiss to the top of her head. "I'm sorry, darling. I can be a jealous idiot where you're concerned. And I'm sorry you were forced to endure that son of a bitch's hands on you. If they ever come here again, I don't want you to be alone with them. It's not safe. I worry what he might do to you. And if he touches you again, I will cut his fucking dick off."

Allison pulled back and peered up at him, her eyes wide with fear. "I don't want you at odds with those men, Jacob.

They're dangerous. Far more dangerous than your grandfather or anyone in the Alliance. I worry for you if you accept Demetrius's offer. And yet I worry what will happen if you don't. They have connections to the men in the shadows, the ones none of the rest of us know—not even your grandfather, Jacob. If they decide to move against you . . ."

Jacob shook his head. "I shouldn't have called them in the first place. My grandfather was right."

Her brows lifted. "I never thought I'd hear you say *that*."

"The Shepherd brothers will have to wait," Jacob told her. "I have other concerns at the moment. Antonovich's stabbing me in the back being a rather important one."

"You'll have to give Demetrius an answer soon," Allison pointed out. "I wouldn't keep him waiting on this. He's not a patient man."

Jacob shrugged. "I'll give it a few days, but then I'll explain to Demetrius that while I appreciate his offer, I can't possibly accept. I'm sure he'll understand . . ."

Chapter Sixteen

"What the hell were you thinking?*"*

Maddie started so violently, the cup of coffee she was carrying flew from her hand in a wide arc, the contents spraying onto her biker boots when the paper cup hit the ground. She turned an irritated look on the speaker, who was leaning against the side of a silver Porsche that seemed comically out of place in the parking lot of the back-road truck stop. "Well, I *had* been thinking how awesome that cup of coffee smelled and how it was going to be *exactly* what I needed for the last hour of my ride. So thanks a lot."

Jack gave her an irritated look. "That's not what I mean, Maddie, and you damned well know it."

She heaved a sigh and crossed her arms. "So, did Finn tell you where I was going? Is that how you found me?" She'd taken the back roads specifically to try to avoid being found if Jack decided to come after her.

Jack pushed off the car and closed the gap between them in two angry strides. He took her by the arms, his grip hard even through her leather jacket. "What did you think I was going to do? Let you fight my battle for me?"

God, even in the darkness his green eyes were mesmerizing, captivating. She wanted desperately to take hold of the front of his silk shirt and drag him to her, lose herself in the warmth of his lips.

"Does it have to be a battle at all?" she asked. "I just wanted to find Antonovich, talk to him, figure out what this game is that he's playing. Whatever happened in Russia is tormenting you, Jack. I just wanted you to have some peace, to be happy."

His grip slackened and he released her arms to take her face in his hands. "And you thought I could be happy without *you*? What you said to Will . . ."

"Was true," she told him, her throat tight with unshed tears as she spoke the words. "We can't have a future together, Jack. There will always be doubt about whether or not our judgment is impaired when the other is in danger. We owe it to our brothers in the Alliance, to the people we're supposed to be protecting, to have our heads in the game."

He closed his eyes and pressed his forehead to hers. He knew she was right. She could tell by the fact that he didn't argue with her, didn't assure her that they would be fine, that they could love each other and still do their duty to the Alliance and to humankind.

"I don't care if you're five feet or five countries away," he told her. "I'm not going to stop worrying. I care far too much. And you wouldn't be here if you didn't care about me too."

She pulled back to meet his gaze. "Of course, I care about you. Are you kidding me? That's why I couldn't let you get yourself killed. And if you take on these people on your own, you won't come out alive. If you want to go after Antonovich and Kozlov and finally put whatever's going on behind you, then you're going to have to let me in."

He pressed his mouth into an angry line. "Maddie—"

She rose up on her toes and brushed a brief kiss to his

lips, which softened at her touch and soon sought hers. She'd only meant to stop his protest against her involvement, but as with every other kiss they'd shared, it soon led to another, now heated and hungry. Her arms went around his waist, pulling him closer.

When he finally ended the kiss, her breathing was ragged, her entire body aching with need for him. "We should go," she panted. "We still have an hour's drive."

"That's a long time to wait," he murmured, his eyes taking on a glint that made her shudder. "And I've already waited far too long to get you in my arms."

She swallowed hard. "Well, then," she rasped, "I guess you'd better follow me. Just try to keep up."

Holy hell.

The drive into Detroit seemed like it took for-fucking-ever. And even now as the elevator crept at an agonizing pace toward their floor, Jack thought he'd crawl out of his skin. If there hadn't been another hotel guest in the elevator with them, he would've punched the emergency stop button and taken her right there.

And damn, but she looked sexier than ever in her motorcycle gear. Her tight leather pants were almost more than he could take. Even now as his gaze skimmed along her curves, he had to covertly shift things around to keep from frightening off the other passenger.

Two floors away from theirs, the elevator stopped and their unwanted companion got off, finally leaving them to themselves. Unable to resist, Jack grabbed Maddie's hand and pulled her roughly to him, claiming her mouth in a harsh kiss. She responded with a moan, pressing her body into his, her hands tangling in his hair.

Now the elevator that had seemed to be moving so

slowly arrived at their floor all too soon. Luckily their room was only two doors down, and seconds later Jack swept her inside, shoving her jacket from her shoulders the moment the door closed behind them. Then, their gazes locked, they moved as one, working together to unbutton his shirt. The moment it hit the ground, she leaned in, pressing kisses to his chest as her fingers fumbled with his belt.

A moment later, he stood before her completely naked, loving the way her gaze devoured him before she pulled her T-shirt over her head and tossed it aside. And when her bra joined her shirt, he closed the distance between them and bent to take one breast into his mouth, teasing and nipping at her erect nipple until she cried out, needing more.

In one swift motion, he grasped her around the waist, lifting her up and falling with her onto the bed. He once more claimed her breast, chuckling as she panted and squirmed, gasping his name. And that only increased as he kissed the valley between her breasts, the silky soft skin of her belly. And when he grasped the edges of her leather pants, he took his time sliding them down her legs, kissing his way along until he reached her ankle, then hooked her leg over his shoulder as he kissed his way back up along her calf, the inside of her thigh.

She cried out, clenching his hair in her fists, when he settled between her legs. He flicked his tongue against the sensitive bud of nerves there, his hands sliding beneath her bottom and tilting her up toward his mouth. When her breath began to saw in and out of her lungs and her muscles tightened, he shifted, sinking in deeper, penetrating her with the tip of his tongue.

She arched up for him, rolling her hips, taking all he could give. And when he moved again, his teeth grazing her clit, she bucked with a cry that filled the room. He drove her through her climax, easing off, then diving in again until she finally clawed at his shoulders, attempting to pull him up to her.

With a reluctant groan, he slid up the length of her body until he was cradled by her hips, pausing only briefly to roll on the condom he'd grabbed during their mad dash to shed their clothes. She was still tight and pulsing when he slid into her. For a moment he was still, savoring the feel of her skin pressed against his, the way her body enveloped him, embraced him in the most intimate ways.

Then he began to thrust slowly, peering down at her as her pleasure played out over her face, searing into his memory the images of her as she looked at that moment. She had said they couldn't have a future. Hell, he'd said as much when he was trying to dissuade her from getting too close to him again. But they had *now*. And as she pulled him down to receive her sultry kiss, he shoved aside any concerns about what the future held for either of them, and let her love wrap around him and warm the cold dread that had settled into the center of his chest.

Later, as she lay in his arms, spent from their second time making love that night, the coldness returned and would've completely engulfed him if she hadn't placed her hand over his heart and lifted her face to offer a sleepy kiss.

"Should we get some rest?" she asked, her voice hoarse from her last orgasm.

He kissed the top of her head and pulled her in closer. "Go ahead, love. I'm not going anywhere. In a few hours, we'll go meet with Antonovich's granddaughter and see what we can discover. But I want you to be careful. If things go south, I want you to forget about me and just do what you need to do to say safe."

She was quiet for a long moment before lifting up on her elbow to look down at him. She brushed another kiss to his lips and caressed the line of his jaw with the back of her fingers. "I'm not worried about *me*."

He turned his face away from her to stare at the ceiling. "I am. Maddie, if anything were to happen to you . . ."

With her index finger she tapped his chin, which was thick with stubble. "Hey. We've had this discussion, remember? I can take care of myself."

He shook his head. "Not against these people, love. Antonovich makes his living betraying whoever he can—as long as he can profit from it. And Kozlov had intended that bomb in Boston for me. He won't stop until he kills me—unless I get to him first."

"Who are these people anyway?" Maddie asked, letting her hand fall away. "Why are they so determined to kill you? And why are you afraid of *them*? I've never known you to be afraid of anyone, Jack."

Jack sighed. He'd never wanted her to know the truth, but if she was going to help him with Kozlov and Antonovich, she needed to fully understand what they were up against.

"My father was from one of the old families in the Alliance," he began. "His line was legendary. And he continued that reputation in his own right, becoming one of the most respected operatives in the Order, right alongside Sean Asher."

"Sean Asher," Maddie repeated. "That's Will's father, right?"

He nodded. "My father's effectiveness made him a lot of enemies, I guarantee you. But he had a lot of allies as well, *confreres* and *consoeurs* he trusted. One of them was a man named Sergei Antonovich."

Maddie's eyes went wide. "The man who wants to kill you was a friend of your *father*?"

He nodded again, starting to feel like one of those bobblehead things on dashboards. "As I've mentioned,

Antonovich was in the KGB, but he was also in deep with the Russian mob. The man would sell out his own mother for the right price. But he'd proven valuable to my father many times, and so my father trusted him right up until the day someone put a bomb in Father's car—much like the one that killed Manny."

Maddie smoothed his chest. "I'm so sorry, Jack."

"We knew it was the Russian mob, but couldn't prove it," Jack told her, covering her hand with his. "And Antonovich was surprisingly quiet on the whole thing, didn't have a single lead for us. Will, Jacob, me . . . We all lost our fathers to these bastards. I guess they didn't want us meddling in their business."

"I'm sensing there's more to the story," Maddie surmised.

Jack felt his expression growing colder, harsher. "Will was certain that there was. He insisted his grandfather—the High Commander of the Alliance—look into it. There were too many things about it—how our fathers were targeted—that pointed to our old enemies the Illuminati. But the High Commander had eradicated the Illuminati, or so he claimed. His pride wouldn't allow him to look deeper."

"So *you* did?" she guessed.

Jack nodded. "Will and I both did, but I was still in the UK, so it was easier for me to insinuate myself into their circles." Here he grinned. "Plus, my Russian's better than Will's. So I poked my nose everywhere it didn't belong, used whatever means necessary to get answers."

He paused, his shame at what he'd done making the words lodge in his throat. But he had to force them out, had to make sure Maddie understood who he really was.

"One of those means included seducing a woman named Natasha, who happened to be the twenty-two-year-old daughter of the head of the Russian mob. She was sweet, beautiful, trusting." He laughed bitterly. "Clearly too trusting if she trusted *me*. Anyway, one night I received word that my cover was blown, the mob was onto me and had put a price on my head. So I left without a word, without a good-bye. I had to abandon my search for answers—and a woman I'd grown to care about."

Maddie drew back slightly at the ominous, bitter tone of his voice. "What happened to her?"

"I later discovered she'd become pregnant with my child."

Maddie blinked at him, clearly not quite sure how to react to the bombshell he'd just dropped on her. He had never mentioned having a child, had never mentioned *Natasha*, for that matter.

He absently twisted the ring on his right hand, which bore the Templar cross, turning it several times with his thumb before continuing. "From what I understand, Natasha hid the pregnancy for several months. If I'd known about it, I would've immediately returned and gotten her to the UK or the U.S.—somewhere that the Alliance could've kept her safe. But I'd been relocated under my alias and was working for your father at that point, so I hadn't heard anything."

"Alias?" Maddie echoed. "What alias?"

He gave her a tight smile. "Jack Grayson is not my real name."

She laughed, a little bitterly, clearly shocked to know the man she'd been so intimate with had been lying to her on the most basic level. He could see in her eyes that she was hurt, angry. "Of course it isn't." She shook her head a little, scrunching up her nose in that adorable way she had, then heaved a sharp exhale. "We'll come back to that little bit of news later. What happened then? How did you find out?"

"I guess Natasha tried to run from her father when it

became impossible to conceal the pregnancy any longer, but she didn't get far before her father's men caught up to her."

"Where is she now?" Maddie asked, her voice barely above a whisper.

Jack's eyes narrowed. "Dead. Along with my unborn child. Her father beat her to death for carrying the son of a sworn enemy. He couldn't find me to kill me too, so instead he hired assassins to go to my family's home and murder my mother and my grandmother and my aunt Eugenia and twelve-year-old cousin Daniel. He also murdered any of the staff who happened to be on hand that day. Luckily, most of them were on holiday, so they were spared. But they returned home to find the bodies of all that remained of my family."

Maddie was speechless, filled with horror. Tears made their way silently to her cheeks as she watched helplessly while Jack struggled with his sorrow and guilt. She wanted to remove the pain she saw etched into his features, the regret that weighed so heavily upon him. But she didn't know what to do except hold him.

He took a deep breath and let it out slowly, continuing with his story. "I received word of their deaths the day after I was called on the carpet for my relationship with you, Maddie. I didn't leave you because I was afraid of retribution for loving you. I left because I was afraid of what you would think of me after I did what I had to do."

Maddie swallowed hard, her head spinning with the information he'd just imparted. "What did you do, Jack?"

He pulled out of her arms and sat up on the edge of the bed, then rubbed the back of his neck beneath the dark waves of hair for a moment before finally continuing. "I buried my family. And then I went to that bastard's home and I shot him in the head while he was eating dinner. But not before I'd killed every single one of his men to get to him."

Maddie sat up and wrapped her arms around his waist, holding on to him, lending him her strength so that he could finish the story. She waited silently.

Finally, he laid his hand on top of hers again and squeezed her fingers briefly. His voice was gravelly when he said, "When I reached his dining room, there were four of his bodyguards there. I shot them, then turned the gun on Natasha's father. And he just smiled at me. The asshole actually *smiled*. It was then that I noticed the boy sitting at the table. Natasha's younger brother. He was terrified, crying. I hesitated, not wanting him to watch his father die. I wouldn't want that for any child. But then I saw movement in the corner of my eye and turned just in time to see the boy's father pulling a gun on me. I reacted."

"Dear God," Maddie breathed.

"As I turned to go, a man came rushing in—Kozlov," Jack told her, his head hanging down. "He glanced at his dead boss, at the boy, and raised his hands before rushing to the other side of the table to grab the child. I let him live so he could take the boy somewhere safe, away from the carnage I'd wrought."

"And now Kozlov is seeking retribution after all these years?" Maddie asked. "Is that what you think?"

He nodded. "The mob boss's brother took over management of their operation. And the Alliance has continued to monitor and interfere with their activities. But I was ordered to stand down and let someone else handle things. Will reassigned me to Chicago, at my request. I wasn't the man you were in love with, Maddie. As badly as I wanted to go back to you, to have a future with you—the Alliance be damned—I couldn't stay. I had a price on my head. I couldn't put you or your family in danger."

She rose up on her knees and turned his face toward her. This time he didn't shrink away. "Jack—"

"Don't," he interrupted. "Don't tell me you understand. Don't tell me that you'll be fine. That *we'll* be fine. Someone has told him where I am, my new name. No one is safe around me now."

"What do you plan to do, Jack?" she countered. "You have to end this once and for all. You can't keep living your life in fear—for me or for anyone else you care about. You need someone to have your back. And if you're going to be too damned stubborn to let your brothers in the Alliance be there for you, then you get me."

He shook his head. "I shouldn't have brought you into this. It was a mistake. I know I agreed to let you go with me tomorrow to confront Antonovich and try to ferret out Kozlov, but now you see why I can't."

"No, Jack, I *don't* see why you can't." He pressed his lips together in frustration and tried to look away, but she held him where he was. "I might not have the history with these two guys that you have, but I was there too when Manny died, okay? I didn't really know him like you did, but no one deserves to go out like that. I won't be able to get that image out of my head any more than you will. Let me help you. As much for my sake as for yours."

He studied her for several moments, his gaze taking in every aspect of her face, lingering upon her lips before traveling back to her eyes. He shook his head as if in dismay. "I don't deserve you, Maddie. I never did."

"Then do something for me," she said, knowing there was no way she could convince him of just how wrong he was. "Tell me *one* thing about you that's true. Just one, Jack."

He gave her a slight smile. "My first name is John. Jack is my nickname and has been since I was in short pants. And everything I feel for you—those are the truest words I've ever spoken." His fingertips caressed her skin tenderly. "I love you, Maddie. I should've told you that so many times before. You are everything to me. And whether you call me Jack Grayson or John Robert Forsythe Estridge, that truth will not change."

Maddie's throat went tight with emotion and for a moment she couldn't speak, her heart too full to even form the words. But then she took his face in her hands, holding his gaze for a long moment, letting the love she saw there envelop her, and whispered, "I love you too."

And when he closed his eyes, his breath leaving his lungs on a sharp exhale, she kissed him, drawing him back onto the bed. And when he lay back against the pillows, she straddled him, kissing and caressing him until his hands began to explore her body, his touch tender and adoring. And when she rose up on her knees to slowly sheath him with her body, the love she saw in his eyes made her heart swell.

As they made love again, she clung to him, sending up a silent prayer that whatever happened the next day, he'd finally find the peace he sought.

Chapter Seventeen

Will made his way down the stairs to the Boston
commandery's headquarters, hidden in plain sight in one
of the fallout shelters that had dropped out of use after the
end of the Cold War. The deeper underground he went,
the more inviting the compound became, until he finally
reached the innermost section, where the ops centers and
private quarters were located. Unlike in Chicago, the
Templars in Boston all had quarters on-site, but then their
homes were scattered throughout the city. The only person
who lived on-site almost permanently was the local commander, Tony Cain, who strode toward Will, extending his
hand in greeting.

"Commander Asher," he said in his deep bass. The guy
had a voice that made James Earl Jones sound like a pre-
pubescent kid, and an authoritative presence that Will
looked for among those he'd tapped to lead the local com-
manderies under his purview. Tony was one of his best and
most reliable appointments by far. "Welcome, sir."

Will gave him a terse nod. "Tony."

"If you'll follow me, sir, I'll take you to Ms. Davenport," Tony told him. "We halted the examiner's session

with Ms. Davenport the moment you alerted us that you'd like to talk to her yourself."

"So how's Claire doing?" Will asked as Tony led him through a labyrinth of hallways.

Tony turned into a hallway with several doors on either side. "Angry. Indignant," he said. "Pretty much what you'd expect. She understands the reason for her relocation, but she's furious about being detained and questioned like a criminal." Tony stopped in front of one of the doors and sent a sidelong glance Will's way. "And sorry to say, but you're definitely persona non grata at the moment, my friend."

"I'll bet." Will raked a hand over his hair, grasping the back of his neck for a moment.

He couldn't go in there. Couldn't face her again. Yeah, okay, so that meant he was being a total fucking coward. But staying away had been as much for her peace of mind as his, hadn't it? At least, that's what he'd been telling himself. Maybe he'd gotten it all wrong. Well, he guessed he was about to find out . . .

Will took a deep, bracing breath, then nodded. "All right. Give me a few minutes with her."

Tony unlocked the door and stepped aside, allowing Will to pass. The room was sparsely but comfortably furnished with a simple wooden chair sitting next to a bed. A table in the center of the room held the only source of illumination—a small grouping of candles that cast just enough light to keep the environs dimly lit and soothing.

He halted when he caught sight of Claire lying on the bed, curled up on her side as she slept, her honey-blond hair fanned out on the pillow, the candlelight accentuating the coppery highlights.

God, she was beautiful—even more so than he remembered, more so than the photos Finn had sent him as part of her dossier.

His chest grew tight at the sight of her, his misgivings about how to handle her situation gripping him once more. He forced himself to move forward and sat in the chair next to her bed. A lock of hair had fallen over her cheek as she slept. He reached out, hesitating briefly before tenderly brushing her hair back, his fingertips skimming lightly across her cheek as he pulled his hand away.

At his touch, her eyelids fluttered open. She blinked rapidly, then gasped, throwing off the blanket covering her, and sat up. "Will."

He managed a hint of a smile. "Hi."

She tilted her head to one side, her brows drawn together in a frown as she reached out with trembling fingers to touch his cheek. When she made contact, he squeezed his eyes shut, her touch sending a jolt of heat through every atom of his body.

"You *are* alive," she whispered.

He grasped her hand and gently pulled it away. "I'm alive."

When he opened his eyes he saw her expression shift, her lovely, full lips pressing into a hard line. And he probably should've seen it coming, but the sting of her open palm against his cheek still jarred him.

"You son of a bitch," she hissed. "All this time you let me think you were dead! Do you have any idea what it was like waking up in that hospital and not knowing where the hell I was? What the hell had happened? And not knowing if the man who'd rescued me—who'd kept me alive for three days in the jungle, for crying out loud—was dead or alive? After everything that happened—what we shared— you just dumped me and vanished without a trace?"

Will rubbed absently at his cheek, still warm from where she'd slapped him. "Claire—"

"And now you have the nerve to keep me locked in here like a goddamned prisoner?" she fumed.

He reached out to lay a hand over hers. "You have to understand, Claire—"

"I don't have to understand *shit*," she spat, shaking off his touch. "I'm an American citizen. I have rights."

Oh, so that's the way it's going to be. Okay then . . .

"We don't work for the government," he pointed out, his tone even. "*Any* government. But you know that, don't you?"

She crossed her arms over her chest and turned her head away.

"What else do you know, Claire?" he pressed. "As I'm sure my colleague has already informed you, I can't let you leave here until you tell us everything."

She laughed bitterly and turned her furious gaze back on him. "So . . . what? You're just going to keep me here indefinitely?" When he responded with only a bland expression, her eyes went wide. "You can't be serious! What about all the promises of a new life? This relocation you keep talking about?"

"We'll make good on that promise," Will assured her. "But if I let you leave here without knowing what else could put you at risk, I don't know who to hide you from."

She arched a brow at him. "Well, I'm sure you guys already ransacked my house and found my notes. And they seized my laptop when I got here. So there's nothing left to tell."

He gave her a tight smile. "Don't be so sure," he argued. "And, trust me, Claire, my method of questioning is more subtle than my friend's. He's good at what he does and he always gets answers—one way or another. And *his* methods are preferable to those of another colleague who's picked up a thing or two from dealing with the yakuza. I'd rather we not have to get to that point. So, let's start with an easy one. What'd you do with the flash drive Tad Ralston sent you?"

"I gave it to your friend," she said. "Jack."

"Yeah, you gave Jack a flash drive," he confirmed. "But it was blank."

She shook her head, frowning. "Blank? That can't be right. Tad told me it contained everything I could possibly want to know about a secret society called 'the Alliance.' I'd heard that mentioned before in the dark ops I'd uncovered. I figured it would lead me to figuring out who you were, what had happened to you. But then Tad started going on about his boss and the Illuminati and I began to wonder if what he was sending me was just a bunch of conspiracy theory BS—until I found out he'd been murdered."

Obviously, Claire hadn't been able to get into the flash drive, because she still thought it contained information. She'd had no idea when she'd handed it off to Jack that it was blank. So their theory had been right. Antonovich had double-crossed Ralston and Hale. They'd all died for nothing.

A quiet knock on the door brought Will's head up. "Yeah."

Tony poked his head inside. "Do you need more time?"

Will shook his head. "No. I found out what I needed to know."

"What?" Claire cried as soon as the door closed and they were alone once more. "What about finding out all I know? What about not wanting to turn me over to the other guy for questioning?"

Will got to his feet. "I was just trying to scare you so you'd tell me what you know about the flash drive. The examiner's actually a really nice guy."

Claire's cheeks flushed with rage. "You asshole. So was the threat about the other guy—the one with the yakuza connection—was that bullshit too?"

"Oh no," Will assured her. "That one was true. So do yourself a favor and answer the examiner's questions."

Claire jumped up and rushed toward Will as he turned away, grabbing his arm to keep him from leaving. "What about *my* questions? I think I deserve a few answers, don't you?"

Will met her pale blue gaze, torn between wanting to drag her into his arms and kiss her—taste the lips he'd tasted briefly once, years before, when they'd both believed death would soon claim them—and his desire to get the hell out of there before she managed to work her way into his heart again.

He sighed. "One question. I'll answer it if I can."

Her expression softened. "Have you ever thought about me since Nigeria?"

"No," he lied. "What happened there was just another mission for me, Claire."

She studied him for a long moment, nodding slowly, her eyes narrowing. Then she grasped the back of his neck and pressed a hard kiss to his lips. It took every ounce of his willpower not to return the kiss. And yet when she pulled back and looked up at him, she shook her head. "You're a bad liar, Will."

Without a word, he turned back toward the door and opened it. But before he left the room, he paused and looked back at her over his shoulder. "Be safe, Claire," he said. "I want you to be happy and have a full life without any of the Alliance's bullshit putting you in danger. Without *me* putting you in danger. You found out what you needed to know. We'll set you up with a new life, a new profession. Any attempt to disclose information about the Alliance will be intercepted, discredited."

Claire's expression twisted with outrage. "You can't do that! I have a responsibility—"

"To whom?" he interrupted. "If you think revealing the truth will benefit anyone, you're mistaken. You'd be causing more damage than you can possibly imagine. Give it up and walk away. I'm afraid I have to insist upon that."

"Or what?" she asked, a twinkle in her eye that looked to him like a challenge. "You'll have to kill me?"

But Will didn't rise to the bait. "I'm not the one you have to worry about."

Chapter Eighteen

Maddie closed her eyes and let the morning sunlight warm her face as Jack steered her Harley through the streets of Detroit, having decided it was far less conspicuous than his Porsche. Her arms tightened around his waist, enjoying the moment of sheer freedom and joy they shared just then—a brief reminder of the days when they'd first fallen in love and their only concern was keeping their affair secret from her father.

If she'd had any idea how her life would change soon after that, she would've spent far more time savoring their moments like this and less time worrying about what the future might hold.

She rested her cheek against his back, reveling in the feel of him, the way their bodies fit together. It was chaste in comparison to their lovemaking the night before, but she felt the same contentment, the same happiness that she'd known as they lay together in each other's arms. Just being together was enough. Knowing he was safe was all she needed. And as soon as they'd dealt with the threat from Antonovich and Kozlov, if Will decided to reassign her to another commandery, at least she'd know that Jack was safe.

All too soon they arrived at the apartment building where Eva Antonovich lived. The stone structure looked like it could've doubled as a set for a gothic horror novel. But the illusion immediately vanished the moment they entered the dingy, poorly lit lobby lined with small brass mailboxes set into the walls. The lone elevator bore an Out of Order sign, so Jack gestured toward the door that led to the stairs. The stairwell was just as oppressive as the lobby, its concrete walls painted a mint green that was dingy and pitted.

"Well, isn't this a charming place?" Maddie mumbled. "You'd think dear old Granddad could afford to help his granddaughter find a decent place to live."

"Maybe she doesn't want his money," Jack suggested, taking the lead up the stairs, his gun held down at his side.

Maddie reached for the handrail but recoiled when a cockroach skittered across the rail where she'd nearly placed her hands. "Well, I think if I lived in a shithole like this, I'd be willing to take a few bucks from the family. My pride only goes so far . . ."

When they reached the third floor of the building and opened the door to the hallway, Jack put out an arm, blocking her way. "Where is everyone?"

Maddie frowned and glanced up and down the hallway, which was as dingy and dimly lit as the stairwell had been. The hair on the back of her neck prickled in warning. "You know," she whispered, "I'm really getting sick of dealing with shit in hallways . . ."

Jack sent an amused grin over his shoulder. "Last one for a while, love. Promise."

"Damned right," she muttered, following him toward Eva's apartment and taking up position to the right side of the door.

He leaned in from his position on the opposite side just enough to knock lightly on the door. His knock was met by silence. He knocked again, a little louder this time. A moment later a tremulous voice asked, "Who is it?"

Maddie shared a glance with Jack and could see he'd also picked up on the fact that something was wrong. "Eva? My name's Jack—I'm a friend of your grandfather. We just need to ask you a few questions."

There was a moment's hesitation, then Maddie heard the bolt lock turning. The door opened a crack, the security chain still in place. A young woman peered out at them through the opening, her wary gaze taking in Jack and then Maddie.

"What do you want to know about my grandfather?" she asked, her voice slightly accented.

"Could we come inside, Eva?" Maddie asked, keeping her tone friendly. "We'd rather not talk out here in the hallway." She offered Eva a smile. "I doubt you want your neighbors to know your business, right?"

Eva studied her for a moment, then closed the door. Maddie heard the security chain disengage, and then the door opened to reveal a lovely young woman with chestnut hair and a heart-shaped face. Her wide gray eyes were still untrusting even as she stepped back to allow them in. She was dressed in pale pink scrubs and sneakers, either getting ready to go to work or having just gotten home.

"Could I get you something?" she asked as she closed and bolted the door. Her invitation seemed more the product of good manners than a genuine offer.

Maddie offered her a kind smile. "No. Thank you."

Eva nodded and took a seat on the edge of a shabby chair in her apartment's sitting area. "What do you want with my grandfather?"

"Have you seen him lately?" Jack asked, glancing around the apartment.

Eva swallowed and shook her head. "No. He doesn't visit often."

"Do you have any other family in the area, Eva?" Maddie asked, watching Jack stroll around the apartment.

"Um, no," Eva assured her. "My parents died when I was young. My grandfather is all I have. He sends me money when he can."

Maddie's brows lifted in surprise before she could check her reaction.

Eva gave her a tight smile. "It all goes toward my tuition. Grandfather wanted me to come to the United States to become a nurse. He wanted a better life for me than what he could give me in Russia. But being an international student is expensive. I'll soon be finished though, and then I can find a better place to live."

"When did you hear from your grandfather last?" Jack asked, opening a door that presumably led to Eva's bedroom.

She sent a nervous glance toward her room and shifted in her chair. "You must understand," she said to Maddie in a low voice, "I love my grandfather very much. I don't want anything to happen to him. What do you want from him?"

"Just answers," Maddie assured her. "Is he in trouble, Eva?"

Eva twisted her hands together in her lap as she glanced between Maddie and Jack. "I don't know. But I think so, yes."

Maddie sat down on the rickety futon next to Eva's chair and put her hand over the young woman's, stilling them. "Honey, just tell us what you know. Maybe we can keep him from getting hurt."

Maddie didn't miss the doubtful look Jack sent her way. And, apparently, neither did Eva. "I don't know anything," she said, pressing her lips together in a stubborn line. "I cannot tell you what I don't know."

"Well then, let me tell you what *I* know," Jack said, his tone harsh. "Your grandfather has double-crossed some very dangerous people, Eva—me included. But, trust me, you'd much prefer I find him before the others do. Because if I have to kill him, it'll be quick and painless."

"Jack!" Maddie chastised. "What the hell are you doing?"

"I guarantee you," Jack continued, ignoring her protest, "the others won't be as forgiving. There's one particular bastard named Kozlov, who has a talent for torturing his victims before he does them in—especially if he has a score to settle."

Maddie gave him a horrified look. Was he being serious or was he just trying to scare Eva into telling them what she knew? Something about the haunted look in his eyes told her that he was on the level, that he'd witnessed Kozlov's handiwork before.

Eva's chin trembled and she turned a beseeching look on Maddie. "I swear to you, I don't know anything. My grandfather didn't tell me what was going on. He didn't say why he was in danger—only that he needed to stay away for a while and that I shouldn't try to contact him. I don't know where he is. I swear to you—"

"Eva."

The woman leaped to her feet on a gasp, clearly startled. Maddie was only a split second behind her, shoving the woman behind her as she brought up her gun. However, she noticed that Jack didn't seem surprised at all by the sudden appearance of the man now standing in the doorway to Eva's bedroom.

He was dressed in a charcoal-gray suit that was expensive but worn. His hair and beard were white, which, along with his stocky frame, made Maddie think of Santa Claus. Not exactly what she'd pictured when Jack had spoken of the former KGB operative.

"Hello, Jack," Antonovich said with a smile as he

slowly entered the room, his own gun trained on Jack. "It's been a long time, my friend."

"Sergei," Jack greeted, his tone even, but Maddie could see the tension in his muscles as he tracked Antonovich's movements. "Got yourself into it this time, eh?"

Antonovich chuckled and responded in Russian, then added in English, "There is no flying from fate, as they say." He shrugged. "It is amazing I have lived this long."

"Where's the flash drive?" Jack demanded. "We know the one you gave to Tad Ralston was blank."

Antonovich's brows lifted, his mouth turning down at the corners in an expression of appreciation. "The Alliance is as clever as ever. Your commander—William Asher—he is young, but he may surpass his grandfather yet."

"Where is it?" Jack demanded again.

"It never existed," Antonovich told him, chuckling again.

"What?" Maddie cried. "What do you mean it never existed? People have *died* because of that flash drive, you son of a bitch!"

Antonovich sent a surprised look Maddie's way, then turned back to Jack. "I like this one, Jack. She has the fire in her belly, yes? Jacob Stone was expecting to receive valuable intelligence that he could use against the ranking Illuminati to assure his rise to power. I am afraid he is quite disappointed to have lost the flash drive—I imagine he will be even more so when he learns there was never anything on it. But what I should say is that I never intended to turn it over to the Illuminati. The data is still safely locked away."

"If you never intended to give them the data, then why approach them at all?" Jack replied. "Why risk making enemies of the Illuminati?"

"Yes, they are not pleased with me," he drawled. "This

is true. But it was time for me to make amends for past transgressions. A man's conscience becomes a heavy burden when he is staring Death in the eye."

"What are you talking about?" Jack pressed.

Antonovich shared a sorrowful glance with his granddaughter. "I have terminal cancer. Maybe just a few weeks left if I am lucky."

"And your way to make amends is getting innocent people killed?" Maddie snapped.

"That was not my intent," he said. "But these games we play . . . they often have casualties. I could not get to Jack without drawing him out."

"I'm not the only one you've drawn out," Jack told him. "Kozlov has tracked you to Detroit. We've always suspected Illuminati ties with the Russian mob. I suspect he's been sent to eliminate us both."

This little nugget of news seemed to cause Antonovich a moment's concern. "When did he arrive?"

"Right after you did," Maddie told him. "Tell us what the hell is going on and we might be able to help."

Antonovich shook his head. "I have no business with Kozlov. I am merely here to see my granddaughter and give her the money she needs to finish school. And to make peace with the man whose father I betrayed." He turned his attention to his granddaughter, who was still standing behind Maddie. "I do all this for you, Eva. You know this, yes?"

Eva sniffed and Maddie felt her nod. "Yes, I know this."

Antonovich then held up his hands and let his gun hang from his index finger. Jack edged closer and took it away, tucking it into the back of his waistband. "Jacob Stone will kill me soon." At Eva's strangled cry, he shushed her gently. "It is all right. I would rather it end this way instead of in a hospital. But I let myself be seen so that I could reach you, Jack. I want you to look after my Eva. I know the Alliance will do right by her. I would not have her pay for my sins."

"You have one helluva a way of making amends," Jack said. "By drawing me out you may've killed us both, Sergei."

"I will do what I can to help you, my old friend," Antonovich promised. "But first, you must agree to my request."

"Of course we'll do everything we can for your granddaughter," Maddie said in a rush, answering for Jack. "You have our word."

He nodded his gratitude, then sighed. "In a safe deposit box in Washington, D.C., the real flash drive is waiting for you to retrieve it. The box is in your name, Jack. I always intended it for you. It will give you and William the answers you seek about your fathers, the proof that the Illuminati is rising once more—"

Antonovich's words were cut off on a gasp as the apartment's window crackled behind them. Maddie saw his eyes go wide with surprise as she instinctively ducked down, pulling Eva down with her.

She looked frantically toward Jack, relieved to find him crouched down as well. But Eva's agonized cry brought her attention back to Antonovich. A dark stain was slowly spreading across his chest. As she watched, his knees buckled and he slumped to the ground.

"Damn it! Jack—Antonovich's hit!"

But Jack was already crawling toward the man. Eva attempted to follow, but Maddie held her back.

"You're in the line of sight," she said, her tone harsh to get the woman's attention as she tried to struggle out of Maddie's grasp. "Stay down or you'll get yourself killed!"

Another two rounds penetrated the glass, shattering a

picture frame near Eva's head and spraying shards of glass. The woman cried out, instinctively backing toward Maddie.

"Any ideas, Jack?" Maddie asked, pressing back against the wall, an arm across Eva's chest to keep her in place.

"It must be Kozlov," Jack told her. "I'll leave first and draw them off. Give me five minutes, then follow. We'll meet up back at the hotel."

Fear for Jack spiked in Maddie's veins. "What? Are you *insane*? They've got a sniper on the building. Odds are they'll have any exits covered, Jack. You might as well wear a target on your back."

"If you have a better idea, Mads," Jack drawled, "I'm open to suggestions. We have to get Eva to safety. I'm the one Kozlov's after."

She pulled her phone from her pocket. "I'm calling headquarters. They can get somebody local to give us backup. We'll just hang tight until they get here."

"Who?" Jack countered. "The Alliance or Kozlov and his men? Because if I don't come out, they'll come in. And then we'll all be going out in body bags. I'm not letting that happen."

"Damn it, Jack!" Maddie spat as he got to his feet. He crouched low as he hurried toward the door.

Several bullets hit the futon, spraying foam padding and fabric. Jack cried out as one struck him in the side. Maddie tried to rush toward him, but this time Eva held *her* back. Jack struggled to his feet, holding up a hand and motioning for her to stay where she was.

"Jack," Maddie said, her voice cracking. She didn't even know what else to say. That she loved him seemed like too much of a good-bye.

He winked at her and attempted his boyish smile, but it was more of a grimace as he pressed his hand against his wound, his fingers already covered in blood. "See you soon."

And then he was gone, leaving only a bloody handprint on the door frame. Maddie suddenly couldn't breathe. Every instinct told her to go after him, to stop him, keep him from getting himself killed.

But then she heard Eva's whispered, "Should we wait like he told us?"

Maddie closed her eyes for a moment, trying to put her fear for Jack aside and focus on her duty to the Alliance and to the frightened young woman at her side. Finally, she nodded. "Yeah," she said. "But when it's time to move, stay close and do everything I say."

As soon as five minutes had passed, they crawled toward the door, but to Maddie's surprise, when they reached Antonovich's body, Eva paused and quickly went through his pockets, grabbing several items from his body and shoving them into her own pockets.

"Eva, what the hell are you doing?" Maddie demanded.

The woman rubbed her cheek against her shoulder, wiping away her tears. "I was told never to leave these items on his body if anything were to happen to him." She sniffed and mumbled something in Russian before bending to place a kiss to Antonovich's forehead. Then she lifted her eyes to Maddie's. "Let's go."

Jack held back a groan as he made his way down the stairs, pressing harder against his wound to try to stanch the flow of blood. It was a flesh wound—albeit one that had taken out a sizeable chunk in his side where the bullet had hit and passed through and was now bleeding like a bitch. The last thing he needed was to pass out from blood loss and leave Maddie and Eva in Kozlov's sights.

When he finally reached the stairwell door that led back to the lobby, he leaned against the wall, grinding his teeth through the pain to keep his shit together. He opened the door just a crack, peering into the lobby. A guy wearing a deliveryman's uniform and a hat pulled down over his eyes entered the building carrying a small package, his intense gaze searching the lobby.

Shit.

Jack rested his head against the wall for a moment, trying to steady the hand holding his gun. He took a deep breath and threw open the door, his gun trained on the deliveryman. "Where's Kozlov?"

The man looked mildly surprised that Jack had gotten the drop on him, but his surprise ended there. "I don't know who this Kozlov is," he said, his words heavily accented. "I am only here to make delivery."

"The hell you are," Jack replied, inching closer, careful to keep his back to the wall of mailboxes. "Get rid of the package. Slowly."

The guy's mouth curved up at one corner.

Fuck.

In the next instant, the guy tossed the box aside and brought up his gun. But not fast enough. Jack dropped, firing off two rounds as he fell, nailing the guy in the center of the chest and sending his would-be assassin's bullet wide, to lodge in the mailboxes behind him.

Jack struggled to his feet, the pain in his side making his head spin, and stumbled toward the door. There'd be more of Kozlov's men coming. He just had to make sure they came for him and not for Maddie.

Still holding his gun, he slid his hand into his jacket to hide it from any curious passersby as he exited the building and made his way down the sidewalk. His unsteady gait drew a few curious looks, but he kept moving forward, eager to get as far away as possible before the sniper could move his position and finish Jack off. Three blocks down, he turned onto another street and sighed with relief when he saw a yellow taxicab idling at the curb.

He picked up his pace, hurrying toward the cab. As soon as he was inside he'd call headquarters and get some backup and figure out a rendezvous point for Maddie to bring in Eva, and—

The screech of tires brought his head up in time to see a black SUV halt a few feet from the cab. Jack bolted toward the cab, but before he could reach it, two men in suits jumped out of the SUV. Apparently spooked, the cab peeled out, cutting off Jack's hope for escape. He spun around, gun raised to take on the guys from the SUV, but not quickly enough. Before he could get a shot off, one of them pistol-whipped him.

Jack staggered, trying to throw a punch, but it went wide, catching one of his attackers in the jaw, but without much force. The next thing he knew, he was being thrown into the back of the SUV.

The vehicle lurched forward, throwing Jack against the door. He sucked in air between his teeth as pain lanced through his abdomen and his vision narrowed briefly before he managed to scoot up against the back of the seat, forcing himself to sit upright and face his attacker. Of course, he knew who it was before the rat-faced bastard in the front seat turned to sneer at him.

"Hello again, my old friend," Kozlov greeted in Russian, his polite tone belying the deadly look in his small, close-set dark eyes.

"Kozlov," Jack ground out. "I'd say it's good to see you, but your hospitality's as warm as ever."

Kozlov's toothy smile widened. "The last time we met, you left many of my friends dead and my employer's son an orphan. Please forgive that I didn't invite you to my home for dinner."

"I'll get over it," Jack assured him.

"We have much to discuss, Ivan—" He closed his eyes briefly and shook his head. "My apologies—I'm afraid I don't know what to call you. Not Ivan Petrov. No, not that. *That* man is a murderer and traitor. John Estridge, perhaps?" He sighed. "No. *He* is no doubt dead with the rest of his family in England. *Such* tragedy . . . Women and children should never be forced to suffer for the crimes of others."

Jack bit back the "fuck you" that rushed to his lips and merely glared at the son of a bitch, subtly noting every aspect of the inside of the SUV, trying to figure out the best way to take out the grinning bastard and his pals.

Kozlov shrugged. "I guess I have no choice then, except 'Jack Grayson.'" He studied Jack with mocking interest. "What will you call yourself next, I wonder?"

Jack managed a sardonic grin. "*Dead*, I imagine."

Kozlov chuckled, his laugh a rough scrape that made Jack cringe inwardly. The Russian switched to English when he continued. "Always the pessimist. That is why my employer liked you, Jack. You were never 'blowing the sunshine up his ass,' as they say."

"No, I left that for you, Kozlov," Jack drawled. "Well, the blowing part, at least."

Kozlov's eyes sparked with anger, but his tone was even when he said, "I'm afraid our last meeting didn't go quite as planned, Jack."

Jack lifted his brows. "No? So where'd your little plan go wrong? Was it the part where you shot at me or the part where you missed?"

Kozlov's expression darkened, and he jerked his chin at the man seated next to Jack. A powerful fist nailed Jack in the jaw, making his vision go dim. He shook his head and had to blink a few times to focus again.

Kozlov sighed dramatically. "It saddens me that our friendship has come to this."

"We were never friends," Jack spat.

Kozlov shrugged. "Too bad. I was hoping that we could come to an agreement. But if you are not my friend, then you are my enemy."

"I'll be sure to have a good cry over that later," Jack drawled.

Kozlov's cruel mouth turned up in a smile that sent a chill through Jack. "Oh, you will cry before I am finished with you, Jack. You were not able to be there to see Natasha's punishment for being a traitor. You could not hear her pleading with her father to spare her life and the life of her son."

Kozlov's words were meant to taunt Jack, but there was something more behind them, an anger that seemed barely restrained. Jack's jaw tightened to the point of pain as he fought to keep his own rage under control.

Kozlov's grin widened. "But don't worry, my friend, I will make sure you stay alive long enough to watch this time."

The heat of Jack's rage dissipated in an instant, the look in Kozlov's eyes chilling him to the bone. "What the hell are you talking about?"

Kozlov gave Jack a pitying look. "Do you really think your friends will abandon you? They will come for you, of course. We will ensure that."

Jack's heart began to thunder in his chest. "Your problem is with me, Kozlov. Leave the rest of the Alliance out of this. I acted on my own in Moscow."

Kozlov nodded. "We will argue that point after I deliver your friends' bodies to the One True Master."

Stone.

"I'm going to take a great deal of pleasure in killing you, Kozlov," Jack ground out.

Kozlov chuckled, shaking his head. "Jack, Jack, Jack. By the time we finish with you and your friends—particularly after you see what we have prepared for your beautiful lover—you will be far too broken to do anything but bleed."

Jack's restraint snapped. He lunged forward, slamming his fist into the head of the driver, sending the SUV weaving wildly and pitching Kozlov into the door. Using the distraction, Jack pounded his fist into the temple of the man next to him with three quick jabs. The guy's head lolled to one side as he slumped against the door. The driver regained control just in time for Jack to nail him again.

But this time, Kozlov was ready for him. Jack caught a glimpse of the gun out of the corner of his eye, just in time to grab Kozlov's arm and slam it against the headrest of the driver's seat. The gun fired, shattering the side window. His fist nailed Kozlov in the jaw and the man released his grip on the gun.

Jack snatched it away and slammed it into Kozlov's head and was turning it on the driver when a searing pain lanced through his side, stealing his breath. He gasped and fell back, glancing down to where the pain originated. A fresh crimson stain began to spread below the bloodied spot where the bullet had grazed him. It was then he saw the knife in Kozlov's hand.

Jack raised a shaky hand and tried to take aim, but the gun fell from his grasp and a sudden jolt of electricity shot through him, making him seize violently. For a few agonizing seconds, he couldn't breathe, couldn't think. The pain abruptly ended and he collapsed against the seat, gasping for air. It was then he noticed that the fucker next to him had come to and tased him.

Kozlov grinned, his smile even more grotesque as the bruises Jack had bestowed began to swell and turn a mottled purple. "Have a seat, Jack," he invited, gesturing with the knife. "We still have a few miles until we reach our destination. You should make yourself comfortable."

Chapter Nineteen

Maddie paced the pavement at the truck stop just outside Detroit, chewing the edge of her thumb as she waited impatiently for her backup to arrive and take over with Eva so Maddie could get back to looking for Jack. She'd tried calling him several times but with no response. And the longer she went without hearing from him, the more her fear grew.

And where in the hell were Finn and Adam? It'd been two hours since she'd called them to report what had happened. That should've been ample time to get their asses in gear. She halted and snatched her phone from her belt, calling Jack again.

This time the line connected. "Oh, thank God! Where have you been? Are you okay?"

"Hello, Ms. Blake."

Maddie's blood turned to ice water in her veins at the deep, thickly accented voice. "Kozlov."

At the mention of his name, Eva jumped to her feet from the curb where she'd been sitting and rushed to Maddie, her hands covering her mouth in alarm. Maddie traded a glance with her, wondering if the woman knew more about what was going on than she'd let on.

"It is lovely to speak with you," Kozlov told her. "I look forward to meeting you in person very soon."

"Where's Jack?" she demanded. "Is he . . . is he alive?"

There was a slight pause, then muffled voices speaking in Russian. Finally, Kozlov replied, "He is alive for the moment."

"What do you want?" Maddie asked, her relief at hearing Jack was alive at war with her fear for what he'd endured at his captors' hands—and what he still might have to endure before she could get to him.

"Nothing you can give," Kozlov told her. "But your lover—he has a price to pay."

Maddie swallowed hard, deciding to try a different tack. "How much do you want?"

Kozlov laughed, the sound rough as sandpaper. "Unfortunately, Ms. Blake, not all debts can be paid with money. Some require flesh and bone."

Maddie choked back the tears that constricted her throat, glad for Eva's comforting arm, which was now around her shoulders. "There has to be something else you want, Kozlov, something else that will satisfy your vendetta."

"What do I want?" he asked. "Why, I want nothing else. This is not about me, Ms. Blake."

Maddie felt panic rising in her chest, her breath going short and shallow. "Then who is it about? Let me talk to *him*."

"You will soon enough," he assured her.

The line went dead. "Kozlov?" Maddie said, her voice catching. "Kozlov!"

"This man Kozlov is a sadistic bastard," Eva told her, shaking her head, her gray eyes glistening with unshed tears. "My grandfather warned me about him. He's the only man my grandfather truly feared. He *will* kill your Jack. Just like he killed my grandfather. Tell me how I can help you."

"Did your grandfather ever say anything about where Kozlov stayed, people he knew? Anything?" Maddie asked, striding back toward the Harley.

Eva shook her head. "No. He only warned me to run if Kozlov ever showed up. He told me stories . . . They made me sick to my stomach. And I'm a *nurse*. There isn't much that turns my stomach."

Maddie felt the bile in her own stomach rise. There was no way in hell she was going to let Jack continue to suffer. If she had to, she'd tear the goddamned city apart to find him.

"Wait," Eva said, her face suddenly brightening. "There is one name I remember—it's a man my grandfather knows. He said he's a politician." She squeezed her eyes shut, mentally searching for the name. "Stone! His name is Jacob Stone."

Maddie couldn't help the bitter laugh that escaped her. Did Jacob's betrayal know no bounds? He'd pissed on his relationship with her father and nearly killed him, and had put Sarah and her son Eli in the center of his grab for power, putting their lives in danger as well. And now he'd betrayed Jack, a man he'd called his friend.

"Do you know him?" Eva asked. "Could you go to him for help?"

Maddie heaved a furious sigh. "Yeah, I know him."

At that moment, a black H2 pulled into the truck stop and drove toward where Maddie and Eva stood. Finn and Adam were jumping out of the vehicle the second it came to a stop.

"Do you have anything on a location?" Maddie demanded.

Finn shook his head. "I reviewed security and CCTV

footage for the time you mentioned. All I got was a black SUV with bogus plates. No hits on any of the men. And then we lost track of them."

"How the hell did you lose track of them?" Maddie questioned, her voice shrill in her desperation.

"These men are professionals," Adam supplied. "They would know how to avoid being traced."

"I talked to Kozlov," Maddie told them. "He had Jack's phone. Could you put a trace on it?"

Finn shook his head on a sigh. "Jack turned off his GPS locator when he left Chicago. He didn't want us tracking him."

Maddie's stomach sank. "Kozlov has Jack, Finn," she stressed. "And he *will* kill him. We're running out of time."

Finn took Maddie gently by the shoulders. "I've got people here in Detroit working on it too, honey. I'd already told my tech team to trace the signal from Jack's phone if any calls went out, so they're going to be trying to triangulate his location as we speak. Without the GPS turned on I can't find his exact location, but that'll give us an area that we can work with. We're going to find him."

"Alive?" Maddie asked. When Finn's gaze became guarded, she added, "I know how that kind of tech works. It takes time—and it's not precise. We could be talking about several square miles."

"I'm going to do everything I can," Finn assured her.

She pulled her hands down her face, her fear increasing with every second they stood there talking. She needed someone to pull rank and get everyone's asses moving quicker. Or she needed someone who wasn't afraid to break a few rules. "Where's Will? Does he know?"

Finn nodded. "He's on his way back from Boston now. He'll be here as soon as he can."

"Then I need you to do me a favor, Finn," she said, sending a meaningful glance toward Adam and Eva.

Adam took the hint and extended a hand to Eva. "Please come with me," he said gently. "We will take you somewhere safe."

Eva nodded and glanced toward Maddie before allowing Adam to hand her into the H2.

As soon as they were out of hearing, Maddie said in a rush, "I need Jacob Stone's phone number."

Finn gave her a sympathetic look. "Honey, I don't have it. Do you think if I did we'd still be trying to hunt him down? The only numbers we had for him have been disconnected. He's most likely using a burner now."

"I have to talk to Jacob, Finn," Maddie pressed. Finn was a freaking genius, for crying out loud—he had to be able to give her *something* to go on. "Please. There has to be some way to reach Jacob. He'll know how to get in touch with the Russians and get Jack back."

"And you think you can just call him up and say please and he'll hand over Kozlov?" Finn asked.

"It's worth a shot," Maddie insisted. "That asshole owes me."

Finn squeezed his eyes shut and riffled his shaggy blond hair in the way she'd seen him do before when he was thinking something through. "Lemme see if I can get a look at Antonovich's phone records. If he was working with Jacob, as we suspect, he might've called him from his cell and—"

Of course!

She pivoted and sprinted to the H2, not hearing whatever else Finn was calling to her. When she pulled open the door she asked in a rush, "Do you have your grandfather's cell phone?"

Eva sat in the backseat with Adam, her hand held gently in both of his, her eyes closed, lips slightly parted. At the sound of Maddie's voice, Eva slowly opened her eyes, her gaze catching and holding Adam's briefly before turning her attention to Maddie.

"Yes," she stammered, her cheeks flushing. "Yes, I have it."

What the hell had she interrupted between the two of them?

Maddie lifted a questioning eyebrow at Adam when Eva slipped her hand from his grasp. But he merely dipped his head slightly. "Shiatsu," he explained tersely to her unasked question. "To assist with Ms. Antonovich's emotional trauma."

"Uh-huh." Maddie turned her attention back to Eva and extended her hand to take the cell phone Eva had pulled from her pocket. She tried to bring up the dead man's contacts, but the lock screen popped up, blocking entry. "Damn it! Do you know your grandfather's code?"

Eva nodded. "My birthday." She rattled off the numbers.

Maddie tapped them in and brought up the contacts, but her momentary elation dissipated in an instant when she saw the names listed there. "Shit. They're all in Russian."

"Here, let me." Eva retrieved the phone from Maddie's grasp. "Dedushka—Grandfather—always changed the names to something Russian in case his phone was compromised." Her brows came together in a frown as she scrolled through the numerous contacts. Suddenly she grinned and tapped the screen, turning the phone to Maddie. "Here. This one. Yakov Kamen—Jacob Stone."

Maddie's heart began to thunder so hard against her ribs that she could barely hear the phone ringing when she dialed the number. And she had to swallow the bile that rose in her throat when a male voice answered with, "I thought you were dead."

Jacob.

"He is," Maddie spat. "And you're going to tell me

where the hell Jack is, or so help me God, Jacob, you'll wish you'd killed me too."

There was a slight pause before Jacob's smooth voice replied, "Well, hello, Freckles."

"Don't you dare call me that, you son of a bitch!" she hissed. "You never cared about any of us. Don't pretend you do now."

"That's not true, Maddie," Jacob told her. "I loved you. I still do. You have to know that. I wish things could've been different . . ."

Maddie closed her eyes. His voice sounded sincere. But as badly as she wanted to believe that the man she'd once considered a brother still cared about her, she didn't trust him. He'd fooled them all too well for too long for her to *ever* trust him again. But as hard as it was to make her peace with his betrayal, she needed him now or the man whose love had withstood all they'd been through would die.

"If you ever cared about me, Jacob," she said softly, playing the odds, "then please help me."

There was silence on the other end, for what seemed like just short of eternity, when Jacob finally spoke again. "Maddie—"

"Please, Jacob," she pleaded. "It's *Jack*. You called him your friend once upon a time."

Another long pause. A sigh. "What do you need?"

"Kozlov," she said. "I want that son of a bitch taken down. Tell me where he is."

"You bastard."

Jacob heaved a sigh and turned away from the window overlooking the ocean to meet the furious gaze of his wife. "I beg your pardon?"

She stood in the doorway, a perfect picture of righteous

indignation, hands on her hips, shaking with rage. "You said you didn't care about Maddie Blake. You lying son of a bitch! What happened to not being responsible for the outcome if she insisted upon playing a role in this 'little drama'?"

"Allison, you're being ridiculous," he chastised, strolling toward her to take her hands. "You have no idea—"

"Don't lie to me!" She snatched her hands away from his and took several quick steps in the opposite direction. "I *heard* you say you loved her, Jacob."

His own anger began to rise at her accusations. As if she had room to talk, when she'd been fantasizing about fucking that psycho Stefan. "I do love Maddie. I have never made a secret of that."

Allison shook her head slowly, her eyes glistening with unshed tears. "And you would choose her over *me*?" she ranted, advancing on him, her hands balled into fists at her sides. "Your *wife*? After all I've done for you! Do you have any idea what I've *sacrificed* for you, Jacob?"

"*Your* sacrifice?" he scoffed. "You want to talk about sacrifice? I might've just sent Maddie Blake to her death!" When she frowned at him, confused, he nodded. "Oh, yes. You heard me. She's willing to put her life on the line for the man she loves. *That's* sacrifice."

"I would do the same for you," she whispered. "You must know that! I would give everything for you, Jacob! All I ask is that you not keep anything from me."

"I have never kept anything from you, Allison," he said, his tone aloof. "I have been honest from the very beginning of our relationship. You have been my confidant, my partner. And I wanted you for my wife as well. Do you think I would've married you had I not recognized your devotion to me?" He took hold of her chin, squeezing hard enough to make her wince. Through clenched teeth, he added, "But, let me make something very clear to you. If you insist upon acting like a spoiled, jealous little *bitch* when I have given you *everything* you could ask for and more, I will find someone else worthy to be at my side when I ascend to power."

Tears spilled onto her cheeks and her voice shook when she said, "Jacob, I love you. I won't allow you to throw away everything you've worked for because of some sentimental attachment. You deserve better. You deserve *more*."

"You're right, I do," he agreed. "But do not *ever* question me again, Allison. Especially after your little encounter with Stefan. Do I make myself perfectly *fucking* clear?"

She swallowed hard and nodded. "Yes. Forgive me, Jacob. Let me make it up to you."

He sighed. "And how exactly do you plan to do that?"

She gave him a tremulous smile. "I have a surprise for you—I wasn't going to give it to you yet, but I think it's time."

He released her chin and let his hand fall away, not sure he should trust the pleading look in her eyes as she grasped the front of his shirt and pressed her body close to his. "All right," he finally said. "What's this surprise?"

Her face lit up. "I'll show you tomorrow."

She turned to go, but he caught her hand, keeping her where she was. He was taken aback by the maniacal look in her eyes as she turned back to face him. He caught a glimpse of something there that he'd never seen before—not in *her* eyes. But he *had* seen that look once before in others—and it scared the hell out of him. "Are you all right?"

Her sorrow had now been replaced by a fanatical mania that made her practically buzz with energy as if she was barely able to restrain her elation.

"I'm just excited," she told him. "I can't wait until you see what I have planned for you, Jacob. I can't *wait* to see the look on your face. I've been planning this for so long . . . It's finally time."

But before he could spare more than a passing thought to Allison's strange behavior, she closed the gap between them and threw her arms around his neck, kissing him with savage need. When the kiss ended, her smile was grotesque, distorted by her fervor.

Jesus Christ. What the hell is she planning . . . ?

Chapter Twenty

"I cannot let you do this."

Maddie threw her leg over the Harley. "If you try to stop me, Adam, I'll put a bullet in you."

"I know you don't mean that, so I won't take offense," Adam assured her.

She lifted a brow at him. "Yeah? Try me."

The man sent a glance Finn's way as if trying to elicit his support, but Finn only shrugged and shook his head. "Sorry, brah, I already tried to talk her out of this half-assed plan."

"If you're both so concerned, then come with me," Maddie said. "Otherwise, continue to sit around here with your thumbs up your asses while I try to actually do something to help Jack."

"We need to discuss our options," Adam told her calmly. "You won't do Jack any good if you are captured as well. You need to pause to consider your options. Your judgment is currently clouded by concern for your colleague."

Maddie's brows shot up, suddenly furious with the man's lack of urgency. "My *colleague*? Are you shitting me?"

"Maddie, honey," Finn said, stepping in between her

and Adam to try to ease the growing tension. "He didn't mean—"

"He's more than a *colleague*," Maddie spat, talking over Finn. "I *love* him. And I thought you all were his brothers, his brethren. You're supposed to care about your fellow Templars. But I guess all you care about is putting the moves on a woman who just saw her grandfather shot to death in her apartment!"

Adam's face went instantly stony at the accusation, the closest thing to a show of emotion that Maddie had seen from the man. He dipped his head in a curt bow, his jaw clenched. "Clearly, you do not value my opinion in this matter. Forgive my interference."

"Jesus," Finn muttered, riffling his hair with agitated movement. "Will both of you just shut the hell up! Maddie, Adam wasn't putting the moves on Eva, for fuck's sake! He was trying to calm her. Maybe you should let him try it on you for five damned minutes so you can listen to reason."

Maddie cocked her head to one side, so not in the mood for Finn's bullshit surfer wisdom. "Wow. Seriously? You're going to leave Jack hanging? After all he's done for the Alliance? What would Will say to that?"

Finn gave her a sympathetic look. "He'd say that the intel on Jack's location is suspect. That the whole damned thing has all the earmarks of a trap. The Illuminati are using Jack as bait—and you're taking it, honey."

Maddie slumped back on the bike. As much as she hated to admit it, Finn was right. "What do you expect me to do? It's Jack. I can't leave him there. He'd walk through fire if it were me. But not just for me, Finn. He'd do it for any of you—and you know it."

"Then let us help you," Finn replied. "I'll get Will on the phone, get his ETA, figure out a plan. Just give me a few minutes before you bolt. Can you do that for me? Please?"

Maddie pressed her lips together for a moment, her thoughts racing, her impatience to get to Jack increasing with every second, making her want to crawl out of her skin. Finally, she jabbed a finger at Finn's chest. "Ten minutes. Then I'm leaving with or without you. And I don't care if I have to kill every single one of those assholes to get to Jack—I will."

When Finn turned away to talk on his phone, Adam took a deep breath and slowly exhaled before turning his attention to the H2, where Eva sat watching all of them anxiously. "What about Ms. Antonovich? We have a responsibility to keep her safe."

"Call the guys at the Detroit commandery," she said. "Let's have them take her into protective custody until we can bring Will up to speed on her situation."

Adam seemed to consider her words for a moment before nodding. "I'll explain the situation to Ms. Antonovich. Considering her family connections, I imagine Commander Asher will want to discuss a relocation strategy after we return to Chicago."

Yeah, he probably would. That seemed to be Will's style. God, at the rate they were going they might as well set up their own relocation colony, for crying out loud. But at least he wasn't offing anyone and everyone who got too close to Alliance. She'd read about some of the Alliance's ops over the centuries. There was a reason the Alliance was still a secret society after all. Will was taking a big risk not eliminating both Claire and Eva. But she had to respect him for not taking such drastic measures without first trying other alternatives. She just hoped it was the right call—for everyone's sake.

Finn tapped the device in his ear as he came back toward them. "All right, kids. Will's en route and is calling in Luke and scrambling a detachment from the Detroit team. And we've got backup meeting us and bringing the mobile command center. We'll set up at the central triangulation point and see if we can zero in on our boy." Here he turned and leveled his aqua gaze on Maddie. "Jacob didn't give you anything besides the fact that Kozlov was still in Detroit?"

She shook her head, wishing like hell the man had given her something—*anything*—more to go on. But it sounded like Jacob honestly hadn't had any knowledge of what the hell Kozlov was planning for Jack. As he put it, asking questions put him at risk. And if someone like Kozlov had been so kind as to take it upon himself to remove a threat to Jacob's safety, then who was he to argue?

But "for old time's sake" and out of the "kindness of his heart"— she'd actually laughed at that one before she could catch herself—Jacob had assured her that Jack was still in Detroit. Beyond that he could be no help. He would leave it to her to determine *where* in Detroit they were holding Jack.

She just prayed they could find him before it was too late. And before she managed to get anyone else killed.

Jack awoke on an enraged roar, the icy water jolting him from his drug-induced, nightmarish slumber, which had featured horrific, terrifying images of Maddie being tortured and murdered over and over again while Kozlov laughed, his sneering, twisted face smeared with her blood.

Still locked in the grip of his fury, he tried to lunge to his feet and go after the son of a bitch and tear him apart with his bare hands, but barbed wire bit into his wrists and ankles, keeping him where he was. He strained against his restraints, his desperation to get to Maddie overriding the searing pain as the barbs dug deeper into his skin.

Kozlov's harsh chuckle finally made Jack go still. "Still you try to escape?" Kozlov said, his tone pitying. "For three hours we have been here and each time we revive you it's the same foolishness."

Jack's chest heaved as he worked to get his breathing—and his thoughts—under control.

Three hours?

He strained to piece together the lost time, but as the memories came rushing back on him, he suddenly wished he hadn't bothered. At least then he wouldn't have been aware of what was coming. And the growing awareness of the pain that wracked his body could've remained a mystery.

Unfortunately, he remembered it all now.

They'd brought him to some kind of abandoned factory—one of many in Detroit, so who knew which one it was. But the place was dark, dank, smelled of trash and mildew and decades of disuse. The machinery had long ago rusted, the factory floor reeking of oxidized metal. But they'd taken him down a set of stairs through a network of hallways that had most likely been offices and storage rooms at some point but were now gaping holes of darkness in the already dark corridors.

They'd had flashlights, but the dark was so deep it seemed to swallow the light. But not in the cold, concrete room where they'd taken him to exact their vengeance—and, apparently, information. It was lit up with portable work lights so bright that Jack had to squint against them as he assessed potential escape routes, but there was only the main door. And he didn't have any weapons to work with, even if he did somehow manage to escape his restraints.

Which, considering the shape he was in and the fact that his clothes were several feet away in a heap on the floor, seemed pretty damned unlikely.

He covertly assessed his injuries. Seeing as how he was naked in the wooden chair they'd secured him to, it wasn't difficult. The barbed wire had torn open his skin down to the muscle. His right eye was completely swollen shut. His nose was definitely broken. He tasted blood but couldn't determine if it was from his split lips or the two teeth he was missing on the right side of his jaw. An assortment of bruises and lacerations on his abdomen told him they'd used him as a punching bag for a while too.

They'd stitched the worst of his wounds—to keep him alive longer and drag out the torture for as long as possible. But some of the crude stitches closing the stab wound had opened back up. At least the repair to the flesh wound from the gunshot still seemed to be holding for now . . .

But the worst pain was in his fingertips where Kozlov's henchman had shoved needles under his nails. He'd rather they go back to using him as a punching bag than have to go through that shit again. Of course, losing a toe wasn't a fucking picnic either, but at least they'd started small . . .

That said, he could feel his body losing the battle. He could only assess the external damage, but he knew the limits a body could take before it went into shock, then, eventually, shut down altogether. And so did they. They could drag this shit out as long as they wanted—or end it just as quickly.

All things considered, Jack wasn't sure which route he'd prefer.

And God knew what the hell they'd given him to try to make him talk. Whatever it was had turned his guts to fire and was making him slip in and out of consciousness—but maybe that was a good thing.

A quiet clatter to Jack's left sent a spike of fear through him. Apparently it was a sound he'd grown to recognize. He turned his head slightly in that direction and saw a mountain of a man with a buzz cut and a long scar running from the corner of his eye down to the corner of his mouth, lovingly caressing an assortment of torture implements—some Jack was familiar with himself from a couple of ops he preferred not to think about.

Fucking karma . . .

Another chuckle from Kozlov drew Jack's attention away from whatever fresh hell was coming. Slowly, he lifted his gaze to meet Kozlov's as the man emerged from the shadows.

He half remembered their questions . . . The data. The flash drive. They still didn't have it. And no matter how many times Jack assured them they could go fuck themselves before he'd tell them a goddamned thing, they just didn't seem to catch on. Of course, hell if he knew where the real flash drive was at this point. Was it really in the safe deposit box Antonovich had mentioned, or was that just a ruse too? The only one who knew for sure was Antonovich, who'd taken that information to the grave.

Unfortunately for him, Kozlov wasn't buying the truth. Which meant Jack had to come up with a damned good lie if he wanted to put an end to this shit . . .

Kozlov crossed his arms over his chest and studied Jack for a long moment. "I can see what you are thinking," he drawled. He began a slow stroll around Jack's chair as if he was assessing a piece of art. "You are saying to yourself, 'If I can just keep this up for a *little* longer, then my friends they will come for me. And I have no doubt you are correct. Your lover will arrive with your friends and deliver themselves into our hands. But the question is, will it be before you are crying like baby"—he paused and put his finger to Jack's temple—"begging me to put bullet in brain to end your pain?"

Jack managed a smirk. "You think you're the first asshole to try to get information out of me, Kozlov? You can't break me."

Kozlov's answering smile seemed genuine, his eyes bright with glee. "Perhaps not. But if you do not tell us what we want to know, I will try the same with your pretty lover. Maybe she is not so strong, yes?"

"Don't you fucking touch her!" Jack roared. "I swear to you, Kozlov, if you touch her, I will rip your fucking heart out of your chest."

Kozlov grinned and swept a hand toward Jack. "I am not so worried at the moment, my friend." He then motioned to his comrade. "If you please, Feliks."

The behemoth playing with his toys immediately turned back to Jack, a sneer draped across his scarred face. The guy's eyes were dull, dead. Jack's gut twisted with dread. He'd seen that look before. People like this had no conscience, no moral compass to even give them pause before committing some atrocity. They were serial killers, henchmen, mercenaries . . . mindless killers who questioned nothing. Hurting others was as mundane and ordinary as eating breakfast or taking a shit.

When Jack glanced down to see Feliks carrying jumper cables attached to a portable battery, he took as deep a breath as a couple of broken ribs would allow and blew it out slowly, steeling himself for the next round.

This is gonna hurt like a bitch . . .

Chapter Twenty-One

"Where the hell is he, Finn?" Maddie demanded, lacing her fingers behind her neck as she paced in the tight space of the mobile command center Finn had called up from the Detroit office, her patience officially at an end. They'd been at it for hours now. God knew what Jack had to be going through—if he was even still alive.

She shook her head and pushed that thought away. No. Not possible. He wasn't dead. He couldn't be. Life couldn't be that cruel. They'd finally found their way back to each other, had finally realized their love for each other. How could he be taken from her *now*? Like *this*?

Finn's eyes narrowed as he scrutinized the map on his laptop screen. "Still in Detroit," he announced, cutting into her thoughts. "I guess that's a plus. But, shit, Maddie, he could be anywhere. They could be holing up in any of the buildings within this radius." He dropped a pin on the map and zoomed in on the several square blocks that he'd highlighted.

"Where would you take a prisoner to interrogate him?" she asked of no one in particular.

"Somewhere secluded."

She glanced over to where Adam had been sitting

silently since they'd arrived at their current location. He'd taken Eva to their brethren in Detroit, leaving her under guard until they could figure out a more permanent solution to her situation.

"Preferably in a building with thick concrete walls," he continued. When she frowned at him, he added, "So no one can hear him scream."

Maddie sank back against the wall of the van, clutching her stomach to keep from hurling. She wasn't an idiot. Her gut told her what they'd be doing to Jack, but hearing it put into words made it all so much worse.

"Nice, brah," Finn chastised. "Show a little compassion, for chrissake."

Adam sent an uncharacteristically apologetic look Maddie's way. "My apologies. My English doesn't always allow me to be subtle. I did not mean to upset you."

She shook her head slightly. "It's okay. What else? What else would you look for in a location?" She didn't know a lot about Adam—hell, no one seemed to. But she did know that when her father had been shot and her nephew nearly abducted, it was Adam that Will had brought in to interrogate her father's bodyguards. And they hadn't been the same since.

"I would want somewhere that was intimidating, unnerving. Either stark and sterile or dark and derelict. In this case, I suspect they'd use an abandoned building—a factory or hospital."

Finn grunted. "Shit, dude—you just described half of Detroit. There's abandoned factories all over the damned place."

Adam inclined his head slightly, acknowledging Finn's point. "Then I would search for one that has very thick walls and few broken windows. And no security."

Finn turned his attention back to his keyboard, typing so fast Maddie couldn't even guess what he'd typed. A few seconds later, his brows shot up and he turned the command center monitor around for them to see. "How 'bout this one?"

Adam leaned forward from his chair to get a closer look and slowly nodded. "Yes. That would be perfect."

"Where is it?" Maddie asked, studying the photos on the screen.

"About three blocks from where I got a ping from the cell towers." He typed again and another website came up, showing more pictures of the structure. "God bless urban bloggers. This guy has all kinds of pictures of the inside, taken just a couple of months ago."

Maddie glanced through the pictures, taking in all the information she could. "Looks like they have three floors and a basement." She pointed to one of the photos. "There's barbed wire around the perimeter, though."

"Not all the way around," Finn pointed out, indicating another photo. "The front gates are gone. And the blogger says they pulled security off the building last fall and are letting the building fall to ruin. Look at all the graffiti. Those are gang tags."

"What kind of entry options do we have?" Maddie asked. "Any more pics of the exterior?"

Finn brought up a dozen others a moment later from the satellite feeds. "Looks like we've got a main exit on each side plus an old loading dock and fire escapes. I don't know that I'd trust those, though—they look like they're one stray cat away from falling off the building."

"How many men?" she asked, her eyes still on the photos, wondering in which of the dozens of rooms Kozlov might be holding Jack.

"There were only a handful on the footage from when Jack was taken, but there are half a dozen cars near

the building. Hard to say how many goons Kozlov has
stationed around the building at this point."

"What's the ETA on Will and the rest of the team getting
here?" she asked.

"Sixty minutes, tops," Finn told her. "And the guys from
the Detroit team are ready to go. They're just waiting for
our orders."

She nodded. "Then let's gear up and go get our boy.
Will is just going to have to catch up."

Finn and Adam traded a glance, but it was Adam who
cautioned, "If we go in without sufficient backup, we could
endanger Jack's life."

She straightened and crossed her arms, glaring down at
him. "They've had him for hours. What do you think
they've been doing to him all this time? What would *you*
have been doing to him? You're the one who reminded me
that these bastards wouldn't want anyone hearing him
scream, Adam."

Adam's normally stoic expression softened. "I know
this is difficult for you, but we must wait for our orders—"

"You don't know shit, Adam," she interrupted.

He sighed. "I know that if you rush into a situation
you put yourself and others at risk—including the man you
love."

"And he's not at risk now?" she snapped.

"And Jack would have you risk your life saving him?"
Adam countered mildly.

Pissed that he was right but still not willing to just sit
around and wait for the others to arrive, she turned to
Finn, hoping to elicit his support. "Finn? What can we do
right now? You're a freaking genius—come up with something. Now."

His wide grin instantly assuaged her panic. "I'm already
on it."

* * *

Jack's chest was heaving, each breath bringing on a fresh wave of agony. Feliks blandly carried his portable battery and jumper cables back to his worktable, shrugging at Kozlov as he passed.

Kozlov nodded in appreciation before slapping Jack on the back, making Jack flinch involuntarily at the contact. "I am impressed. You have—what is the expression?— *balls of steel.*"

"You can suck my *balls of steel,*" Jack ground out through clenched teeth.

Kozlov chuckled, something darker than usual creeping into his laughter. "I will leave that to my little friends."

Jack lifted his head, wishing his could see better out of the one eye that wasn't swollen shut, but his sweat-soaked hair was matted to his face, obscuring his vision. He glanced around the room, wondering what the hell Kozlov was talking about.

As if sensing the question in his expression, Kozlov gestured toward the shadows. A man whom Jack vaguely remembered from the car ride came forward, carrying a small wire cage. Inside were several rats. And from the way they clawed at the cage, clambering to get out, screeching and bruxing their incisors, they were pissed-off rats.

"Although," Kozlov continued, "I imagine they will start with that open wound. This was a favorite method for interrogation and torture during medieval times—but I'm sure you know that. You were always a good student of history. You knew all about *our* history before you infiltrated our family, before you forced yourself on my cousin—"

"*What?*" Jack interrupted, outraged at the accusation. "What the hell are you talking about, you sick bastard! Natasha and I cared for each other. I *never* forced myself on her or any other woman. Who the hell told you that?"

Kozlov's expression hardened. "You used her, seduced her. It is no different in the eyes of our family. Would she have been lured to your bed had she known the truth?"

Jack glared at him. "And yet if she was a victim as you claim, why kill her? Why kill my unborn child?"

Kozlov rushed forward with an enraged cry, clutching Jack's throat and bringing his face close to his. "It was not *your* child in her belly, you bastard. But her father thought it was. And he killed her for it."

Jack studied Kozlov for a moment, the truth dawning on him. "The baby was yours."

Kozlov shoved him away with another roar of anger—and sorrow. Jack's chair teetered on its legs but didn't tip, so he was able to see Kozlov's brief, furious pacing before the man charged Feliks, barking at him in Russian with such fury, the man instantly exited the room, followed by the asshole who'd carried in the rats.

"My mother was a distant cousin of the family," Kozlov said, still pacing, each movement agitated. "Natasha was not even really a relative, but her father saw it that way. He refused to let me marry her. We tried to stay apart, but we couldn't. She even had affairs with other men." He sent a murderous look Jack's way. "But when you left so suddenly . . . She always returned to me."

Jack didn't even know what to say. The guy was still mourning the woman he'd loved all these years later. Jack could see the anguish behind his anger. If their situations had been reversed and Maddie had been murdered, taken from him so cruelly and senselessly, Jack couldn't have said he'd be any less vengeful. Hell, he'd taken out the Russian mob's leader when someone he'd had a short affair with had been murdered—he hated to think what he'd do if he lost Maddie.

"Sounds like I did you a favor taking her father out," Jack finally said. "Saved you the trouble."

Kozlov grunted. "Perhaps. That is why I have not come for you sooner."

"So then, why now?" Jack asked.

Kozlov sent a brief glance his way. "My assistance was requested in intercepting the data Antonovich sold to the American politician."

Jacob. I should've known that asshole was behind this.

"What's in it for you?" Jack pressed. "Money? Let me go and the Alliance will triple whatever Stone has offered."

At this Kozlov stopped his pacing and turned a maniacal look on him. "Money? Yes. Of course money. But Stone has offered more than that. He offered a place of power at his side when he ascends as the One True Master."

"And you believe him?" Jack countered. "Jacob will say whatever he has to in order to get what he wants. But he is just a pawn in the Illuminati's game, an insignificant player on a board that is far more complicated than he realizes."

"Perhaps," Kozlov conceded. "But not for long. Soon he will ascend and we Faithful will know the full measure of his benevolence."

"You're fucking delusional," Jack told him. "Jacob will put a bullet in you before he'll share any of his power."

Kozlov shrugged. "If that is the Master's will, I will accept it."

"Jacob will never ascend in the Illuminati," Jack insisted. "He has fed you a line of bullshit. He's a politician, Kozlov. He'll say whatever he must to get what he wants. The Masters will never relinquish their power. They would die before allowing all they've worked to rebuild to be wrested from their grasp."

Kozlov's cruel mouth curved into a menacing grin. "This is the first word of truth you have said today, I think."

Jack licked his dry, cracked lips, wishing it had done a

damned bit of good before he managed to ask, "What are you talking about?"

Kozlov picked up the cage of rats, turning them a little, studying them a moment before he replied. "I received a call from the Mistress to encourage my haste. The Master will ascend tonight, and I must prove my loyalty in order to take my place among his most trusted."

The maniacal gleam in Kozlov's eyes sent a chill through Jack. Exactly what the hell was Jacob planning? And how many innocents would pay the price as a result?

"Now," Kozlov said, setting the cage of rats on the table and opening the cage door, "which one should we start with?" He extracted a particularly large brown rat and closed the cage door, much to the ire of the others. The rat squirmed and screeched, clawing at the air as Kozlov carried it toward Jack.

"Fucking hell," Jack muttered under his breath, his heart pounding. He tried to swallow but found it impossible. He frantically assessed his wrists and ankles again, searching desperately for a way to break free of the barbed wire. But it was too tight and dug deeper into his flesh as he renewed his struggles to break free.

"So, tell me, Templar," Kozlov said. "Where is the flash drive my Master desires? I will give you ten seconds to tell me before I allow my friend here to go exploring. And every time I ask and you refuse to answer, I will release another of his comrades."

"I told you," Jack said, his throat tight, his gaze locked on the squirming rat, "I don't know. The one we intercepted was blank."

Kozlov nodded. "Very well."

As Kozlov took a step forward, holding the rat by the tail, preparing to drop it on Jack's lap, Jack pressed back into his chair in a futile effort to avoid what was coming.

A sudden beeping brought Kozlov up short. Frowning,

he fished his cell phone from his pocket with his free hand. "What do you want?" he demanded in Russian. "You are interrupting." There was a short pause, then Kozlov chuckled. "Excellent."

He pocketed his phone and offered Jack an amused grin. "It seems your friends have arrived. Shall we see which ones live long enough to actually find you?" He cast a glance toward the rat. "I think I will leave my little friend here to keep you company while I attend to our guests."

"Jesus," Jack muttered as Kozlov tossed the rat. It rotated in midair and landed with an angry hiss before skittering off into the shadows. When Jack looked back toward Kozlov, the man was gone.

Maddie drew her knife across the throat of the guard stationed just inside the east door, glancing up to see if anyone came rushing in at the sound of his surprised cry when she'd grabbed his head and pulled it back to expose this throat. She eased the man's body down to the ground, suppressing a groan at the deadweight in her arms. "I'm in."

"Damn it, Maddie," Finn admonished in her earpiece, "I had a plan."

"Yeah, well it was a shit plan, Finn. We were supposed to go in the door with no one guarding it."

Maddie glanced toward Adam, who'd already dispatched the other guard. With the windows darkened by decades of dirt and grime, little sunlight made its way into the abandoned car factory, and the darkness concealed more than it revealed. She motioned for Adam to follow her and crept along the wall in the shadows, feeling more than hearing him behind her. The guy was a freaking ninja.

"I can't help it if Kozlov has a bunch of vampires

working for him," Finn continued. "The dudes had zero heat signature."

"They're not vampires, Finn," Maddie whispered, rolling her eyes as she cleared the narrow corridor that led to the factory floor. "Your equipment's faulty."

"Hey, now," Finn quipped. "There's nothing wrong with my equipment, honey. And if you hadn't hooked up with Jack you'd know that by now."

Maddie smiled, glad for Finn's humor just then. It kept her mind off of what she feared she'd find once they managed to locate Jack. "Guess I'll just have to live with the fact that you're the one that got away."

His answering chuckle broke off abruptly. "Look alive, kids. You're coming up on a whole cadre of Koslov's boys."

"Cadre?" Adam whispered.

"What?" Finn replied. "Should I have called them something else? What's the technical term for a group of Russian mobsters who secretly work for the Illuminati — which officially doesn't exist? A gaggle?"

Maddie sent a look over her shoulder at Adam, shocked to see the man was actually grinning, but it instantly vanished when he saw her studying him. He jerked his chin, motioning for Maddie to go farther down the corridor. She nodded, then lost sight of him as he slipped deeper into the shadows.

Yep. Ninja.

"What's the ETA on Will and the others?" she asked softly, exiting the corridor and entering an area of the factory that still housed the abandoned equipment and a few random parts that hadn't yet been stripped or removed by looters.

"Will's on his way," Finn told her. "Should be here in ten. And I've got Luke suiting up now with the guys from Detroit. They're taking point."

She moved quickly across the open space, keeping close

to the wall and watching for any movement above on the suspended walkways and observation points. Of course, considering the state the structures were in, someone would have to be a freaking moron to set foot on them.

"I'm approaching the east stairs," she announced softly. "A little shock and awe for a diversion would be great right about now."

There was a slight pause. "Hang tight, Maddie. Detroit team's preparing to storm the castle."

She shook her head. "Storm the castle, Finn? Really? You've watched too many—"

"Shit. Heads up," he said, cutting her off, his tone suddenly serious. "You've got three dudes about two hundred feet to your left when you exit the stairs, Maddie."

She liked snarky, irreverent Finn a helluva lot better . . .

Maddie took a deep breath and let it out slowly as she began to descend the stairs. "Copy that."

She crept down the stairs, her back to the wall, keeping her gun trained on the semidarkness below. There had to be a light source somewhere below because a faint but harsh yellow glow produced just enough light to keep her from having to switch to her night vision.

Suddenly a barrage of gunfire rang out above her and a deafening boom sounded, vibrating through the concrete under her feet and raining down dirt and concrete. She sent a nervous glance behind her to what she could still see of the factory floor.

"Diversion worked," Finn announced. "We've got everybody scrambling toward where the Detroit team breached. You're good to go."

Maddie exited the stairwell and cleared the corridor. The men who'd been there must've hurried off to assist the others on the main floor just as Finn had predicted. "All clear, Finn. Where now?"

"Looks like I have a lone figure about fifty yards south

from your current location. That's probably our best bet. Didn't even switch positions at the sound of the breach, but the other one with him just left the room heading in the opposite direction."

"Good enough for me," she said, heading in the direction Finn had indicated. But after only about half the distance, the corridor ended, coming to a T with another corridor. "Dead end. You're going to need to guide me in. Am I going east or west from here?"

She heard him clacking on the keyboard and then a juicy curse. "Okay, looks like you need to head west." More clacking. "The blueprints of the building show there's a series of rooms along this corridor with multiple parallel and adjoining corridors. It's a fucking maze down there, so watch your back. I'll watch for any heat signatures on the scope, but they could literally pop up from anywhere."

"Great," she muttered. "If demons and zombies start jumping out at me, I'm holding you responsible, Finn."

"Holy shit," he said. "Was that a *Doom* reference? That's it. You *have* to marry me now."

She grinned as she headed down the hallway. "Okay, approaching another intersection. Where now?"

Suddenly a cacophony of gunfire and explosions sounded over Maddie's comm and in the factory above her. She cried out as the sound assaulted her ear and concrete and debris crashed down behind her, blocking her retreat.

"Finn!" Maddie yelled. "Finn, do you copy? What the hell's going on?"

More chaos on the comm.

"Finn!" she repeated. "Do you copy?"

Nothing.

Shit.

She was on her own.

Cursing under her breath, Maddie hurried forward, her

heart pounding, fearing that her route to Jack had been cut off by whatever the hell was going on upstairs. She'd just reached another intersection of corridors when she heard Finn's voice, the communication garbled and breaking up.

She pressed her fingertips against the device in her ear, trying to make out what he was saying, but all she could catch were a few random words—but they were enough for her to figure out what he was trying to tell her: Abort mission. Then it was Will's voice in her ear. The transmission was just as bad. But the message was the same.

She clenched her jaw and shook her head. "Sorry, Commander, but screw that." Moving forward, she murmured, "Don't worry, Jack, I'm not leaving you behind."

Chapter Twenty-Two

"Get them out right fucking now!" Will demanded. "That whole section of the building's structure is compromised. I want everyone out of there."

"The Detroit team's already out," Finn told him. "Luke's putting three men into position around the perimeter to watch the exits for any of Kozlov's guys who might still be alive, but I'm not getting a whole lot of movement. Handful of people max. But I still haven't received any word from Adam or Maddie."

"Didn't I give you orders not to go in until I got here?" Will roared, the vein in his temple pulsing with anger.

Finn had the good grace to at least look contrite. "Maddie didn't want to wait. They'd already had Jack for several hours."

Will massaged the knot forming in the back of his neck, not sure if he should be furious at his team for disregarding orders or pissed at himself for trying to deal with the Claire situation on his own instead of trusting the Boston team to handle it. If he'd delegated like he should've, he would've been in Chicago when everything went to shit.

"It wasn't your call to make, Finn."

"You're right," Finn agreed. "It wasn't. It was yours. But

you weren't here and we weren't waiting." The kid set his jaw and met Will's gaze. "It was *Jack*. And if you'd been here there's no way in hell you would've waited for backup. You would've been in there right along with Maddie. So instead of chewing my ass out, brah, why don't we focus on getting our people out before more of them get killed?"

Will stared at the guy for a moment, finding it hard to believe he'd just been schooled by a twenty-six-year-old kid whose main ambition in life was to catch the perfect wave. And yet schooled he'd been. The kid had a point. And if he kept it up he might end up being one of the best recruits Will had ever brought on board . . .

"So what do we have left to work with if you send me in?" Will asked, his tone gruff, but not as harsh.

Finn's brows shot up, clearly surprised at Will's change of plans, but then he shook his head, surveying his control board. "My gear's still in working order, but the readouts I'm getting are shit. I still have the blueprints, but Luke said there were cave-ins when Kozlov's explosives detonated. I have no idea how to guide you through if I don't know what you're going to encounter."

Will checked the clip in his SIG, then grabbed the M4 he'd set aside when he'd entered the mobile command center, and examined the magazine before slamming it back in. "Guess we're just going to have to improvise."

Never in his life had Jack felt so helpless, so hopeless. Kozlov had been expecting the Alliance—Maddie—to come to his rescue. He'd depended on it. And as much as Jack hated the thought of being gnawed to death by rats, his larger concern was for Maddie and the others. But unless he could get out of this fucking barbed wire there wasn't shit he could do to stop what was going down.

As if the little bastard had been listening to his thoughts, the rat Kozlov had tossed into the room slunk out of the shadows, sniffing the ground, slowly making its way toward Jack's chair.

Jack cursed under his breath. This wasn't exactly how he'd imagined his final hours. Dying in a failed op certainly had always been a possibility, but not in this way—strapped to a chair, naked, beaten, and disfigured by sadistic assholes. But even worse was his concern that in their efforts to rescue him from death, others of his brethren would pay the ultimate price. Jack had always been prepared to lose his life—but never the lives of others.

He zeroed in on the rat, which was dashing back and forth between the splatters of Jack's blood on the floor, sampling them all in a frenzy.

With any luck the explosion he'd felt rock the building a few minutes before would be followed by another that would go ahead and bury him and prevent anyone—prevent *Maddie*—from finding him this way.

He'd rather she remember him as she'd last seen him, remember the moments they'd shared together, the love he'd never adequately been able to express. He didn't want her final image of him to be of a man tortured and mutilated. He knew from experience that that kind of memory would haunt somebody forever. He'd rather she not find him at all.

A soft shuffle of movement in the hallway brought Jack's head up toward the door. A moment later, the heavy latch ground, metal upon metal. Jack's heart leaped into his throat, momentarily cutting off his breath, when the door swung open and revealed Maddie's beautiful face. But his relief and the rush of love that brought tears to his eyes vanished when he saw the look of horror and anguish in her eyes as she spotted him.

So much for his last wishes . . .

With a strangled cry, she rushed forward, smacking away the rat that had reached Jack's injured foot before dropping down in front of him. "Oh my God, my God. Jack. Oh, baby." Tears trailed down her cheeks as she took in the extent of his injuries. Her hands came up to touch him but hovered aimlessly as if unsure how or where to begin. "What the hell have they done to you?"

"Maddie," he said, his voice as stern as he could manage. "There are wire cutters on the table."

She launched herself to her feet and rushed to the table, holstering her sidearm and snatching up the wire cutters. She ran back to his chair, making short work of the barbed wire, wincing with him when she peeled the wires from his skin. Finally released from his bonds, Jack slumped forward, his arms and legs momentarily useless. He most likely would've tumbled from his chair had Maddie not caught him in her arms and tenderly cradled him against her for a moment.

When his muscle control returned, Jack pulled back enough to attempt a smile, but considering the way her chin trembled at the sight, he'd apparently failed miserably.

"C'mon," she said, averting her gaze and attempting to drape his arm around her shoulders, "we've got to get you out of here. It sounds like all hell is breaking loose upstairs."

He managed to get to his feet, but his legs felt rubbery beneath him and he had to lean on Maddie more than he would've liked. She groaned, accepting his weight, and tried to help him toward the door. Each step was agony and new sweat prickled his skin, mixing with his blood. Maddie's hold around his waist slipped and Jack lost his footing, coming down hard on one knee.

Maddie was on her knee next to him in an instant. "Finn!" she barked into her comm. "Finn, do you copy, damn it? I have Jack!"

She hissed a curse and turned her attention back to Jack, gently cupping his cheek and attempting to meet his gaze. "You have to do this, Jack. I can't carry you out of here."

"Go," he told her, shaking his head. "Just leave me here with a gun. I'll find my own way out, but I don't want you staying here with me and risking yourself. I'll be right behind you."

"Bullshit," she spat, her voice tight with emotion. "I'm not leaving you. Not ever again, Jack. Do you hear me? I love you. And I want to spend the rest of my life loving you. I can't lose you now."

She leaned in, brushing a tender kiss to his bruised and bloodied lips, careful not to hurt him, then tightened her grip around his waist. Seeing the trust, the faith in her eyes made Jack's chest ache and his throat grow tight.

"You won't," he promised. "I'll never be parted from you again, Maddie. I swear it."

As one, they stood, pausing a moment to let Jack get his footing, then slowly made their way toward the door.

"Wait," Jack gasped, gesturing toward the table where the tools of his torture still lay. "My clothes. And gun."

Maddie eased out from under his arm and gathered up his things, helping him throw on his pants and a shirt as quickly as his injuries would allow. When she handed him his gun, it nearly slipped from his fingers, but he regained his grip and held it down at his side as they cautiously entered the hallway.

"Where to?" he asked, glancing up and down the corridor.

She shook her head. "No clue. The way I came in is blocked. And I can't raise Finn on the comm."

"Then I guess we go the other way," Jack told her. "Lead on."

He felt Maddie take a deep breath before starting down

the hallway. The meager glow that had been provided by
the light in the room waned with each step and soon they
were in total darkness.

Maddie shifted, adjusting her night vision. "Just step
where I tell you."

"I was supposed to be the one protecting *you*," he murmured. "How did we manage to get ourselves in this
position?"

She chuckled softly. "A new position now and then
keeps things interesting."

He couldn't help but smile even though the movement
brought on a fresh wave of pain. "Well, then, I have quite
a few we can try . . ."

Maddie laughed, the sound coming out more like a
strangled sob in her relief at having Jack back in her arms.
When she'd opened that door and found him beaten and
bloody, his injuries too horrifying to fully assess at a
glance, she'd felt fear like she'd never known before.

With every step she'd been preparing herself for what
she might find, but actually seeing him that way . . . the
man she loved, the man whose strength and seeming in-
vincibility she depended on . . . it shredded her. If she'd
ever had any doubts just how deeply she loved Jack, they
vanished at that moment. She didn't have the words to de-
scribe it—nothing seemed even close to adequate.

"Well, we'd better get moving then," she told him,
taking a turn down a hallway that she hoped would lead
them toward a stairwell. "I seem to recall this secluded
beach near my family's lake house that would be a great
place to try out some of these new positions you're talking
about."

Jack chuckled, a disheartening ghost of his normal
laugh. "Seems fitting. That's where you first kissed me."

"I'm pretty sure *you* kissed *me*," she teased, her heart breaking for the time they'd lost, their stubborn refusal to admit their love for one another until it was almost too late.

"Hey, get a room, you two."

Maddie gasped and released her hold on Jack's hand to put her fingertips to her comm. "Finn? Where *the hell* have you been?"

"Sorry," he said. "We were experiencing some technical difficulties. Sounds like you've located our boy."

"Yeah, but he's in bad shape," she told him. "Get us the hell out of here, Finn."

There was a slight pause before Finn said, "I'm not sure which heat signature is yours. I have three groups of two showing up. Any idea where you are?"

"Still underground," she said, but as soon as the words came out of her mouth, a set of metal stairs came into view. "Check that. We're headed up."

She led Jack up the stairs, careful to take them slowly. He wasn't even groaning with complaint, but she could see the pain he was suffering in spite of his efforts to hide it from her in the darkness.

"Okay, I've got you," Finn told her. "When you get to the top of the stairs, head to your left. The other way is toast from an explosion Kozlov's men rigged. Took out at least two of ours from Detroit, and another guy may not pull through."

When Maddie cursed, Jack glanced her way. She was glad he couldn't see her expression. "Copy that. Left it is."

As soon as they reached the top of the stairs, Maddie ditched her night vision, glad for what little ambient light was streaming in. "Okay, Finn—"

Gunfire erupted, pinging off the metal structures and sending up sparks in the semidarkness. She heard Finn saying something, but she didn't quite catch it as more gunfire rang out, reverberating in the vast openness of the factory floor. Instinctively, Maddie crouched, dragging Jack with her as she sought somewhere to take cover. But as they dove behind the remnants of one of the factory's conveyor belts, a searing pain tore through her leg and side, and she tumbled to the ground, dragging Jack down with her.

"Shit," she hissed, pressing her hand against her side as they worked to drag themselves into a sitting position behind the conveyor belt. She reached up to her ear to contact Finn, but the device was gone, having fallen out at some point when they were being shot at.

As hopelessness began to settle in, she let her head fall back against the metal, and closed her eyes, panting through the pain.

With Jack in his current condition there was no way they could make a run for it. Hell, she probably wouldn't get ten feet either before Kozlov's men mowed her down. And shooting it out with Kozlov and however many of his men remained was risky. But it looked like that was going to be their only option.

Maddie opened her eyes and turned toward Jack, her eyes holding his for a long moment, then followed his gaze as he looked down at her stomach and thigh, assessing her injuries. She was losing blood fast. With trembling fingers she reached for the tourniquet attached to her gear, but her grip fumbled as she attempted to tie it around her thigh. Fortunately, in spite of his own injuries, Jack's hands moved in swift, sure motions.

Maddie groaned through clenched teeth as he tied it off. She cursed under her breath, chastising herself for not being able to remain silent.

"So close to escape," Kozlov called out, his voice echoing in the openness, making it impossible to locate his position, "only to have your path blocked at every turn. It seems almost too cruel."

Jack's fingers closed around hers, giving them a comforting squeeze. She turned her head so she could see him, could look into his beloved face one last time. If she had to die that day, at least it would be beside him.

"I love you," he whispered, offering her a sad smile. Then, before she realized what he was doing, he lifted his arm in the air, his gun raised in surrender.

"I'm coming out!" he announced.

"No," she rasped, clinging to his hand, trying to pull him back down as he struggled to his feet. "Jack!"

"Let's end this, Kozlov," Jack continued, his hand slipping from her hold. "Just let Maddie go."

By some miracle, the asshole didn't take a shot at Jack. Instead, she heard his deep rumble of a laugh, which sent a chill down her spine.

"Jack, please," she pleaded. "Don't do this."

"And why would I do that?" Kozlov asked.

Jack glanced down at her, his brows furrowed. "The last wish of a dying man."

Maddie pushed up just enough to peek over the conveyor belt and saw Kozlov strolling toward them, his gun trained on the center of Jack's chest.

"I could agree to this ridiculous bargain," Kozlov mused, his lips curving into a sadistic grin. "I am certain Feliks would enjoy another session with you. But what guarantee do you have that I will let your woman live?"

Maddie's gaze snapped to Jack in time to see his deadly smirk. "This."

Jack dropped his arm and fired so fast, Kozlov didn't even have time to react. She whipped her head around on a gasp in time to see Kozlov drop to his knees, a rivulet of blood making its way down the center of his forehead to the bridge of his nose before he listed to his side and crumpled to the concrete floor.

In the next moment, Jack's knees gave out and he dropped to the ground beside her, wincing in pain and mumbling a string of curses as he curled into himself. Maddie was reaching for him when a click brought her head around.

A massive man with blood spatters covering his shirt towered over them, a gun in his hands. In the next moment, he staggered backward as if convulsing. But the report of the M4 reached Maddie's ears as crimson stains spread across the man's chest.

And yet the man somehow recovered his footing and raised his gun again, staggering toward them. Before he could get a shot off, the side of his head exploded, spraying the nearby machinery with gray matter.

A moment later, Adam stepped into view, his gun at his side. Hurried footsteps rushed toward them, and then Will was vaulting over the conveyor belt and dropping down in front of them. He set aside his M4 and hurriedly assessed their wounds, barking orders at Finn and the rest of the team.

Maddie closed her eyes again. Her body felt light, like she was drifting away. But then the familiar weight of Jack's arm encircled her, holding her close, keeping her with him.

"Don't let me go," she murmured.

She smiled when she heard his whispered response. "Never."

Chapter Twenty-Three

Jacob extended a hand to Allison, helping her from the limousine. "I must say, darling," he drawled as he pulled her arm into the crook of his elbow, "when you said you had a surprise for me, this was not exactly what I'd anticipated. But at least now I know why you insisted on bringing a full security detail with us."

He eyed the half dozen Faithful whom Allison had persuaded him to bring along with them. They stood at attention, their eyes hidden behind their dark sunglasses, even though the sun was sinking below the horizon. "Always good to have a little extra muscle when I'm entering the mouth of hell."

She beamed up at him. "I think you'll enjoy this more than you think."

He eyed the steps to the abandoned observatory where his grandfather and the other Illuminati held their court. "Being called to the carpet by my grandfather has never been one of my favorite pastimes."

"He didn't call this meeting," Allison told him, tugging him up the steps. "I did."

Jacob's steps slowed, his blood running cold as he turned his gaze on his wife. "You did *what*?"

She arched a brow. "I called the meeting. I thought it was time that you discussed a few things with the entire council. They have ignored you for far too long, Jacob. It's time to make a statement."

Jacob jerked her to an abrupt halt. "What the hell is that supposed to mean? What have you done?"

She sighed and gave him a patient look, stopping just short of rolling her eyes. "We're just going to have a conversation." She patted him lightly on the chest. "And I'm sure you'll be more than satisfied with the outcome."

Jacob grunted, knowing his grandfather far too well to believe that any conversation that involved Jacob's place among the Illuminati would end well. More than likely this little stunt of Allison's was going to end up getting him exiled completely instead of only partially. In fact, hadn't his grandfather been more than clear on that issue during his last little visit to the court?

He was on the verge of demanding they leave that very moment, but as soon as the thought crossed his mind, he realized standing up the council would be just as detrimental to his future. They didn't take kindly to being inconvenienced—pompous asses, the lot of them.

He spat a curse, then took a deep breath, pausing a moment to straighten his cuffs and smooth his jacket before squaring his shoulders and offering his arm to Allison once more. "Well, then, I suppose we shouldn't keep the council waiting."

They entered the building, their detail following a few steps behind. Jacob had to admit, he and his entourage were an impressive sight as they entered the inner sanctum. Light from the torches that blazed in their wall mounts danced eerily upon the cavern walls like worshippers caught in the grip of orgiastic ecstasy.

He suppressed a shudder of foreboding and turned his attention to the raised platform at the other end of the room.

All five members of the council sat at the stone dais, their faces hidden in shadow beneath their black hooded cloaks. *Ridiculous*. As if he didn't know what every single one of them looked like, for fuck's sake. He'd grown up having to endure their tedious conversations at council dinners at his grandfather's home in Georgetown. Before each of them lay a silver dagger, a symbol of the blood oath they'd taken when they'd ascended to the council.

And at each end of the dais stood the sentinels, ever watchful, ever silent. They never moved unless ordered by the council. No one but the council knew who they were, knew their names, saw their faces. Once Jacob's father had called them assassins; he had refused to elaborate when Jacob pressed him for more information. In Jacob's mind, these men were the *true* mystery of the Illuminati.

"Jacob," his grandfather drawled, drawing his attention. "I believe it was you who called this meeting via your secretary—"

"His *wife*," Allison corrected, her tone icy.

The man grunted, clearly unimpressed with Jacob's choice of brides. "As I was saying, I believe it was *you* who had the audacity to call us here, so get on with it."

Jacob cleared his throat, not quite sure what to say, seeing as how he was as much in the dark as they were. "Good evening, gentlemen. I appreciate your taking the time out of your busy schedule to—"

"Yes, yes," his grandfather interrupted, waving Jacob's words away. "Did you come here to kiss our asses or did you actually have something to discuss? If this is about the debacle with the Russians earlier this evening—"

"Sorry?" Jacob interrupted. "What debacle?"

Angus Stone laced his fingers over his stomach and leaned back in his chair, nodding. "Good. Plausible deniability. Excellent execution. That look of complete bewilderment will serve you well—you've certainly had enough practice perfecting it."

Jacob blinked at him, wondering what the hell he was talking about, but forced a smile and inclined his head, acknowledging the compliment. "At least we can say I've learned something from you over the years."

"Although I don't care much for your methods, Jacob," another of the council members added before his grandfather could respond, "I appreciate your using our enemies to eliminate the Russian problem. Kozlov was becoming too much of a renegade. His whole operation was growing difficult to control. Now that the Alliance has taken him out along with several of his men, we can install our own choice to run the business dealings in that area of the world."

Kozlov is dead, then?

That meant his last direct link to the flash drive had been erased. Only the woman—Claire Davenport—remained. But she wouldn't be as easy to get to, that was for damned sure. Will would have her under lock and key—provided she even knew anything. He'd have to resolve that loose end soon.

But tonight, there was something else brewing. He could feel Allison practically buzzing with anticipation. Her lips were pursed, unsuccessfully attempting to hide a smile.

Jacob laid a hand over his heart and offered a slight bow. "It is my pleasure to serve."

"And yet he has served faithfully without the recognition

he deserves," Allison told them. "As one of the Faithful, I beseech you to at last name Jacob One True Master."

There was complete silence in the chamber except for Jacob's sharp intake of breath. *Holy fuck.*

As fear of how the wrath of the council might play out and his fury with Allison for putting them in this position wrestled for dominance, the silence stretched on. His mind raced in an attempt to find a way to downplay her request, to apologize for overstepping his bounds and for flouting protocol in pretty much the most insulting way imaginable.

Jacob swallowed hard, then smoothed one of his brows, not surprised to find it damp with nervous perspiration. "Gentlemen—"

Allison stepped forward and leisurely strolled before the dais, the sharp clack of her stiletto heels making him flinch inwardly with each step. "Before each of you is an envelope. Inside is a card bearing a single question. A simple yay or nay is sufficient—I'll even let you write your response if you'd prefer not to speak."

She motioned to the security detail, who immediately moved into position behind the men—with no interference from the sentinels.

What the hell?

It was their job to protect the council, to eliminate any perceived threat. So why the hell were they just standing there, passively observing the drama playing out before them without even taking a step to bar the guards from ascending to the dais?

When none of the councilmen made a move to comply, she halted and tilted her head to one side, giving them a chiding look. "Really, gentlemen. What can it hurt to grant the whim of a pretty woman, hmm? I assure you, I'd be most grateful if you'd humor me on this one tiny, insignificant thing." She clasped her hands together, feigning a demure pose. "Please?"

God, she's good.

Finally, one of the councilmen reached for his envelope with an annoyed sigh. The others immediately followed, except for Jacob's grandfather. Jacob could practically feel the man's furious glare from beneath his hood.

Oh, yeah, this isn't going to end well at all . . .

Upon opening the envelopes, the men exchanged concerned glances with one another before turning their attention almost as one to Allison. Her smile grew at their reaction.

"You have to make a decision regarding Jacob's future with our organization. And your response to the question on that card will determine your own future as well."

"This is ludicrous!" Angus Stone roared, slamming his fist upon the marble. "Who the hell do you think you are, you pretentious bitch?"

Allison ignored him, instead addressing the other men, her tone particularly unyielding when she said, "What say you, gentlemen? As you can see, it is time for Jacob to ascend to the role for which he was destined. Will you offer your support?"

"Yes!" the first one cried. "Yes, of course."

The other three also assented without hesitation, their voices raised in what Jacob would've called hysteria had it not seemed so absurd. His gaze flitted among them, trying to figure out what in the hell was going on.

Allison turned her attention to Angus Stone, waiting expectantly. When he still refused to respond, she sighed. "You know a vote such as this must be unanimous. If one of you votes against Jacob, I'm afraid that means you all stand against him."

"Angus," one of them pleaded in a harsh whisper. "Answer the goddamned question for chrissake."

But Angus still refused to budge. "I won't be bullied in my own inner sanctum."

Allison huffed in a pretty pout. "Well, that's unfortunate, isn't it? I'd really hoped this would go differently." She spread her hands. "I'm sorry, gentlemen. I'm afraid you leave me no choice."

"Allison . . ." Jacob cautioned, confused by the rising panic, the desperation he sensed among the council.

But before she could respond, Allison motioned toward the sentinels. Immediately, they unsheathed the daggers at their waists.

Suddenly, Jacob realized what was about to happen. "No! Don't!"

But before the words even left his mouth, one of the council members leaped to his feet, snatched the dagger before him and lunged forward, plunging it into the center of Angus Stone's chest.

A wordless cry of shock and horror erupted from Jacob. Instinctively, he moved forward to stop the man, to aid his grandfather, whose hood was knocked from his head by the attack, revealing his astonishment. But before Jacob could take more than a step, his guards were upon him, holding him back.

And as another councilman leaped to his feet, plunging his own dagger into Angus Stone's chest over and over again, Jacob realized this was why Allison had brought the extra security—to hold him back, to keep him safe as the four councilmen murdered his grandfather in a frenzy while the sentinels looked on.

"Oh, shit," Jacob muttered, his voice catching in his throat. "Oh, God."

Jacob tried to look away, but when he closed his eyes, Allison grasped his chin. "Do not look away, my love. This is all for you."

Jacob sagged as his grandfather went limp in his seat.

And yet still the others took turns stabbing him until finally they came to their senses and backed away, the daggers falling to the ground with a clatter that echoed in the chamber.

Slowly, they descended from the dais and pulled back their hoods, revealing faces now splattered in gore. Jacob's stomach heaved. He managed to stay on his feet, but only with the aid of the hands that grasped his arms, keeping him aloft.

One by one the council members took a knee before him and bowed their heads. And then his own guards followed suit.

The sentinels followed, pulling back their hoods to reveal their faces to him. To his horror, they were familiar. Demetrius and Stefan Shepherd. This was what Demetrius had meant when he'd pledged his support. And now Jacob was as beholden to them as they were to him.

Last to kneel was Allison, her face beaming with pride as she lifted her gaze to his.

"The Illuminati council and your Faithful servants bow to you, Jacob Stone," she said. When he could no longer stand the shock that shook him to his bones, Jacob dropped to his knees among them. But Allison grasped his hands in hers and brought him back to his feet. "Arise and take our place on the dais, One True Master of the Illuminati."

Taking slow, shaky steps, Jacob allowed her and the others to lead him to the dais. His grandfather's body lay in a heap where someone had shoved it from the now vacant chair. And Jacob was too shell-shocked to resist when they seated him there. The arms of the chair were warm and wet beneath his palms.

Bemused, Jacob lifted a trembling hand to find it covered in blood.

"What have you done?" he murmured, still staring at the carnage, unsure whether the question was for Allison or for him. "What have *I* done? It wasn't supposed to be like this."

"I have secured your position as One True Master," Allison said, strolling along the length of the dais, her finger skimming across the surface of the table, leaving a long, crimson line as she smeared his grandfather's blood across the marble. "Now you will receive the respect and admiration you deserve. And soon the entire world will be at your feet."

He closed his eyes briefly, his chest going tight as the weight of the path he'd set them on fully pressed down upon him. His mouth was dry, his throat tight when he finally spoke. "What was in the note, Allison?"

She smiled, a disturbingly sinister gleam in her eyes. "I explained that the sentinels awaited my command to slit their throats if they sided against you."

"And what was the question?" he asked, no longer certain of his wife's sanity.

Allison bent forward from behind the chair and whispered in his ear. "'*Do you want to live?*'"

"What now?" he asked, all feeling and emotion draining away as his entire body went numb.

"Now, my love," she whispered in his ear, "you lead the world to enlightenment."

Chapter Twenty-Four

Will Asher crossed himself and rose from where he knelt next to the tomb of Ian Cooper. The knight in medieval garb carved into the stone sarcophagus was new, but the style—a knight lying on his back with his sword upon his chest—harkened back to a time when the Knights Templar had fought for the church, believing their mission righteous. How quickly that had changed when those for whom they'd fought turned on them, declaring them heretics.

As Will stood near the newest of the tombs, he surveyed the others in the room. They'd used this particular church in Chicago for all their burials in that region for as long as he could remember. Some of the sarcophagi held the bodies of fallen Templars dating back over a century. He looked out over them, mentally calculating how many had been laid to rest under his watch. Only a handful. But each one weighed heavily on his shoulders. And he wondered if it ever got easier.

He hoped not. It shouldn't be easy to lose a brother, a friend. If he ever reached the point when it did, he'd know it was time to step aside and let another take his place.

He already worried at how easily he'd walked away

from Claire again. How simple a thing it had been to create a new life for her, send her away to start over—regardless of how she felt about it. He hoped she'd know happiness, but he had a feeling that the woman would continue to be a thorn in his side.

Eva Antonovich was an entirely different matter. Her status in the country made things a little more complicated, but they'd soon find a suitable situation for her. In the meantime, she was staying at the compound. Considering their recent ops, having a nurse on staff might not be a bad thing . . .

Will would've liked to speak to those who'd come before him—Hugues de Payens, Jacques de Molay—to ask them if they would've continued their mission, persevered in their desire to protect the innocent, had they known that the Order would one day be reviled by those who had once championed it. Would they have stayed their course, knowing that those they'd called brother would one day betray them?

The Alliance had long ago severed all ties with the church and had redefined its mission to protect all people of the world—not just a select few. They had realized after the Order was disbanded and their Grand Master burned at the stake that no one group should hold all the power, no one entity should rule over all.

The Illuminati had attempted to challenge that position, had sought to create the New World Order through tyranny, but the Alliance had been there to stop them, to maintain a balance. Or so he'd thought.

Will looked down at his hand, in which lay the flash drive they'd retrieved from Sergei Antonovich's safety deposit box in Washington, D.C. He inhaled a deep, bracing breath and blew it out slowly, wishing he could disregard the information he'd discovered there. It was ironic how one tiny little piece of plastic could have such enormous ramifications.

He closed his hand around the flash drive, then placed his other hand on the carved knight, whose face bore a striking resemblance to the man Will's team had lost just a few short weeks before. "I will make your death count for something, Ian," he vowed, his voice echoing in the burial chamber. "I swear it."

Will sighed and made his way through the tombs, reading the names as he passed, committing them to memory so that they'd not be forgotten. Finally, he came to the one he'd visited more times than he could count. Sean Asher's sarcophagus was so like the man, sometimes Will half expected for his father to sit up and have a conversation with him, to actually answer the many questions Will had posed to him over the years, wishing he was still able to answer them.

He needed that advice now more than ever. They were at a crossroads. The choices the Alliance had before it would decide the fate of all of them. And the next move he made was bound to burn some bridges.

Well, one good thing about burning bridges—the only way you can go is forward.

Making his decision, Will left the burial chamber, his feet feeling as though they, too, were encased in stone. Each step was heavy as he made his way to the ceremonial chambers aboveground in the newly constructed offices adjacent to the church where his grandfather and the Grand Council waited.

While the burial chamber was entrenched in tradition, the meeting space for the Grand Council was sleek and modern. The men who sat at the table wore three-piece suits and ties; their only noticeable connection to the Alliance was the ring bearing a Templar cross that each of them wore on his right hand.

"Commander Asher," one of them greeted hesitantly, eyeing Will's jeans and black leather jacket with obvious censure. "We didn't have you on the agenda for another twenty minutes. But since you're already here . . . What brings you to this meeting of the Grand Council?"

Will slapped the flash drive down on the table and slid it across the wood. It came to rest in the center, directly across from his grandfather. "This."

They exchanged confused glances, one of the other council members finally asking, "What is it?"

"Proof that the Illuminati are rising," Will told them. "Names, dates, documents, email records. There's intel going back decades—including the documents they stole from us during the Cold War. Didn't know about that breach? Well, my father did. And he died for it. It's all there. Read it. And then deny the truth."

One of the council members leaned forward, obviously interested in what Will had to say. "But we were assured that the Illuminati had disbanded, that we had eradicated their leadership, leaving them powerless."

Another nodded. "Their assets were seized. I saw to it myself."

"This is absurd," the High Commander scoffed.

"You can't continue to ignore the truth," Will argued. "Too much is at stake."

His grandfather heaved a bored sigh, disregarding the flash drive. "William, we have indulged this erratic behavior long enough. We've already made a special concession to allow you to bestow membership upon a woman whom you've made an initiate, defying centuries of tradition. And now you have the audacity to storm in here, demanding we take action on evidence that is questionable at best? Had the Illuminati been re-forming, we would've known about it. You can't seriously believe that they have existed secretly, undetected all this time?"

"*We* have," Will shot back.

This seemed to hit home. Seeing he'd made his point, Will turned and strode toward the door. "Read it," he called over his shoulder. He paused in the doorway to offer one parting shot. "And give me a call when you're ready to do something about it. I'll be waiting."

Maddie swept her hair up from her neck, pinning it into a loose knot like the one she'd worn the night of the Boston gala. She picked up another hairpin from the few scattered upon the top of the vanity and slid it into place, offering Jack a soft smile when she caught his reflection in the mirror.

"You look beautiful," he told her, not bothering to disguise the rough edge of desire in his voice. He came forward, his gaze holding hers in the mirror. Unable to resist, he bent to kiss the side of her neck, his hands resting lightly at her hips.

She moaned softly and closed her eyes, leaning into him. "If you keep that up, we'll be late for my celebration dinner."

"Would that be such a horrible thing?" Jack asked, kissing the back of her neck, eliciting another little moan of pleasure.

His arms slid around her, pulling her closer against him, still careful of the area where she'd been shot. They'd both recovered from their wounds, but the scars—both physical and emotional—would take a while to heal and might not ever fully disappear.

But the experience had brought them together in a way that Jack hadn't expected. He'd been raised never to *need* anyone—to develop friendships and relationships, certainly, and even to love, as he'd known his parents had loved one another. But to need another person . . . it wasn't to be imagined.

But in those moments when they'd held one another, battered and bleeding, he'd realized just how much he needed Maddie. His life simply wasn't complete without her in it. He'd tried for years to fill that void, to explain it away, pretend there wasn't a huge gaping hole in his heart. But life was too short, time too precious. She'd taught him that with her unwavering love.

As if she sensed his thoughts, her fingers brushed over the scars at his wrists. When he glanced up, he caught a glimpse of the sorrow in her eyes before she forced a smile and grabbed another hairpin.

"I'm fine," he assured her. "You know that, right?"

She sighed and leaned back against him, meeting his gaze in their reflection. "I know. But I still have nightmares almost every night. I've chosen this path, Jack. I want to continue my father's legacy with the Alliance. But I don't know if I can ever see you like that again."

He gave her a crooked smile. "Trust me, I have no intention of *going through* anything like that again."

She linked her fingers with his and pulled his arms tighter around her.

He gave her a gentle squeeze. "Hey, this is supposed to be a happy occasion. Do you have any idea how proud I am of you? Of all you've accomplished? You've made history, Madeleine Blake."

This actually brought a flush to her cheeks and an uncharacteristically uncertain smile to her lips. "I did, didn't I? I'm guessing the Grand Council is still reeling from Will's announcement."

Jack chuckled. "Well, he didn't really give them any choice in the matter, did he? I think we will see a lot of changes within the Alliance now that we have proof the Illuminati are a threat again. We've sat on our laurels for decades, believing that the worst threats were isolated groups that could be managed; but we can't afford that complacency any longer. Danger could come from any quarter at this point."

Maddie laughed. "I guess the conspiracy theorists weren't completely off their nut," she said, attempting to fasten the clasp of the necklace he'd given her so many years ago.

"Here," he murmured, taking over with the clasp. When he'd successfully linked the delicate chain together, he pressed a kiss to the nape of her neck. "There. Perfect."

She gasped a little at the contact and shuddered. He pulled back at her reaction, unsure if his kiss had been welcome.

They'd yet to do more than hold each other or share the occasional kiss since their ordeal. At first it was because they were in the process of healing, but then there was a hesitancy, an uncertainty. Whether it was the result of the trauma they'd experienced or something else, he couldn't tell. He didn't push, letting her set the pace.

"I'm sorry," he told her sincerely. "I didn't mean to make you uncomfortable."

She reached behind her and took his hands, bringing them back around her waist. "You didn't make me uncomfortable. You never have. I just needed a little time to come to terms with things, relearn how to let myself enjoy the moment instead of worrying every second about what the future might hold."

He pressed his lips to her neck, letting them linger, then swept them across her skin, loving the way his touch made goose bumps rise on her arms. "And now?"

"Mmmm." She closed her eyes, grinning, as he trailed kisses along the curve of her throat to her bare shoulder. "I'm enjoying this moment very much. You?"

He would've responded, but at that moment, her hand drifted down to cup him through his slacks and the words he'd been about to utter died on a groan. And when she guided his hand down to her thigh, he didn't even bother trying to form a coherent thought.

As his hand grasped the hem of her dress and slid it up over her hips, his other hand drifted up to cup her breast, his thumb grazing her nipple through the material, eliciting a gasp.

But when his hand slid between her legs and found she'd been wearing nothing beneath her cocktail dress, his breath left him on a sharp exhale. As he caressed and teased, her hips writhed with his touch, arching into him only to arch back against his groin until he was grinding his teeth to keep his shit together.

"Jack," she panted, guiding his hand deeper. "I want you inside me."

Thank Christ . . .

With his free hand he unfastened his belt and slacks, letting them fall to his ankles, freeing his erection. He continued to stroke and caress her when she bent forward, bracing her elbows on the vanity, her panting now replaced with moans of need.

He grasped his shaft and thrust between her folds until he grew slick. Then he pressed in gently, entering only far enough to stimulate the sensitive flesh there. Maddie cried out as her muscles tensed.

He continued to thrust, entering a little more each time, the sweet sounds of her pleasure bringing him to the brink.

"Ah, God, Maddie," he groaned when she tensed and cried out in release. His arm went around her waist, keeping her pressed against him.

Then he thrust deep, grasping her hips as he withdrew and thrust again, his tempo increasing slowly until he felt his own release coiling at the base of his spine. Then he thrust once more, shouting as he came.

For several breathless moments, they remained motionless, allowing their ragged breathing to slow. Finally, Jack withdrew on a groan. But before he could say a word, Maddie reached behind her, unzipped her dress and pulled it over her head, tossing it into the adjoining bedroom.

"What are you doing?" Jack asked, taking in every gorgeous inch of her.

Maddie stepped forward and pulled off his tie, tossing it aside, a slow, sultry grin curving her lips. "We should probably shower again, don't you think?"

Jack didn't even bother arguing. He dragged her into his embrace and kissed her, hungry for more.

Maddie took Jack's face in her hands and dragged him to his feet, grateful her back was pressed against the shower wall after the orgasm she'd just experienced. They'd been gentle with one another at first, concerned and careful of their still tender wounds, but now that she had Jack back in her arms, the desperation and fear for him that she'd been trying so hard to suppress came rushing to the surface, and this time there was no gentleness as Jack joined their bodies.

She urged him on, her nails digging into his skin as she hung on to his shoulders, loving the way they fit together, the way they clung to each other. Making love to Jack had always been an amazing, mind-blowing experience—but now it also made her feel alive in a way she'd never felt before.

And in that moment between them, there was no fear, no sorrow. Only life—complete and perfect.

When they finally managed to drag themselves from

the shower, they still paused to kiss, touch, caress, share a loving glance as they hurried to dress and make themselves presentable once more.

Damp curls still clung to Maddie's neck when Jack led her into the party already underway downstairs. Her sister, Sarah, was bustling around, coordinating the caterers, making sure that the champagne was flowing and the hors d'oeuvres plentiful before dismissing them.

Maddie hadn't considered the logistical difficulties in planning the evening's festivities until her sister had described the fifty-page document she'd been given after volunteering to serve as hostess. Although each individual had been carefully screened and hand-selected from the catering company owned by a trusted *confrere*, they were still outsiders and would be sequestered in Jack's guesthouse until they were needed. Maddie could only imagine the nightmare Sarah was in for when it came to planning her and Luke's wedding.

When Sarah saw Maddie, she gave her a radiant smile. Maddie's younger sister looked amazing, her thick waves of auburn hair arranged beautifully, her black dress clinging to her figure in a way that drew more than just Luke's admiring gaze.

"I was beginning to wonder about you two." Sarah grinned, winking at them.

"God, are we that transparent?" Maddie whispered, suddenly feeling a little self-conscious.

Sarah hugged her and kissed her cheek. "Only because it's easy to see how incredibly happy you are."

Maddie hugged her back, having to blink away the tears that suddenly blurred her vision. "Thanks, sweetie. Love you."

Sarah drew back, grinning from ear to ear. "Love you too." She then turned her smile on Jack and hugged him, pressing a kiss to his cheek as well. "Everything's ready, Jack."

Sarah grinned at her sister again before drifting away to stand with Luke and their father, Senator Hal Blake, saying something to them that Maddie wasn't able to catch over the murmuring of the various conversations.

She sent a quick glance around the room, taking in the numerous faces—some familiar from her time with the Alliance; others familiar because of her father's political connections, who'd apparently been allies of the Alliance; others entirely unknown to her. She imagined they were the most trusted *confreres* and *consoeurs*. But before she could ask Jack to introduce her to the people she'd yet to meet, he took her hand and pulled her into the center of the foyer.

"Good evening and welcome," Jack said, his voice easily heard over the din of the guests. They immediately grew quiet and turned their attention to him.

Maddie stepped closer to Jack, suddenly feeling exposed.

"Thank you for joining us on this momentous occasion," Jack continued, nodding his thanks as someone handed him a champagne flute. "Tonight we celebrate Madeleine Blake and her initiation into the Alliance. I couldn't be more proud to serve at Maddie's side and to welcome her into the order."

He raised his glass, prompting the others to raise theirs in solemn salute.

"But I hope we'll soon have something more to celebrate," Jack continued, handing his glass off to one of the other guests.

Maddie sent a suspicious glance his way. "Jack . . . ?"

He lifted her hand and pressed a kiss to her fingertips. "Maddie, the day I met you I didn't even know what to think. I just remember being utterly captivated by this woman who at such a young age could enter a room and command it as if she were royalty. And I fell in love with you before I even knew what was happening. Although we were separated by time and distance and circumstances, it seems fate had other plans for us—for we always seem to find our way back to each other."

Maddie's eyes began to sting as tears blurred her vision. She dabbed gently at her cheeks to remove the few tears that had escaped, her heart beginning to pound.

"And it took nearly losing you, nearly losing my own life," he continued, "to make me realize that you are the person I want at my side for whatever precious moments we still have left—as my lover, my partner, my friend."

Maddie's heart swelled with joy as Jack eased down on one knee and took her hands in his. "Maddie, my love, earlier tonight you made a vow to the Alliance. Now, *I* would like to make a vow to *you*. I promise to love you for the rest of my life, to worship and adore you, and to endeavor every day to be the man you deserve. Will you marry me?"

Although Maddie had suspected that this was where Jack was going with his speech, hearing the words still left her breathless. And for a moment, she didn't respond, too full of emotion to speak. But then she took his face in her hands and nodded. "Yes, Jack. I'll marry you."

He was on his feet in an instant, grabbing her around the waist and pressing a hard kiss to her lips to the delight of the crowd, who clapped and whistled in approval.

Her arms still encircled his neck when he set her back down on her feet and kissed her again, this time tenderly, taking his time. When he at last lifted his head, their friends and family rushed forward to congratulate them with hugs and handshakes and, in Finn's case, a heartfelt *"Dude . . ."*

Even Will offered her a warm hug and a kiss on the

cheek. "Congratulations, Maddie." He then gave her a sly smile. "Try to keep him in line, will ya? I haven't had much luck in that regard."

She returned his smile, not missing the hint of sorrow— or maybe it was envy—in their commander's eyes. She'd learned a lot about Will in the year she'd been with the Alliance, but she had a feeling her knowledge of the complicated man merely scratched the surface. Perhaps someday there'd be someone who could get through that tough exterior and truly discover the man she'd only caught glimpses of in rare moments like this . . .

It was sometime later before Maddie and Jack finally had a moment to themselves again, and Maddie had to admit she was relieved when Jack took her hand and swept her out onto the veranda where a small bistro table held two flutes of champagne. Strands of lights wound through the pergola, casting a soft glow around the patio and giving the stunning arrangements of flowers an almost fairy-tale quality. The heady fragrance wafted to her on the breeze and she closed her eyes, breathing in the beauty of the moment.

When she felt Jack's arm encircle her waist, she opened her eyes and smiled up at him. "Thank you for this. I couldn't have imagined a more perfect evening."

"It's not over yet," he assured her. He released her and took a step back and reached into his jacket pocket, withdrawing a small velvet box. He opened it to reveal a stunning emerald ring.

"My God, Jack," Maddie breathed as he slipped it onto her finger. "It's gorgeous."

He lifted her hand to his lips, pressing a kiss to where the ring encircled her finger. "Rumor has it my ancestor took this emerald from among the Templar treasures that were secreted away after the order was dissolved, and when he fell in love and married, he had it set into a pendant for his bride. It has passed down through my family, but I thought the stone would make a fitting engagement ring—should you agree to have me. But if you don't like it, I will have something else made—"

Maddie silenced him with a kiss before murmuring, "It's perfect."

"I can't take all the credit for that," he admitted, pulling her back into his arms. "Sarah helped me pick out the setting a week ago."

She laughed, shaking her head. "You are just *full* of surprises."

He gave her that cocky, debonair grin she adored. "I'm glad you think so. Because I just might have a few more planned . . ."

She arched a brow. "Is that right?"

"Mmm-hmm." The gold flecks in his eyes seemed to dance with mischief. "Would you like a hint?"

She eyed him warily. "I don't know . . . Maybe just a little one."

His grin widened, and he leaned down to whisper in her ear as if afraid the guests might somehow hear what he had to say. Or maybe he just liked the way she shuddered when his breath skated across her skin. And if that hadn't made her shiver with anticipation, what he shared about his plans for them later that evening certainly would have.

She returned his grin with a wicked little smile and draped her arms around his neck, pulling him down for a kiss that let him know she might have a few surprises of her own in store . . .

Have you read *Deceived*,
the first in Kate SeRine's Dark Alliance series?
It's available now from Zebra Books,
wherever paperbacks or eBooks are sold!

"Dark, dangerous, edgy, and deliciously sexy!"
—Julie Ann Walker,
***New York Times* bestselling author**

"Kate SeRine knows how to pack a punch!"
—Donna Grant, *New York Times* bestselling author

Luke Rogan's assignment is simple: secure young
Elijah Scoffield and his mother and bring them back to
headquarters—just an ordinary mission for an operative
of the Dark Alliance. But Elijah is no ordinary kid. He's
the grandson of one of the country's most influential
politicians—a man privy to the Alliance's most valuable
secrets, including its centuries long connection to the
Knights Templar. And someone else is attempting to
capture the boy—someone who's proven he doesn't
give a damn about collateral damage . . .

Heartbroken at the lies that tore her world apart,
Sarah Scoffield will do anything to protect her son—
even if that means teaming up with a deadly stranger.
But Sarah soon finds herself falling in love with her dark
hero. And as danger stalks ever closer, the fiery desire
that claims them awakens in Sarah passions she'd
thought dead and buried long ago . . .

"You look like you could use something warm to drink."

Luke's head snapped up toward the sound of the voice. Behind the counter of a homemade wooden booth that sported cartoonishly large red apples painted on the front was a woman so striking Luke actually felt his chest grow tight. Her lips curved into a smile, bringing dimples to her cheeks. Long dark auburn hair spilled over her shoulders, framing the curves of the full breasts beneath the crimson turtleneck she wore. He was so taken aback by her loveliness, it took him a full twenty seconds to realize he was staring at Sarah Scoffield. Holy hell . . was it really gonna be that easy?

"Yes, I'm talking to you," she teased with a laugh, motioning him over. "I guarantee this is the best apple cider you've ever tasted, and all proceeds go to Bakersville schools. I promise you won't regret it!"

Luke sauntered over, unable to repress a grin. Sarah Scoffield was even more breathtaking the closer he got. And the picture her sister had sent didn't even begin to do her justice. Looking at her standing there smiling at him with those adorable little dimples, her wide dark eyes sparkling, Luke began to think this job might not be so bad after all.

What the hell was wrong with her?

Sarah wasn't the kind of woman to hit on a complete stranger, and yet here she was flirting mercilessly with the man on the other side of the booth. She'd seen him skulking through the crowd, his height and powerful build making him hard to miss. And that profile—she couldn't remember the last time she'd seen a man so heart-stoppingly handsome. And when he'd turned toward her and pegged her with that dark stare of his . . . well, it'd been a long time since she'd felt her heart skip a beat, let alone since she'd felt the other areas of her anatomy sit up and take notice.

As he came toward her, Sarah busied herself filling a paper cup with cider to hide her sudden onset of nerves. By the time she lifted her eyes again, she was able to steady her hands as she handed the cup over.

He took the cup from her, his fingers brushing over hers briefly during the exchange. As he lifted it to his lips, he peered over the edge and took a careful sip. "You're right," he drawled. "I don't regret it one bit."

Dear Lord . . . that *voice*! It was deeper than she'd expected and velvety smooth. She felt the heat rising to her cheeks and offered him a nervous smile. "I'm Sarah," she said, extending her hand. He took it in his massive paw and gave it a quick shake, but he didn't immediately release her, continuing to hold her hand gently in his grasp.

"Luke," he replied. "Can someone fill in for you here, Sarah?"

"I . . . uh . . . I'm supposed to be working here for the full hour. Sorry." She drew back slightly, but his grip tightened on her fingers, keeping her where she was.

He leaned across the counter until his lips were close to her ear. "Sarah, I need you to come with me."

Sarah's blood suddenly ran cold with fear. "Listen," she stammered. "You've got the wrong idea. I didn't mean—"

"Your father sent me, Sarah," he interrupted. "You're in danger."

"My father?" she scoffed. "Not very likely."

Luke glanced around as if expecting danger to close in on them at any moment. "There was an incident earlier today. Your father was injured, and your sister—"

"Look," Sarah interrupted, finally pulling her hand from his grasp. "I don't know who you are, but this isn't funny. And, by the way—it's a *lousy* pickup line. Now, if you'll excuse me, I have a job to do."

Luke downed the cider and grabbed his wallet from his back pocket, fishing out a couple of hundred-dollar bills and handing them to her. "For the cider."

She cautiously reached for the money. "It only costs a dollar."

"I'm guessing it'll cover what you would've sold for the rest of the hour," he said. "Now, I need you to come with me so I can get you and Eli to safety. I'd rather not have to throw you over my shoulder and drag you outta here kicking and screaming to do it, but I will. I'll do whatever I have to do to keep you safe. Where's your son?"

Sarah's fear was replaced by anger. "What the hell do you know about Eli?" she demanded. "You touch one hair on his head, and I swear—"

Luke cursed and strode around to the back of the booth, gently but firmly taking hold of her elbow. "Lady, I'm not the one you need to worry about."

Sarah's breath caught in her chest. At least a foot taller than she was, Luke towered over her, his powerful body crowding her as he pressed close. She put a hand against his muscled chest to stop him from getting any closer and was surprised to find his heart beating as fast as hers.

Dear God. He was looking at her with such intensity, she almost expected him to kiss her. And something told her it wouldn't have been a tentative, uncertain kiss.

"Everything okay, Mrs. Scoffield?"

Sarah started and tore her gaze away from Luke's—which was far more difficult than she would've thought—to give the man in the booth next to hers a smile. "Yes, Mr. Thomas. Everything's fine." She turned back to Luke, narrowing her eyes at him. "Just who the hell should I be worried about? What was this *incident* you seem to know all about?"

"There was an attempt on your father's life," Luke told her in a low rumble. "I'm sorry."

"What?" She pegged Luke with a pointed stare, her anger and disbelief making her tremble. "Prove it. Prove to me that my father sent you. Prove that *any* of what you're telling me is true."

Luke heaved an exasperated sigh and took out his phone and turned it toward her. "Here."

She read the text message from the phone number she recognized as her sister Maddie's: **Pic of Sarah and Eli. Please bring them home safely. Dad in surgery.**

Sarah immediately called out, "Mr. Thomas! I need to take a break. Could you watch the booth for me until Mrs. Smith gets here?"

Luke didn't wait for Mr. Thomas to answer before grabbing Sarah's hand and pulling her along behind him. "Where's the boy?"

"The haunted house." Sarah gestured toward a sprawling historic home down the street that was converted into a house of horrors every year to the delight of people all over the county. She'd held firm about Eli not going, planning to have him sit with her at the booth until she was free to go with him, but then Hunter's mom had informed her that, contrary to what Hunter had hoped, she and her husband *would* be joining the boys at the festival and keeping watch over them.

Luke picked up the pace, his powerful strides forcing Sarah to take three steps to his every one. She struggled to keep up with him, her long denim skirt and brown knee boots not really suited for jogging. But as her fear and panic ramped up, she surged forward, now dragging Luke behind *her*.

"Betsy," Sarah panted when they reached the wrought iron gates, recognizing the girl taking tickets as one of the high school girls who'd babysat for her during staff meetings. "Have you seen Eli?"

The girl blinked at Sarah—well, at Luke, really—but finally seemed to snap out of it and nodded. "Uh, yeah. He went in, like, a few minutes ago, I think. Haven't seen him come out yet. But, you know, I'm not like watching for him or anything."

Sarah bolted up the steps, ignoring Betsy's protestations about tickets, and heard Luke's heavy footfalls right behind her. "Eli!" she called when she burst inside. "Elijah!"

Luke grabbed her arm and pulled her to a stop. "Sarah—"

"Let me go, damn it," she yelled over the spooky music and artificial sound effects of creaking doors and demonic cackles. "You told me my son's in danger. Well, I'm going to go find him."

Luke pulled her a few steps toward the wall and deeper into the thick curls of artificial fog to let another group of people pass, then grasped the back of her neck and bent to speak directly into her ear, "We're not the only ones looking for him, remember?"

Sarah shuddered at the warmth of his breath on her ear and forced herself to focus on what he was saying.

"We don't want to lead them to Eli." He drew back just enough to peer down into her face, and his hand drifted from the back of her neck to cup her cheek. "Now, follow me—quickly, but calmly."

Sarah nodded and let him take her hand as they hurried through the darkness, lit only by disorienting strobe lights. They searched the faces of those they passed, looking for Eli in the crowd. Whenever she saw one of the children she recognized, she tried to ask if they'd seen her son. Those to whom she could make herself heard could do little more than nod and point, their voices lost to the noise.

More than once, costumed performers dressed as grue-some zombies, mangled murder victims, or ghosts with hollowed-out eyes leapt out at them, startling a cry from her. But Luke barely flinched. It seemed the man was com-pletely immune to fear. Which made Sarah wonder just how the hell her father knew him.

The aura of danger that surrounded Luke was unlike any she'd seen before—and did nothing to assuage her fear for Eli's safety. If her father had sent someone like the man beside her to protect them, then the people he feared were coming for them had to be pretty damned frightening.

Her panic increasing with each passing moment that Eli wasn't with her, Sarah tightened her grip on Luke's hand. Finally, as they made their way through the crowded third-story hallway, she thought she suddenly caught a glimpse of Eli. Without thinking, she bolted forward, squeezing her way through the crowds, frantic to keep him in sight as he and the Smith family made their way toward the back stairs.

She was just about to dart down the darkened stairwell after them when a group of giggling girls emerged from the room to her right, clogging the passageway. Sarah el-bowed her way through them, drawing angry protests that were thankfully drowned out. She raced down the stairs, which were dimly lit by a dull yellow bare bulb at the top landing and another, blinking, fizzling bulb farther down below, like something out of those creepy slasher films from the eighties.

Her heart pounding, she took the stairs as fast as she could. As she made the first landing, she came to an abrupt halt with a loud scream, not having expected to encounter a performer sprawled on the floor as if he'd been shot in the head. A shockingly realistic splatter was painted on the wall a couple of feet above him and smeared down as if he'd hit the wall when the bullet struck him and slowly slumped to the ground.

After the initial shock, Sarah moved to go around when something about the man's face suddenly struck her as familiar. It was in the next instant that terror gripped her, making her knees momentarily weak. The man wasn't a performer. It was Mike Smith—the father of Eli's friend Hunter and the man who was supposed to be watching out for her son.

Sarah forced her feet to move, tripping over the body and nearly tumbling down the stairs. Her heart was racing, her pulse pounding so loudly in her ears she no longer could hear the haunted house sound effects bleeding through the walls into the stairwell.

Dear God.

Mike Smith was dead. Shot in the head. And the person who'd committed such a horrific murder was there in the darkness somewhere. With her son.

Sarah didn't care anymore about being quiet. All she wanted was to get to her child before it was too late. She bolted down the stairs, screaming for Eli at the top of her lungs. When she reached the bottom of the stairs, there was a heap lying in the shadows. Heedless of her own safety, she rushed forward, dropping to her knees. She reached out a trembling hand and rolled the body over.

Sarah gasped, choking back a horrified sob when she saw the wide, unblinking eyes of Patricia Smith. And beneath her lay the huddled form of a little boy with dark hair. Sarah placed a hand on his shoulder, expecting to find him dead as well, but he screamed and pulled away, cowering with his arms over his head.

"Hunter!" Sarah cried. "Hunter, honey! Where's Eli? Where'd he go?"

Hunter couldn't stop screaming, the poor boy too traumatized to respond. Fighting back the scream of frantic need to find her own son, Sarah managed to scoop up Hunter and was attempting to stand with him in her arms to take him with her when strong hands wrested the boy from her grasp.

Her protective instinct on overdrive, Sarah lashed out, kicking and clawing at the man.

"Sarah!"

The deep voice broke through her rage, bringing her assault to an abrupt halt. Her relief at seeing Luke was so intense she had to choke back a sob, but the desperate need to get to her son kept her on her feet. "He's gone," she told Luke, her voice quavering. "And Patti and Mike . . ."

Without a word, Luke rushed through the back door and into the night, the traumatized little boy still in his arms, his piercing gaze searching the darkness, his expression deadly. Sarah's own eyes darted around, desperately trying to spot Eli.

"Oh my God! What's happened?"

Sarah's head snapped toward the voice and recognized the woman rushing toward them as a fellow teacher at the elementary school. "Helen, have you seen Eli?"

The older woman shook her gray head in confusion. "Yes, dear, I believe I saw him run out of here a moment ago. Was headed toward the midway. He must've been darned scared from the haunted house tonight. He was running like the dickens."

Luke gently handed Hunter over to Helen, pushing away the rush of emotions and horrifying images that came flooding in on him from his own childhood trauma. "There's been a murder. Call the police."

He didn't wait for the woman to respond before taking off after Sarah. Damn, the woman was fast! But he had to believe if it'd been *his* kid in danger, it would've taken an act of God to keep him from getting to his child, so he could understand her desperation. But that same love and protective instinct was going to get her killed if he didn't reach her.

Fortunately, his long strides made up for her head start. By then, they were almost to the midway, and he heard Sarah's strangled cry as she poured on a fresh burst of speed, racing past the curious festival attendees who sent confused glances her way. Luke caught sight of the little boy at almost the same moment as Sarah. But he also saw the wiry guy in a gray hoodie moving in from the boy's flank.

Sarah reached her son just before the other man, scooping him into her embrace and pivoting to shield him with her body. Luke kept running, throwing himself into the would-be kidnapper and taking him down to the ground before the guy even realized what'd hit him. But it didn't take the attacker long to recover his wits.

Luke saw the gun just as he reared back to drive his fist into the guy's face. He grabbed the man's wrist, slamming it against the ground with one hand and connecting with the guy's jaw with the other. As the gun finally slipped from the attacker's hand, Luke felt the man squirm beneath him and heard Sarah's cry of warning just in time to roll away and avoid the sharp blade of the hunting knife that the guy had apparently hidden away in a sheath at his calf.

"Who the hell are you working for?" Luke demanded as the guy squared off against him, hunched over, teeth bared.

The attacker swung his arm, slicing through the air as he advanced on Luke, damned near catching him with the tip. Luke jumped back at the last second, catching the guy's arm as he swung past him and twisting him around into a choke hold, pressing the knife to his throat.

"I said, who the hell are you working for?" Luke growled.

The guy chuckled darkly, leaning into Luke to avoid the blade at his throat. "I serve the One True Master. And if you kill me, more will come. We will know your secrets, Templar."

Luke was about to ask how the hell the bastard knew who he was when the guy started convulsing. Sarah hastily stumbled backward with Eli, shielding his eyes.

Luke cursed under his breath and released the man, letting him fall to the ground, where he continued to convulse and spew white foam, which was soon tinged dark with blood. Luke's stream of ripe curses grew louder and more colorful when he realized the motherfucker had poisoned himself, taking the coward's way out instead of allowing himself to be questioned. When Luke regained his composure, he glanced up to encounter the horrified stares of the crowd of people who'd dared to approach now that the assailant was on the ground. More than a few of them were on their phones, no doubt already calling 911.

Luke lunged forward and took hold of Sarah's arm, quickly leading her and Eli from the scene before the police could show up.

"Where are we going?" Sarah demanded after a few yards, digging in her heels and pulling him to a stop. "We need to stay here and tell the police what happened! You heard what that nutjob said—more will be coming."

Luke relaxed his grip and glanced down at her and then into the wide dark eyes of her son. The boy was mute with terror, but tears hovered on the edges of his long black lashes as if he was holding them back with sheer will-power. The last thing the kid needed was to hear his life was in danger, but something about the way Eli looked at him—a mixture of fear, disbelief, and awe—told him the boy could take it.

"It's because more'll be coming that I need to get you two outta here," Luke told them. "Eli, you think you can hang in there for me, buddy? You're safe right now, but I want to keep it that way. Will you trust me for a little while, help me get your mom somewhere safe?"

Eli nodded. "Yeah." He blinked a few times, swallowed, and glanced at his mom before squaring his shoulders and nodding again. "Yeah. I'm good. Let's go."

"Good man." Luke clapped him lightly on the back before meeting Sarah's gaze. "How about you?"

"I don't even know who you *are*," she breathed. "Not really. You say my father sent you, but how can I know that for sure? How do I know I can trust you any more than *that* guy?"

Luke sighed. Hell if *he* knew how to convince her to trust him. If she'd met him five years earlier, he would've told her she couldn't. He hadn't been worth trusting back then, and he probably had no right to ask a young mother to put her life and the life of her son in his hands even now. But as he stood there looking into Sarah's gaze, so fierce, so indomitable, and yet frightened and vulnerable, he somehow knew he'd give his very last breath to protect her and the boy.

"You *don't* know you can trust me," he finally answered. "But if you want to survive, Sarah, you're gonna have to."

Connect with

More by Bestselling Author
Hannah Howell

Available Wherever Books Are Sold!

Check out our website at
http://www.kensingtonbooks.com

More from Bestselling Author
JANET DAILEY

Calder Storm	0-8217-7543-X	$7.99US/$10.99CAN
Close to You	1-4201-1714-9	$5.99US/$6.99CAN
Crazy in Love	1-4201-0303-2	$4.99US/$5.99CAN
Dance With Me	1-4201-2213-4	$5.99US/$6.99CAN
Everything	1-4201-2214-2	$5.99US/$6.99CAN
Forever	1-4201-2215-0	$5.99US/$6.99CAN
Green Calder Grass	0-8217-7222-8	$7.99US/$10.99CAN
Heiress	1-4201-0002-5	$6.99US/$7.99CAN
Lone Calder Star	0-8217-7542-1	$7.99US/$10.99CAN
Lover Man	1-4201-0666-X	$4.99US/$5.99CAN
Masquerade	1-4201-0005-X	$6.99US/$8.99CAN
Mistletoe and Molly	1-4201-0041-6	$6.99US/$9.99CAN
Rivals	1-4201-0003-3	$6.99US/$7.99CAN
Santa in a Stetson	1-4201-0664-3	$6.99US/$9.99CAN
Santa in Montana	1-4201-1474-3	$7.99US/$9.99CAN
Searching for Santa	1-4201-0306-7	$6.99US/$9.99CAN
Something More	0-8217-7544-8	$7.99US/$9.99CAN
Stealing Kisses	1-4201-0304-0	$4.99US/$5.99CAN
Tangled Vines	1-4201-0004-1	$6.99US/$8.99CAN
Texas Kiss	1-4201-0665-1	$4.99US/$5.99CAN
That Loving Feeling	1-4201-1713-0	$5.99US/$6.99CAN
To Santa With Love	1-4201-2073-5	$6.99US/$7.99CAN
When You Kiss Me	1-4201-0667-8	$4.99US/$5.99CAN
Yes, I Do	1-4201-0305-9	$4.99US/$5.99CAN

Available Wherever Books Are Sold!

Check out our website at www.kensingtonbooks.com.